ALSO BY ART BOURGEAU

The Seduction

WOLFMAN

A NOVEL

ART BOURGEAU

DONALD I. FINE, INC.
New York

Library of Congress Cataloging in Publication Data

Bourgeau, Art.
Wolfman.

I. Title.
PS3552.0833W6   1989   813'.54   88-45846
ISBN 1-55611-120-7
Manufactured in the United States of America
10 9 8 7 6 5 4 3 2 1

This novel is a work of fiction. Names, characters, places and
incidents are either the product of the author's imagination or
are used fictitiously. Any resemblance to actual events, locales,
organizations or persons, living or dead, is entirely coincidental
and beyond the intent of either the author or publisher.

DESIGNED BY IRVING PERKINS ASSOCIATES

TO DONALD I. FINE, WITH THANKS

Ralph Waldo Emerson said it best. "Our chief want in life is somebody who shall make us do what we can."

1. *And in the second year of (his) reign, Nebuchadnez-zar dreamed dreams, wherewith his spirit was troubled, and his sleep brake from him.*
2. *Then the king commanded to call the magicians, and the astrologers, and the sorcerers, and the Chaldeans, for to shew the king his dreams . . .*
3. *And the king said unto them, I have dreamed a dream, and my spirit was troubled to know the dream.*
4. *Then spake the Chaldeans . . . O King, live forever: tell us thy servants the dream, and we will shew the interpretation.*
5. *The king answered and said to the Chaldeans, The thing is gone from me: if ye will not make known unto me the dream, with the interpretation thereof ye shall be cut in pieces, and your houses shall be made a dunghill.*
6. *But if ye shew the dream, and the interpretation thereof, ye shall receive of me gifts and rewards and great honor . . .*

Daniel: Ch. 2, Vs. 1-6

CHAPTER 1

L ORING WEATHERBY took his tea and moved to the club chair that looked out the window at the park trees. It was four days now since the crash of the stock market, and he had not slept once since then. Outside it was still dark, the trees merely more shadows in a land of shadows ranging from dark gray to black.

The house was quiet. There were no sounds of people sleeping, pets snoring or even clocks ticking. The only sound was his own breathing. The only light a glimmer from the kitchen. Loring took a sip from his tea and sat down in the club chair.

The chair was his favorite possession. It had come from an auction at Freeman's, and before that from a parsonage, as attested to by a small brass plaque on the rear leg. The leather was old and cracked but not torn, and the parade of clerics whose backs and bottoms had graced it before him had given it a shine more than skin deep. A shine that seemed to go down, down, down, like a warm red bottomless oxblood pool.

The house was cold. He pulled the collar of his silk brocade dressing gown tighter to keep out the chill and settled back to wait. The four days of sleeplessness had taken a toll, and there was nothing so much that he wanted as to walk away from everything around him. To be released. To chase rainbows or butterflies. To be carefree. But he knew it was not to be.

The stock market crash had come on Thursday last. It had started in the morning with just a downside trickle. A little profit-taking. A minor market adjustment. Nothing to be concerned about, but by afternoon a hurricane through downtown Philadelphia could not have wreaked more financial havoc. Blue chips, high flyers, utilities, transportations, mutual funds, even over-the-counter penny stocks were savaged. Nothing was spared. Fortunes were wiped out in minutes.

He settled deeper into the chair, its warmth for a moment taking his mind off the past four days. True it was nothing more than the leather reflecting his own body heat, but in the darkness it seemed a powerful circle that surrounded and kept him safe from the cold of the house. He allowed himself to relax with it and for a moment tried to envision the faces of the clergymen who had enjoyed it before him. Good men, kindly men, like Father Frank and Father Mike at St. Ignatius.

Outside, the darkness was giving way to the gray of the false dawn. The shapes of the trees were becoming more distinct. Gone were the leaves. The late autumn rains had seen to that.

What was left was a January landscape in November. One that would have depressed many, but not Loring. Winter was his element. He was strongest in cold.

The grayness drew his focus outward and brought his mind to the present. He reached for his tea and raised it to his lips before he realized the cup was empty. For a moment he was confused. The cup had been full when he sat down. Then he smiled. The chair, it always felt so good. After he sat down it had probably lulled him into that half-asleep/half-awake state where people did things without thinking and he had drunk it without conscious thought. Four days without sleep could make one forgetful. At least of the little things.

He picked up the cup and saucer and went to the kitchen for a refill. As he pushed open the door the light above the stove seemed to blind him. He stopped and looked away, blinking rapidly until the sensitivity of his eyes diminished. Then he crossed the kitchen and poured more Earl Grey, being careful not to look at the clock on the stove. It was Monday, that was all he needed to know. The rest would come soon enough, he told himself as he felt his stomach begin to tighten, the first stirrings of the cramps and the pain Monday pressures always brought.

He added cream and sugar to his tea and stirred with the spoon nestled on the saucer. In the light it was obvious he was a handsome man, with blond hair and aristocratic, chiseled features that in profile seemed to belong on a coin.

He was above medium height and lean. Under his robe he was nude, his skin alabaster white and smooth. He had the muscle definition of a swimmer: light and graceful rather than the heavy slabs of a wrestler or football players. But this morning he felt tired, leaden, older than his thirty-one years, a feeling he tried to shake off. Time was a game men played with other men. To give it, take it away, control was the key

11

to winning because time was life. Time was money. But it is no more than the passage of suns. It was not God.

He took a sip of his tea. After the crash on Thursday had come Friday. A day for digging out and placing the blame, except there had been no relief. The market began where it had left off and continued downward, dropping hundreds of points throughout the day. By mid-afternoon one broker was heard to remark that he felt like he was on an elevator whose cable had snapped and he was just watching the floors fly by. Another one updated the old, old garment district joke: "What's the only thing worse than Thursday? Friday." No one laughed. By closing, over twelve hundred points had vanished in two days.

Loring took his cup and returned to the living room. The room was now light enough so that everything was visible. The house was a single story cottage, the living room long and narrow. One side was almost entirely taken up by windows that looked out on the woods of the Wissahickon. The leather chair sat near the windows. One end of the room was dominated by a fieldstone fireplace, well-worn furniture was clustered around it. The furniture had the look of a men's club, a room of leather and wool, a room for winter. The rest of the wallspace was covered in bookcases, filled to capacity. There was no television in the room or the house for that matter. He did not like television.

He carefully set his cup down on the desk before turning on a lamp and going to a bookcase filled with matching volumes. He selected two. At his desk he removed three files from the lower righthand drawer, an exercise he had repeated throughout the weekend as he steeled himself for today.

The books were filled with graphs. He opened them to places already marked. Pushing his blond hair out of his eyes he studied first one and then the other to be certain they were what he wanted. Satisfied, he turned his attention to the files. Each was also filled with graphs. The graphs in the first file represented the ups and downs of his clients' portfolios. The second represented the ups and downs of the market as a whole, and the third represented the events of the past days.

One of the graphs in the books represented the growth of Iowa corn since the year 1976; the other represented a graph of sunspots for the same period. He compared these graphs with those in the file folders. They matched. He was right. He knew it. All he had to do was stick by his guns and not be afraid of what happened last Thursday and Friday. Gazing at the old inkwell on his desk, he tried to clear his mind.

Loring Weatherby was a chartist, or so he told himself. He believed the world operated on a higher order than chaos, even the stock market, and that to be successful one had to find the beat, to get in sync with an all-governing internal rhythm. The trick was to discover the rhythm. To that end some years earlier he had joined an institute in St. Louis whose sole function was to provide people of a like mind with graphs charting the ebb and flow of virtually everything chartable, from Florida orange production, to female babies born in Hawaii, to the sale of men's felt hats in New York City, to Ohio State football. For him there was a link, a key, a thread that ran through it all, tied it all together. And from these mountains of graphs he had found that key, at least he thought so until last week.

Outside a bird landing on the feeder attached to the window distracted him. He stopped and watched it feed. It wasn't much of a bird. A drab winter sparrow, was all. Barely enough to hold in your hand, but one cheerfully pecking away at the unexpected bounty in the feeder. Then a blackbird arrived. Even though there was enough seed for both and a dozen more like them, the blackbird did not peck at the seed, it pecked at the sparrow until it drove it away.

Loring felt anger. He did not want the blackbird in the feeder, not like that. It had to go. He reached across the desk and rapped on the window with his knuckle. The blackbird looked up from its feeding but didn't fly away. For a moment man and bird stared at one another. The bird's eye was black and soulless. Loring rapped on the window again. This time the bird raised its wings in flight, but there was no haste, no fright in its departure. Loring watched for a few more minutes. The sparrow did not return.

His mind turned to the task before him. It has not been an accident but the product of months of intense research when he discovered that the graphs of the stock market's performance matched the graphs for sunspots and Iowa corn production beginning almost a dozen years earlier. That was the beat, the rhythm he needed. All that was necessary was to put his clients' money into stocks that were known to be market sensitive, then to sell and repurchase as the graph dictated. It had not been foolproof. Nothing could allow for minute day-to-day fluctuations, but on the whole he had made a great deal of money for his clients with his method.

He closed the books with a sigh and went to his bedroom to dress for work. Friday's trade papers had blamed the computer for the crash. As the drop began it was fueled by the automatic sell-orders stored in it. It was a crash caused by technology. The Wall Street *Journal* quoted several sources but took no stand. The people there, Loring was sure, knew better, knew that the computer was the effect not the cause.

He pulled on a heavily starched white shirt with a medium-spread collar, made for him like all his shirts by Vittorio, an aging shirtmaker on Seventeenth near Locust. From his closet he chose a Brooks Brothers charcoal pin stripe suit and red-and-blue suspenders.

He believed the real cause of the crash was too much prosperity. There was no room to trade. Prices were too high. No one was making any money. Things had topped out, so a few money managers began dropping large blocks of stock in an effort to stimulate some downside action, and then to buy back, making a profit on the spread. The result had been larger than anyone could have dreamed. Over twelve hundred points lost in two days.

Many of his clients had been hurt badly. They had panicked against his advice to hold tight, and they had turned their portfolios into ashes. Others had listened, even bought what he had advised and were now in a position to regain their losses and turn short-term profit phoenixlike. But he was concerned about the losers. Somehow he had failed them, when the chips were down he hadn't come through.

How could he know? He kept asking himself through the long, sleepless weekend. Men against Order. They should not have prevailed but somehow they did. Not right. They were screwing around with things bigger than themselves. So little regard for transcendent forces could bring everything tumbling down.

Once during the weekend he picked up his Missal and felt guilty because he had not been to church in so long. He opened it at random. The thought for that Sunday advised that the days were evil and that numberless sins cried for punishment. He had tried to pray but had stopped himself. Best not to concern God. Right would win out. Be careful what you ask for because you might get it. He heeded the voices. Well, not really voices, he assured himself. Just thoughts that sounded like voices . . .

From his jewelry box he selected a set of gold cufflinks

formal in design and slipped them through the cuffs of his shirt. He was almost finished knotting his tie when the sound of the phone startled him. Instinctively he looked at his watch. Not quite seven-thirty. Who would be calling him now? The phone rang again. In the quietness of the Wissahickon it sounded like a jackhammer.

He ignored the phone beside the bed and walked into the living room to use the one at his desk. He hated the phone beside the bed. The idea of chatting from even the edge of the bed made him feel guilty, like a malingering invalid.

"Hello." From the other end he heard a female voice say, "Loring, hi. How are you?" His sister's voice. She still had that distinctive breathless quality, but today her voice sounded different, metallic and faraway, as if they were talking from parallel dimensions of different time and space with an orange juice can and string between them.

"Karen, what's wrong? It's not even six-thirty in Chicago . . ."

She laughed, the sound like someone raking a thumb down the teeth of a comb. He looked down at the phone and mentally cursed it.

"Nothing's wrong, silly. I'm just calling to invite you to my wedding."

"Your wedding?"

"I was afraid of that, you didn't get my letter, did you?"

"What letter?"

"I knew it, the goddamn mails. I won't go into how wonderful he is because mom and dad are on the extensions . . ."

Before he could ask who "he" was, as if on cue he heard a second female voice and a male voice say nearly in unison, "Hi, son," and he heard himself say, "Hello." This inspiring exchange was followed by a moment of silence in which they waited for him to say something else.

When he didn't he heard Karen start again with something about the world passing her by at age twenty-seven, and how she'd met Charles, a broker like Loring, and they could play squash together when he was out for the wedding, but he blocked out most of it.

He was furious that she had called the man on the line "dad." He was their *stepfather*, not their father. Their father was dead. Dead.

She was chattering on. "Anyway, as I said in the letter you never got, the wedding is December 28th. Charles is like you about remembering important dates. This way, right in the middle between Christmas and New Year's, he won't have any excuse for not remembering our anniversary. And, Loring, I want you to come to the wedding."

"Charles?"

"Yes, I just *told* you, the man I'm going to marry!"

"Everybody is going crazy with the plans," interrupted his mother. "It's going to be a beautiful wedding."

"That's right," added Malcolm, his stepfather. "While you're here we want you to stay with us. It'll be just like old times . . ."

Loring was staring out the window as he tried hard not to visualize their faces. Karen, because he missed her; the others because he did not. What was he getting himself into? Outside, the blackbird returned to the feeder. The sight of his arrogance added to Loring feeling somehow put upon from all sides. Even a damn bird . . .

"When did you say?"

"The twenty-eighth. December 28th. Aren't you listening to a word I've been saying?"

"Yes, of course. I'm just preoccupied. The market crash, you know." He took a deep breath. "Karen, I'm sorry, but I can't be there. That week I've chartered a boat out of Barbados, I'm taking three couples—my best clients—sailing. But I'll be with you in spirit—"

"Son, can't you change your plans?" his mother said. His stepfather was silent.

He would not be intimidated.

"I'm sorry, I *can't*. I hate to do this but I have to go, I have a meeting in town. The market crash . . ."

He left the house as quickly as possible, afraid the phone would ring again, got into his maroon Mercedes and headed for the office.

Traffic was light until he hit the river drive, then slowed to a crawl as yet another facelift on the Schuylkill Expressway poured thousands of extra commuters from outlying suburbs like Conshohocken and King of Prussia onto the winding road. As he finally inched his way past the Art Museum he was still thinking about the phone call.

Other than Karen, who had come for a weekend visit some five years ago, he had seen his family only twice since he'd left home for prep school at St. Ignatius in Villanova at age fourteen. Shortly after that his stepfather had moved the family and business to Chicago. They had come east for his prep school graduation and his graduation from the University of Pennsylvania, and both times had been pure hell. Memories faded, feelings didn't. He had not once been to Chicago, he had never seen their house, he had never seen his room. And he was glad of it.

There was a line of cars at his garage on Fifteenth Street, but the attendant saw him and waved him ahead. On the walk to his office in the Penn Center complex he glanced at his watch and saw it was a few minutes past eight. The partners' meeting would already be underway. He started to walk faster, his Burberry open and blowing slightly in the cool morning breeze.

In the conference room of Cartwright, Blanchard & Haynes the air of the meeting was tense. Most of the eleven partners were in shirtsleeves, their jackets thrown around the high backs of the conference room chairs. The table was littered with styrofoam coffee cups. Two of the partners were smoking cigars, several others cigarettes.

William Blanchard, a stocky, powerfully built man in his early sixties and the managing partner, was on his feet at the head of the table. When he saw Loring enter he looked over the tops of his reading glasses and said, "Good morning." The simple greeting carried a note of disapproval that the youngest partner in the firm was the last to arrive at so important a meeting.

The meeting lasted another half-hour in which the more senior partners took turns bandying phrases like trade deficit, economic reports, computer problems, echoing the industry party line begun on Friday about what had caused the crash.

"Loring, are we boring you?" William Blanchard said.

Several of the partners were looking at him now. Financial wizards, one and all. This morning he saw them for what they were. No wizards. No Merlins, Beelzebubs or Asmodeuses. Gray, gray cattle.

"No," he said.

"Then perhaps you'd share some of your thoughts on the market with us."

He waited. One beat, two, three. He was no longer part of the hurricane, he was past the winds, *he* was the eye.

"Each of you seems afraid to confront the truth. The market is pure. It is nature. It is jungle. A struggle of good against evil. What it boils down to is—you can't take losing."

"If we're the losers, who are the winners?" asked Paul Shelby, the next youngest partner and Loring's only real friend in the firm.

"The people who made all the money that everyone else lost last week." He paused to savor the crystal clarity of his thoughts. "We all know it's out there. It's up to us to go out there and bring it back."

The puzzled looks did not surprise him. They were weak on concept, they needed specifics to act.

"Toward this purpose, I think communications stocks will be the first to turn around. They were hit hard on Thursday, but those stocks are now more undervalued than much of the rest of the market. They will rebound quickly."

He stood. "If you'll excuse me, I'll get to work. I want to get on the phone to my people and let them know what's happening. This is like a Christmas sale, and I don't want to miss out on the bargains."

○

The market opened stable. For the first hour of trading it held its own. Then around ten o'clock it started to move up slightly, and everyone in the office began to breathe a bit easier.

Loring's phone was quiet. He had executed all his trades for the moment, and used the lull to catch up on some financial reports. He opened one of the lower drawers of his desk. There, resting on top of the financial reports, was his sister Karen's letter.

He picked it up and looked at it carefully. How did it get there? He turned it over. It had been opened. Not by him, he was sure. If he had he would remember it. Then by someone else, but why? He took the letter out of the envelope and began to read it. It was written on blue notepaper with a small spray of gold flowers in the corner, and it covered some six or eight pages. It was a typical happy letter from a young woman about to be married. Why would anyone here want to tamper with it, he thought as he slipped the letter back into the envelope. Then he noticed the address. It had not been sent to the office. The envelope bore his home address.

Fear fluttered inside him. Something was wrong here. Suddenly the office no longer seemed friendly. He left his desk and went to the men's room. It was empty but he made a pretense of washing his hands in case anyone should come in . . . If the letter had come to the office it could have gone to the wrong mailbox. Simple as that. And whoever opened it would have realized the mistake and slipped it in his desk without calling undue attention to himself. But the home address put it in a very different light. Was someone at the office having his mail intercepted? Someone curious about how he developed his stock ideas?

He shook his head. "You give your ideas to whoever needs them. Nobody's tampering with your mail. You just blocked it out of your mind after you read it because you didn't want to go, and you knew there would be hard feelings over it. That's all."

He chuckled softly like a man who had just told a funny story on himself, and turned the water off. As he dried his hands he felt better. Today was going to be fine. Walking down the hall to the office he thought about the Caribbean. He could hardly wait. If he had ever needed a vacation it was now.

O

At 10:48 the market rally ended. Prices began to fall. Not at the rate of the previous Thursday and Friday, but by 11:15, not quite thirty minutes later, it was down over twenty-five points. If it kept on at that rate by closing it could be down as much as two or three hundred more points. The office began to hum with the tension.

Loring forgot about the letter. His phone began to ring almost continually. He reassured, cajoled, begged, wheedled and pleaded with client after client. Anything that would keep them from panicking and making the worst decisions of their lives.

Between calls he recognized what had happened. The money managers who he knew had precipitated the crisis in the first place were in a strong cash position, having gotten out early and high, and the short rally was due to them doing a little bargain hunting. Now they were finished for the day, and without them the market was collapsing again.

He closely watched the ups and downs of his morning picks. A little rally after breakfast, then it was over in time for lunch. Against the eroding market his communications stocks were performing well. Just before noon an announcement came over the wire hinting that the federal government was considering the licensing of several giant communication companies into the cable television business, and that they would be allowed to use the fiber optic capabilities of their existing telephone lines as the medium for bringing their product to market.

Loring laughed when he saw it. He knew there was no truth in it. It was just the government's way of warning the television networks that they should steer any blame for this crisis away from the administration, unless they wanted hell to pay, but the market responded positively to it as the one good piece of news of the hour.

Now was the crucial time. For the next few minutes— maybe a half-hour, maybe an hour—his stocks would start to move up, but he knew they wouldn't hold, probably not even past two o'clock. Like surfing, the trick was to get the most out of the wave and get off.

He punched in the symbol for Federal Telephone & Telegraph. It was up a quarter on bid, a half on asked. Which was two on the day for a stock selling in the nineties. The symbol for Armstrong Communications, a conglomerate that owned a number of independent southern telephone companies, was slightly behind, selling up three-quarters on the day, but the bid was up three-eighths and the asked was up three-quarters. If he went in now and split the bid and asked, settling on a half, he could likely get out at one and a quarter up on stock selling in the forties. A handsome profit.

The sound of the phone interrupted his calculations. "Loring Weatherby speaking," he said without taking his eyes off the screen.

His sister's voice, tearful. "Why do you hate me? What have I ever done to you to make you—?"

"I don't hate you, you know that," he said, trying to keep his eye on the screen.

"All you ever think about is yourself. I ask you to come to my wedding and you're too busy ..."

She was wrong. He had tried to explain before but she could never seem to understand. *You* were fine, but you were connected to *them*, too, and I hated that. I had to shut you out, too ...

"No, Karen, you know that ..." he said.

She paid no attention, and on the screen disaster struck. Someone had had the same idea and beat him to it, splitting the bid and asked on Armstrong Communications at a half. Now the three-quarters asked was a memory. He punched in at a half to sell too, but it wasn't accepted. He backed off to three-eighths, but still nothing.

And Karen still going on about "the most special day of my life, I wanted my family together, the four of us, you and me and mom and dad—"

"Don't call him that," he heard himself say as he watched the screen.

"Why do you always have to act like this? He's been a good father ever since daddy's death . . ."

Defending them, like always, he thought. On the screen new sales figures were showing. Not as good as he had hoped but something. No bid was showing. He punched in a quarter. It was not accepted.

Then he remembered Federal Telephone & Telegraph. In the turmoil of Karen's call and Armstrong Communications' decline he had forgotten it. He covered the mouthpiece of the phone and yelled to Paul to check Federal Telephone for him.

Paul yelled back that it was still up a half but the two points had gone. Everything was crumbling. He'd had two winners in hand and had missed the beat, he'd missed the rhythm. Karen's fault. He took his defeat, punched in even for the Armstrong. It was accepted, and for the day he got out up three-quarters, but he still felt he had failed. He punched in the symbol for Federal Telephone, made the sale order and took his lumps there, too. This time it was flat, no profit at all.

He turned from the screen. Karen was still there . . . "Loring, the other day I was going through my bureau and I found a picture that you drew. It was from the year daddy died. It was a picture of a picnic. Do you remember it?" He didn't answer. "You drew the three of us, you and me and mommy sitting on a blanket that looked like one of mom's tapestries. The sun was shining. Everyone was smiling. Wolf was with us and playing with his ball. Over in the corner you drew an ant carrying off a sandwich on his back and he was smiling. Do you remember?"

24

Loring kept still. He saw the picture in his mind, and it was enough.

"And do you remember how when you went to St. Ignatius, before we moved to Chicago, I would come and visit you every Thursday, and how Father Mike would let us go into Villanova? We would walk around looking in all the stores and have hamburgers . . ."

"I remember," he said into the mouthpiece, his voice raspy now.

"I want you at my wedding, I *need* you there . . ."

He knew it would be a mistake. No good would come of it. It would be a retreat to the past, to dredge up the moments he'd spent years trying to forget. But he could not bring himself to say no again, to hurt her. He said he would come but wouldn't stay with *them*, his mother and stepfather. At least she seemed appeased some and he escaped the phone.

When he looked up Milt Lewis was passing his desk. "You okay, Loring?"

"Yes, of course. Why?"

"Hey, you look sort of strung out. It's been a bad day all around. Take it easy."

The market continued downward until closing. There was nothing to do but watch. The final total showed fourteen hundred points down since the crash began.

○

Loring didn't stay for the cleanup. As he pulled on his Burberry he looked at his calendar. The only note that remained was for him to pick up a suit that was ready at Treadwell & Company.

Should he put it off? No, the time is now. Do it and get it over with.

As he headed for the elevator Paul Shelby joined him. They had an easy closeness without much socializing. It had to be that way. They were too different. As Paul, who bore a startling resemblance to Henry VIII, was fond of saying about their relationship, "Loring, you're Catholic with a capital C. I'm a Hedonist with a capital H, a man born with a silver spoon up my nose."

As they walked across the lobby Paul said, "Did you get the two points on Federal Telephone?"

Loring thought about lying and saying that he had. "No, I was in East Berlin."

"What? What the hell do you mean by that?"

Loring walked through the lobby's glass doors and into the afternoon coolness. He looked around. It was still cloudy but no rain. A block away at City Hall, scaffolding surrounded the statue of William Penn on top of the building. A citizen's group was trying to raise money to finish the project, and a young woman approached him, offering to sell him a button attesting to this fact. He gave her three dollars but did not take the button.

Paul shook his head as they walked west on Market. "You're a soft touch, fella ... Anyway, how come you missed the two points on Federal Telephone? That's not like you—and what's this East Berlin business?"

Loring paused at the corner. "The Communists had me. The points were in West Berlin. There was a wall between us and I couldn't get over it today ... It's a game. Sometimes I go over, sometimes I tunnel under, sometimes I go around, and sometimes I don't get through at all. That's when they find me hanging from the barbed wire."

Paul laughed. "God, isn't that just like you to turn the market into a damn Cold War video game. You're right, though. That's about as close as it comes to reality sometimes. But what put you on the other side of the wall today?"

26

They started up Sixteenth Street. Loring didn't want to talk about it but he knew Paul wouldn't leave it alone.

"My sister's wedding ... she called. We had some words and it messed up my timing on the sale."

"Hey, it's not the end of the world ... you at least got out even, didn't you? That puts—no pun intended—you ahead of the game."

Loring knew Paul didn't understand. He didn't understand the market. He didn't understand the jungle. What happened was very important. Time and timing. Timing was the pulsebeat between the "T" and "E" in time. When that got out of rhythm confusion reigned, and everyone lost.

He heard Paul say, "I take it you don't want to go to this wedding ..."

"You take it right," said Loring.

They stopped at the corner of Sixteenth and Chestnut. There wasn't much to look at there except a square block hole in the ground where another office tower was going up.

Paul looked at his watch. "How about a shooter before the after-work crowds hit?"

"I don't think so," said Loring. "I've got to pick up a suit at Treadwell, then I'm going to head home."

"That's crazy, by then it'll be rush hour and you know what a madhouse Kelly Drive is with the expressway torn up. Tell you what, I'll go with you to get your suit, and then we'll go over to Mace's Crossing for a couple of unwinders."

All Loring wanted to do was to pick up his suit and head home, traffic or no traffic, but he heard himself say yes.

As they turned onto Walnut Street Paul said, "None of my business, but why don't you want to go to your sister's wedding? Bad blood between you?"

Not that simple, thought Loring. "No, nothing like that, she just sprung it on me and I've got a boat chartered out of Barbados that week."

Paul let it go.

O

Treadwell & Company was in the same block with Nan Dus-kin. Before it became a haberdashery the building had housed a bank. That was in the 1870s. Since then it had guided "gentlemen" for over a century in the proper way to dress.

They marched through the first floor, heels clicking on the marble floors, to the suits in the rear of the store.

Claude, his regular salesman, looked up from The Wall Street *Journal*. "Mr. Weatherby, nice to see you. You're here to pick up your suit, I presume," he said. He pulled off his glasses and stuck them in his pocket. "I've had it ready since this morning. This way, please . . ."

As they crossed to the fitting room Claude continued, "It's been very quiet for us these past few days. The market crash, you know. Many of our regular clients have been busy . . ."

Loring grunted noncommittally. Treadwell & Company intimidated him. No matter what suit he was wearing when he was in the store, it always seemed wrong and shabby. No matter how neat his hair, it seemed to need a trim or a wash.

Claude held back the curtain as Loring and Paul entered the fitting room. Loring had been there many times and had never given the room a second thought. But today he stopped still and looked around with a growing sense of fear and new awareness . . . The muted lighting . . . the mahogany paneling . . . the heavy drapes . . . the hexagon of mirrors . . . suddenly he felt like this was the room behind the door in a funeral home. The one with "No Admittance" on it. The one where they dressed the bodies.

The suit could wait. He turned to go but Paul was there, smiling. Loring stopped, confused. Paul wouldn't be smiling if anything was wrong.

28

Paul was speaking to Claude. ". . . Just slip him into it and give him the stick of chewing gum or whatever and let us go. We want to get to Mace's Crossing while there's still room at the bar."

Claude managed a smile, but his eyes were cold. Which made Loring more uneasy. About what, he wasn't sure, but the feeling was there. More than unease. Fear . . . He looked around again. Take stock of your surroundings, know the enemy. Enemy? Strange word to pop into his head now. Guido, the tailor, was standing by. He had the coat to Loring's suit in his hand. The pants were draped over his arm. Around his neck dangled a tape measure. For some reason the sight of the tape measure made Loring apprehensive. Why?

He took the trousers and went to the dressing cubicle. "Just get it over with," he told himself.

He willed his mind blank as he returned for the tailor to check the fit. I'm not here, he thought, standing in front of the mirrors. Guido knelt in front of him to check the cuffs— and Loring saw a pinprick of light moving like a shooting star through darkness. He understood, though it was a hard-earned lesson. His mind was the universe, and he was moving to a place where he was safe. He felt Guido's hands move up his leg to check the inseam.

"No, no," he muttered as he steeled himself. The unwanted touch made him think of the morning and the phone call. His stepfather's voice . . . The suit was wrong, the wedding was wrong . . .

"I'm sorry. What was it you said?" asked Claude.

Loring only looked at him.

"You were just mumbling something but we didn't get it," Paul said, looking intently at him.

Loring felt himself blush. "Oh, that, I was just thinking about the market today. I guess I was doing it aloud. Sorry."

Paul smiled and turned to Claude. "That's my boy," he said.

"Always working, always thinking. Actually he's the brains of the outfit. Without him I'd never make a dime. Now slip that coat on him so we can get the hell out of here. I'm getting drier by the minute."

Loring needed a moment to regain control. He went back to the cubicle and took his time changing into his regular trousers. Alone was the best way, the only way. When you're alone there is no threat. All that's there is time. Spend it wisely, as St. Paul said. The thought comforted him.

He returned and took the jacket from Claude. Guido helped him on with it and he allowed himself to be led into the lighted area of mirrors.

He noticed the mirrors formed a hexagon around him. Three in front. Three in the rear. Six by three. Three sixes . . . the mark of the beast. *No*, he thought to himself as he stood on a small platform about ten inches higher than the floor around him. Forget about this business of sixes. Forget about everything. Just get your suit fitted and get out of here. Don't stop downstairs to pick out a tie. You can do that later. Just get the suit and then go have a drink with Paul. Relax. That's what you need. You need to relax.

He heard Paul's voice: "Looks good. Maybe you ought to take it to your sister's wedding." He applied a smile, looked at himself in the mirrors. Parts, angles, angles of parts winked back, but something was wrong.

The coat didn't fit. It was too large for him. He looked at the sleeves in the mirrors. Far too long. They needed to be taken up at least an inch and a half. Maybe it's the way I'm wearing it, he thought, as he shrugged his shoulders and tugged at the lapels to make sure it was correct.

He dropped his hands to his sides and looked in the mirrors to check the sleeve lengths again. If anything, his adjustments had made matters worse. Now the sleeves seemed to cover his hands, leaving only his fingers exposed. He adjusted the coat again. It seemed far too roomy.

"Claude, I think you've made a mistake," he said. "This isn't my coat. This one's too large." Not wanting to cause Claude undue embarrassment he added, "It's the same *kind* of suit. You probably picked up the one next to it."

Claude whipped out his glasses and checked the sales slip with Guido.

"No, Mr. Weatherby," he said, "the ticket is right. You're a forty-one long. This is the correct suit." He added, "The trousers were right too."

Loring tugged it together in front. He could see in the mirrors that there was enough excess material to turn it into a double-breasted. Any fool could see it. The suit was just too *large*.

"It doesn't fit," he said.

Claude sighed and looked at the sales slip again. It made Loring angry. He wanted to shout out, "Don't look at the paperwork, look at the suit," but he didn't. Instead he said, "I'd like to try another suit."

Claude was not pleased and managed to convey it. "*Certainly,* sir," and turned to go.

Guido was at the ready with the requested second suit. He and Claude exchanged looks as he slipped the coat off the hanger.

Loring stepped off the platform in the lighted mirror area and into the dimness to exchange the coats. Claude accepted the offending garment while Guide held the new one open for Loring to slip on. The way Guido tugged and smoothed reassured Loring that he had been right and the new coat was going to look much better.

But when he stepped up on the platform surrounded by the hexagon of mirrors he saw he was wrong. In his reflection the new coat was worse than the first. Not only did the sleeves appear to cover his hands, fingers and all, but the coat seemed to reach halfway to his knees.

"What's wrong with you people? This one's worse than the first ..."

Claude stepped to the edge of the platform. "Come here and let me check the sleeve tag."

While Claude checked the tag Loring caught Paul's eye with a look that seemed to say, "I don't understand what's happening." Paul smiled. "It looks fine to me. They both do." Claude agreed.

Loring stepped back to the center of the platform and looked at himself in the center mirror, although in doing so he saw his reflections bouncing back and forth from the other five mirrors. The coat was still too large. He looked like a teenager wearing something which belonged to his father—and then he understood. It all made sense.

It was the mirrors. It was like being in a hall of mirrors in a sideshow. What did they say about magic tricks ... all done with lights and mirrors? Only this time *he* was the light, and they were the audience and they were draining him, sucking him dry ... and he was shrinking ...

He saw his eyes widen in his reflection and tried to calm himself but could not. He felt like a prisoner, held there by bonds of force. Words from Revelation came to mind: "One woe is past; and behold there come two woes more hereafter ..."

His heart began to pound. He could hear it. Holy Michael, the Archangel, he began to pray, defend us in battle, be our safeguard against the wickedness and snares of ... He stopped. No more words would come.

Keeping his eyes on the mirrors he forced himself toward the edge of the platform, his heart pounding louder and louder

32

as he stepped carefully off it. He was wrong. To be alone was no protection. He knew better than that. Then where?

Guido slipped the coat off him, and Paul stepped up with his old jacket and Burberry. "Are you okay?" he said, the worry clear in his voice.

Good old Paul. He could have hugged him at that moment. Even though Paul didn't understand, at least he was there with his support. But no words would come.

Paul had reached out and touched his arm now. "Loring ..." His touch seemed to break the restraint and Loring was able to speak. But his heart was still pounding, and he had this awful fear—of death. So strong that it was like a smell, a noxious enveloping black cloud ...

The thought of being alone was terrifying. He forced calm into his voice as he said, "I'm not feeling too well, Paul. Would you go with me to my doctor's? He's just around the corner."

Paul nodded and helped him on with his coat.

That night the wolf came to Loring in a dream.

CHAPTER 2

THE WIPERS made a clicking sound as they swept back and forth across the windshield. The one on the driver's side was worn, leaving a crescent-shaped smear on the glass with each stroke, making it difficult to see.

Nate Mercanto looked at his watch, a Seiko, a gift from his brother. Three-thirty a.m. His shift was not even half over. Eight o'clock seemed a world away.

The radio in the blue-and-white was quiet. It had been that way since he had come on duty at midnight. The rain had helped create that. Not that there was ever much happening in the vastness of the Wissahickon section of Fairmount Park. It wasn't like Central Park in New York, he thought. No muggers, no purse snatchers, no street gangs. No action of any kind. Just peace and quiet. Which was why the men of the Park Squad were known throughout the department as "squirrel chasers."

Through the night he had used the slack time to do his *ki* exercises, the meditative part of his Aikido training. They were simple breathing and concentration exercises, Buddhist in origin, designed to give the fighting spirit a sense of inner peace. Done correctly they could make even a trip to the dentist bearable by sharpening and refocusing the practitioner's mental focus away from the unpleasantness at hand. In the quietness of the third shift they were the only way he could keep his mind off Rudy Gunther's death.

He pulled into the parking lot near the entrance to Forbidden Drive. The white limestone gravel of the lot reflected his headlights upward, making the rain shimmer like a curtain of Christmas tree icicles. Beyond that all was dark.

For a moment he relaxed his concentration, and that night came back to him, as always. It had happened near South Street while he was working undercover and had discovered Gunther breaking into a parked car. When he identified himself as a police officer Gunther attacked him, and during the fight Mercanto shot him. It sounded simple but it wasn't.

The officer who headed the investigation for Internal Affairs had recommended suspension. "A hothead," was what he had called Mercanto. The suspension was granted, and it was months until the FOP lawyers could plead his case before the American Arbitration Association. He was found blameless and restored to duty, but those intervening months had changed him. As the suspension time dragged by he had been forced to admit there was some truth in the allegations against him. He had not contained the situation, not called for backup.

36

He had violated procedures, let his ego rule his head. A man was dead, and he was at least in some measure to blame
.

He drove slowly, peering through the rain. There was no need to hurry. It was not until he was about halfway down the parking lot and beginning to make his turn that he saw the car—a black BMW. It was parked in the lower corner of the lot and was facing the Wissahickon Creek.

"Probably just some folks making out," he muttered to himself. He drove closer, stopping the blue-and-white a discreet distance away to give whomever was in the car a chance to rearrange any clothing, and get themselves together.

He got out, shoving his nightstick into the ring on his belt, and picked up the five-cell flashlight from the front seat. He looked back at the walkie-talkie lying on the seat. Should he bring it? No, he could handle it. If there was trouble, this time he would back away . . .

The chill of the rain felt good. Bracing. He pulled his cap lower on his face and switched on the flashlight. As he started toward the car he turned up the collar of his leather coat to keep the water from running down his neck.

The heavy double-breasted coat with its two rows of silver buttons always made him feel a little like a movie version of a Nazi U-boat commander. In fact, with his dark looks and perpetual five o'clock shadow, at thirty-three he looked more like the swarthy captain of a Greek freighter.

Under his feet he heard the crunch of the gravel as he closed the distance to the BMW. To his left he heard the sound of Wissahickon Creek bubbling over the rocks. He could not see it. It was about fifty yards lower than the parking lot and in darkness. Up ahead he sensed rather than saw the entrance to Forbidden Drive, a dirt lane cut through the forest that paralleled the creek and was closed to cars. The Park Squad patrolled its length on horseback from here in the Valley

37

Green section all the way to Lincoln Drive. To his right, about halfway up a steep and wooded hillside, he could make out the bare outlines of a white farmhouse that was a French restaurant called Maison Catherine. There was no light inside, it had long since closed for the night.

When he made the same rounds on the other two shifts Catherine Poydras, the owner, would often bring down coffee for him and they would chat for a few minutes. She had owned the restaurant for over twenty years and knew everything that went on in the Wissahickon section of Fairmount Park.

A noise to his left startled him. He turned and flashed his light, holding it well away from his body. The light showed a garbage can. It was full. On the ground, next to a rock, he saw an empty Miller Lite bottle. He shined the light back up the can and saw several others heaped loosely at the top. Probably it just rolled off from there and hit the rock—then he heard the second noise.

It also came from the area of the garbage can but further back. In the woods where his flashlight beam would not reach. It was not a single noise like the first but a series of shuffling, scuffling sounds, as if someone or something was headed down the hill toward the creek. As he walked toward the can he figured that it was probably nothing more than someone's dog all set to have a little sport with the can until he had been disturbed. A far cry from the kind of noises he'd known when he worked undercover.

He bent down and picked up the bottle, placing it back in the can and directed his light into the woods behind. The noise stopped. He moved the light from left to right but couldn't see anything. The darkness and woods were too thick.

"Go on home, boy. You've got no business out here in the rain on a night like this." From the way he said it, it wasn't clear whether he was talking to the dog he imagined out there in the darkness or to himself, but suddenly the rain didn't feel good to him anymore.

He wondered why the presence of the police car hadn't caused some activity in the BMW. Maybe asleep. He started back toward it.

About fifteen feet from the car his light picked up a dark shiny stain on the ground, roughly circular in shape and two inches in diameter. A couple of feet closer he saw another one, this one slightly larger, then a third still larger. Someone's car has a bad oil leak, he thought.

He raised his flashlight to play on the black BMW. Still no sign of movement inside its dark, rain-streaked windows. He moved to the right so he could come up on the driver's side from the rear, transferring the flashlight to his left hand as he did. His right hand touched the snap on his holster. As he did he thought of Rudy Gunther and pulled his hand back.

"Don't be so jittery," he muttered to himself.

He approached the car and shined his light at the back window but couldn't see through the window's dark tint. He let the light play up the side of the car. The other windows were similarly tinted. No wonder he didn't see any movement inside the car. He shook his head. Most cities had ordinances against windows tinted this dark. Why didn't Philly? He stepped closer and tapped the window on the driver's side with his flashlight.

"Hello in the car," he called out.

No response.

He thought for a moment about moving up and shining his light through the windshield, decided that was stupid, he'd be giving someone a clear head-and-chest shot.

"Hello in the car, this is the police," he called out and rapped the window harder with his flashlight.

Still nothing.

Mercanto shrugged his shoulders to relieve the tightness. It was a movement like a fighter would make. Maybe the car's empty, he thought, but who would park a BMW in a deserted spot like this? That was just asking for someone to steal it or trash it.

Taking a deep breath and letting it out slowly *ki* style, he transferred the flashlight back to his right hand and reached for the doorhandle with his left. If there was a problem behind those windows he was going to be in trouble with both hands occupied like that. Might as well be holding two bags of groceries.

"Let's get it over with," he muttered, and pulled the doorhandle. The door did not budge. Locked. He felt a sense of relief, and anger. Someone *did* leave it parked here. Stupid ass.

But to be sure he moved around the rear of the car to check the passenger side. Which was when he saw the door ajar.

It wasn't open much, maybe six or eight inches. He shone the light on the ground. Near the door were more stains.

He moved the light back to his left and reached for his gun. Presenting as little target as possible he reached out and shoved the door open wider with his foot. The inside light did not go on. He hesitated, then moved.

The smell registered almost before the sight. The air was thick with it. The metallic smell of blood. And fainter the smell of burned gunpowder. And fainter still the rose-ash smell of charred flesh.

His light illuminated the front seat. Behind the steering wheel was a man of about forty with a neatly trimmed mustache and no beard. His head was back against the headrest like he was sleeping, but his eyes were open, staring up at the roof.

Mercanto quickly shone the light into the backseat. Empty.

He flashed it again on the man. His hair was wet. Clearly visible in his right temple was a small black hole, and from it a line of blood had dripped down his cheek and neck, losing itself in his collar. Mercanto directed the light beyond the man's head and onto the window beside it. The window was clean. No blood or brains on it. Which meant no exit wound, making the gun most likely a small caliber pistol, probably a .22 since they were so common. Short and sweet. No muss, no fuss. Then he remembered the smell . . .

He started to move the beam down the man's body. He was wearing a raincoat and under that a blazer, navy-colored, and a gray-and-black-striped shirt, European in cut, and a dark, narrow tie.

It was then he saw the cause of the smell

The man's right hand was resting palm-up on the seat. Only there was no palm. The skin and the flesh had been torn away. Through the pool of congealing blood where the palm had been Mercanto could see the whites of the bones leading to the fingers.

Blood was spattered on the leg of the man's gray trousers. Mercanto let the light follow the splatters. The leg of the trousers appeared to be ripped near the inside mid-thigh, and more blood leading to a dark pool between his legs, staining both trouser legs.

Mercanto did not like his back to the dark. Pulling away from the car he played the light over the front seat and the floor mats below. There was no sign of the weapons. Neither the gun, nor whatever else had been used.

He felt shaky as he looked around at the darkness. In his decade of police work he had seen many dead bodies, but the shock of the mutilation had broken through his professional distance, making it personal.

The rain seemed colder. His beam showed the water was

already breaking up the stains on the gravel. He still had his gun in his hand, and he kept it there as he started back to the blue-and-white.

The radio snapped and squeaked, its reception and transmission made worse by the weather, as he called in, but the warmth of the car felt good, a shelter from what he had just seen. While he waited he tried to make some sense of this. He did not go back to the BMW, he might disturb some piece of evidence if he did. His first duty here was to secure the crime scene. Well, he had done that.

Most crimes, he knew, were simple. They showed a certain pattern, even orderliness, but this one . . . He thought of the body. Death was almost certainly caused by the gunshot wound. He stopped himself. Why did he think that? The mutilation of the hand and thigh would have involved arterial bleeding that could have caused death. He remembered the victim's face. It was strangely peaceful. No sign of the agony that would have shown itself if the mutilation had taken place before death. In fact, as Mercanto thought about it, there wasn't even a look of surprise. Damned odd.

So what was the sequence of events, as the manual liked to call it? The wound was in the right temple. The mutilation was on the right side. Which would indicate the killer was sitting in the passenger seat when it happened. No surprise on the victim's face might mean that he knew his killer, that he even drove his killer here. He shook his head. What about the kind of rage that caused the killer to mutilate the body so violently. It *must* have shown itself before the act. But the face of the dead man didn't lie. It was peaceful, no surprise, no agony.

He drummed his fingers on the rim of the steering wheel. All right, look at it from a different angle. The killer finished up, then what did he do? If he came with the victim how did he get away? A second car, an accomplice? Or did the killer meet him here? A romantic encounter, maybe? One that went off the rails? Sex crimes often involved mutilation. The anger there was so great.

Looking back at the BMW as a focus point, he began his *ki* breathing exercises again, but this time the relaxation did not come. As his mind cleared, instead of the usual sense of peace he felt a building sense of anxiety, of urgency. He turned in the seat to stare out the back window. Alarm bells seemed to be going off in his head. He opened the door quietly and got out.

He did not turn on the flashlight but tried to stare into the darkness. No sign of anyone. Of anything. But he still *felt* something. The rain blowing in his face. Don't be funny. All right, then, think, think back.

And turning back to the car he saw it. The door—he had left the door ajar on the blue-and-white. Not much, only a few inches, but just like the killer had done.

Had the killer felt this urgency? Was that what he was feeling? Not on *his* part but on the killer's. So ...? For a moment nothing came, his mind was a blank. He turned slowly away from the blue-and-white and stared toward the BMW.

The killer had come out of the car on the run, leaving the door open behind him. Why? He was afraid, but why? What scared someone mean enough, vicious enough, to do this kind of crime? Scared him enough to make him bolt and run. Discovery. Headlights. Car sounds, that's what probably did it.

But where did he go? How did he get away? His car maybe? No, he didn't think so, but for a moment he didn't know why. Then he remembered ...

"The stains on the gravel, of course. The killer was covered in blood," he said out loud.

He hurried back to where he had first seen the stains between the garbage can and the car. They were almost gone now from the rain. There were two more still visible but fading in the direction of the garbage can. As he neared the can he remembered the sound of the beer bottle that had startled him earlier. After that, the sounds in the woods. What if it wasn't a dog, what if it was the killer?

At the can he shone the light all around on the ground, half-hoping he was right, half-hoping he was wrong. Nothing caught his eye. He moved a few steps down the hill. Still nothing. A few more steps brought him to the woods between the parking lot and the Wissahickon Creek. Nothing A waste of time. Maybe it was the killer. Maybe not. All he could do was to put it in his report.

As he turned to start back up the hill he saw another stain. He bent and touched it to be sure. It was sticky. He shone the light on his fingertips, they were a dark red brown. He sniffed them. There was no oil smell. He took a deep breath and let it out slowly and softly as he reached for his gun.

The woods were not Mercanto's element. The advantage was with whomever was in there. He switched off the light and tried to be quiet, but the cracking, rustling sounds he made as he walked through the trees and underbrush sounded like cannons going off. Under his breath he said, "Sucker, you aren't any better at this than I am. I heard *you* all the way up the hill."

He paused every few feet and listened. He knew the killer had a gun. To use his flashlight would be to make himself a sitting duck. He was nervous, but he kept his mind on his "one point," the spiritual center of the body and the origin point of his *ki* strength. It let his other senses work without mental interference from him. Gradually he began to feel what was happening around him. The woods were not quiet. There was the rain, the wind and all sorts of rustling and bumping from it. Natural noises, noises that belonged there. Behind them, much fainter now, much further away, he heard noises that did not belong there. Those shuffling, scuffling noises. The same he had heard when he arrived.

He turned his head in the direction he thought they were coming from but he wasn't sure. Without sight, direction was tough to determine. Was the killer still on this side of the creek or had he crossed over? No . . . the killer still had to be on this side of the creek. The only place it was shallow enough to cross along this stretch was on the rocks at the falls near Devil's Pond further down. That was probably where he was hiding.

Up above he heard the sound of cars arriving and voices calling out to him. He called in reply to keep himself from being shot by accident and started up the hill, but before he did he looked in the direction of Devil's Pool and said quietly, "It's you and me, you and me . . ."

At the top of the hill he saw squad cars and the first unmarked car. The unmarked car would be Homicide, and he walked toward it now to make his report.

When he saw the balding detective who was giving orders, he stopped. He knew the man. His name was George Sloan, he was the head of Seven Squad, the man who had suspended him.

Sloan turned and saw Mercanto almost at the same time. In the shadows it was difficult to see the expression on his face, but his voice left little doubt.

"They said it was you," he said. "Make your report and get out of here."

Mercanto knew Sloan still hadn't forgiven him for causing

the department trouble, bringing an investigation down on their heads. But this was carrying it pretty damn far . . . "You don't have to worry, Lieutenant. "I only found this one. The killing happened before I got there."

CHAPTER 3

DR. MARGARET PRIEST walked her patient to the door. She was sorry to cut their session short, but Estelle's phone call earlier had ruined her concentration and it wouldn't be fair to the young woman to continue today.

They stopped at the door. "Traci, thank you for understanding," she said. "Next session I'll give you some extra time, I promise." She paused. "Even though it seems painful, I think we're making excellent progress."

She saw the young woman relax some. "I'm glad you think so . . . and I hope *you* get whatever it is straightened out."

○

Alone, Margaret began to pace. The office, normally comfortable to her with its soft grays and blues, now seemed cramped, confining.

Where did Estelle get off, calling her and saying those things. Didn't friendship mean anything to her? This was not a goddamn sofa she was talking about . . .

Margaret noticed her cigarette half-smoked in the ash tray. She picked it up. It was all so casual, the way Estelle had said it. So ladylike. "Adam is having an affair," she'd said. Friend to friend. Just thought you'd want to know. How come she left out "a word to the wise"? The bitch.

Margaret stubbed out her cigarette and tried to make some sense of her own feelings. She was angry . . . no, angry was too sterile a word for what she was feeling. *Pissed off* was more like it. Pissed off at Estelle. Ten years of marriage to Adam had shown he wasn't like that . . . mercurial, emotional, that was part of being married to a poet. But he was *not* unfaithful.

Trust counted. People couldn't be together twenty-four hours a day. She opened the vertical blinds behind her desk and stood looking out across Walnut and Chestnut to the Market Street skyscrapers extending the Penn Center complex almost to 30th Street Station. Plus, *if* he was going to have an affair, there was no way he would do it with a student. He had too much pride for that. How many times had she heard him deride other professors for just that sort of behavior, their lack of integrity . . .

There had to be a better explanation for it. She turned and looked at the phone on her desk. No, she wouldn't call him. He was having trouble with his work and she wouldn't bother him. No reason.

She turned back to the window. Her thoughts made her feel

small, even petty. Not her way ... but what *was* the way? She folded her arms. Okay, what would she tell a patient in a situation like this? Suffer in silence? No. To suppress feelings, not to rock the boat? That, she pontificated to herself, would be a classic neurotic conflict between feelings and social acceptability. Neuroses ... Freud said they reflected failure in the sex life. She allowed herself a half-smile. Well, that was one area of their marriage that had never been a problem. They'd always freely given to one another, no fear or restraint there. So why now?

"Why, indeed?" she said aloud as she made a decision.

Reassurance. Every marriage needs it. She picked up the phone to dial his office in the English department at Taft University.

He answered on the second ring. "Hi, darling," she said. His deep voice brightened and her doubts began to fade immediately. This wasn't the voice of a man having an affair. "I had a few minutes between patients and thought I'd give you a call. How's your day going?"

She heard a sigh. "Fine, until a student showed up for a lunch date I'd forgotten. She'd asked me to read some of her stuff and chattered on and *on* ... wrecked the morning, made me feel like you with a patient ..."

Margaret smiled. There it was, the logical explanation. Just like she told her patients ... better to confront fears. "Was her work any good?" Why did she ask that?

"Sophomoric. Teen-age ramblings about Tibet and being an ancient queen."

"Well, I hope the afternoon goes better for you. Which poem are you working on?"

"The one about the young boy seeing the rockets come in at the beginning of the Tet Offensive."

She knew the poems about his Vietnam time were like

reopening an old wound. She heard the bell in her reception room. "Darling, I've got to go, my next patient is here. Love you."

"See you tonight," he said.

As she hung up she felt much better. The tightness, the upset were gone. She would have no trouble concentrating now. She smoothed her skirt, adjusted the collar of her blouse and started for the door. This would be the new patient, the one who had called.

She had given no thought to what he might look like, but at first sight two things struck her. His blond, rather aristocratic handsomeness and the visible tension in him, evident even in the way he was sitting. "Mr. Weatherby, I'm Dr. Priest," delivered in her quietest most reassuring tone. . .

The sound of her voice startled Loring. He turned. Standing in the doorway was a tall woman in her late thirties. Her shoulder-length hair, highlighted by a touch of streaking, was light brown and hung loose, framing her face, which had a touch of roundness coming with her age. Her lips weren't too full and seemed more likely to smile than frown. Her nose was broad at the bridge, her brows full, her skin soft and pale. But her eyes . . . they hit him . . . large blue eyes, knowing intelligent eyes . . .

She turned and started back into her office. Loring got up and followed her. He could hear her walk, hear the rustle of nylons against her skirt. Since his call he'd thought a good deal about what she would look like. Nothing he'd imagined prepared him for . . . for her femininity that seemed overpowering . . .

He stood beside one of the chairs in front of her desk while she closed the door and then pulled the blinds, darkening the room to a soothing quietness.

She sat behind her desk. "Please sit down." He did, scarcely daring to breathe.

"Before we get into any specifics, let's talk for a few moments. Have you ever been to a therapist before?" He shook his head, no words came. Why was he so damn nervous? Before he'd come he'd made up his mind not to be that way. Had even allowed himself an extra measure or two of belladonna. She smiled now. A warm genuine smile. "I'm not the dentist," she said.

Her words, her tone relaxed him a little. "Then you aren't going to give me nitrous oxide," he said, trying to go along.

Another smile. "No, unfortunately it doesn't work for me. I'd like to ask you a few questions..." And she led him through name, address, birth date. When she asked about medications he lied about the tension-relieving belladonna and said "none." When she asked about his family he balked. That wasn't what he was here to talk about.

"They're in Chicago. This doesn't involve them."

She did not press it. "Let's talk a moment about what we try to do here. People come because they're dissatisfied with part of their life. Something's causing too much pressure. Depression, or stress—"

"With me it's *work*-related," Loring said quickly, wanting to dispel any thought she might have that he was crazy or something. "Things have just gotten out of hand and I need to talk it out. That's all. Stress, right."

She nodded. "If you decide to start therapy we'll talk about a lot of things. Sometimes it can be unpleasant, even painful. It helps some—to remember that when you come here you can say anything, tell me anything without worrying about it. It's all about opening up."

Loring looked away from her. He saw the couch along one

side of the room. In spite of her soft words it reminded him at that moment of the rack. "I'm not going to lie on that," he said, nodding toward it.

"That's okay."

He kept his eyes on it like it was an enemy to be watched. A vision came to mind of Dr. Priest standing at the head, a mask covering her soft features, her breasts bare, and he felt himself laugh before he could stop it.

"What's funny?" she asked, not looking toward the couch but keeping her eyes on him.

Her question embarrassed him. He couldn't tell her that. The idea that he'd thought of her like that . . . undressed . . . he couldn't bring himself to think the word "sexually" . . . made him feel ashamed. This was obviously a good woman, everything about her said it. Still, he really wanted to tell her what he was thinking . . .

After a moment he said, "I guess patients lie to you."

"Sometimes."

He was silent then: "There's something I'd like to ask you . . ."

She waited.

"When I called for the appointment you didn't seem surprised . . ."

"Your doctor told me about you. I was expecting your call."

Loring sat upright. Suddenly he thought of the letter he'd found in his desk, the one from his sister addressed to his home. This wasn't right. He felt his heart start to pound. "What did he say about me?" His voice seemed unnaturally high when he said it.

"He told me your name and that you might call."

His chest felt tight, the way it had felt in the fitting room. He wasn't sure he wanted to know the answer but he said, "What else?"

"That you'd been under a great deal of stress . . . you've just said it yourself."

Loring shook his head. "He shouldn't have, not without my permission. He had no right to go around talking about me . . ."

He looked about the room. Coming here was a mistake. There was no help here. Just get out and go home. No one can help you but yourself. Don't let her get you under her thumb like . . .

"Mr. Weatherby . . ." She repeated his name. "Let me explain something. I don't accept patients off the street. All of them come from referrals. Your doctor behaved in a routine manner. He didn't violate your confidence . . ."

Something in her tone, a note of . . . strength . . . combined with the softness made him look at her again. Their eyes met, and she held his gaze. Her eyes were not penetrating. The opposite. Their blueness reminded him of fine china and cloudless skies. Corny but true. When he looked at them he felt . . . felt she was offering him something. Maybe some relief? But what would she want in return? Strange thought, but even as he thought it he felt himself begin to relax again and the fear, tension, began to recede some. He saw that *she* saw this as she gave him another smile. Christopher Marlowe's words came to mind. "Was this the face that launched a thousand ships and burnt the topless towers of Ilium . . . ?" Come on, she's no Helen of Troy . . .

He said the only thing he could think to say. "Are you a Freudian?"

"Somewhat. Freud is the father of modern analysis, so we're all Freudian in that sense. But there are others whose work is important, too. I'm eclectic, I suppose."

Vague as it was, the answer seemed to satisfy him, to somehow go to his discomfort. At least he didn't want to leave.

53

"Do you ever fail with a patient? Not help them, I mean." Said more to draw her out and hear her voice than for her answer.

"Yes," she said. "Therapy involves many things. It's not foolproof, but I don't think that's something we should worry about now." She paused. "Do you mind if I smoke while we talk?"

"No, go ahead." She was asking him. Good. He watched her put the cigarette between her lips and light it.

"Would you like to talk about what's especially bothering you?" she asked.

He felt the edge return. "My doctor didn't tell you . . . ?"

"No," she said, and he breathed easier again. It was his story. He would tell it in his own way.

"Well . . . I don't know exactly how to begin." She made no effort to help him. He watched her draw on her cigarette and exhale the smoke. The delicacy of it sent a slight chill up his spine. He tried to collect his thoughts. "The incident . . . I guess you would call it . . . happened when I went to pick up a suit." He paused. She still didn't say anything. "When I went to try it on . . ." How could he tell this? More than anything he did not want to humiliate himself in front of this woman, have her laugh at him. Even though he'd only been with her a few moments something about the way she looked at him made her opinion of him important . . . "I mean, there's really not too much to it. It was the stress of the day, the stock market crash. I was edgy, a little nervous, and the suit was too big. I . . . I overreacted . . . I guess you'd call it."

She drew on her cigarette again and exhaled, the tendrils of smoke carrying a hint of her perfume to him.

"How did you overreact?"

He began slowly. Remembering was surprisingly painful. "The day had gone pretty badly from start to finish. I left the office early with another broker. We were going to have a drink. On the way we stopped at Treadwell's to pick up a suit that was ready for me. We went into the fitting room and I tried it on. When I stepped in front of the mirrors . . . they have mirrors that surround you . . . the suit seemed much too big. Not just a size or two. It was like they'd given me a suit for a basketball or football player. I thought they'd made a mistake, but when I complained they looked at me like I was nuts or something."

"You say it seemed too large. Was it?"

He looked around for something to fix on and saw her tap the ash of her cigarette into a large crystal ashtray on her desk. The blue-whiteness of the glass was cooling. "That's when things began to get out of hand. I insisted that they bring another suit. When I tried it on it was worse than the first." He knew how weird this all must sound. It did even to him and he had lived it. Nothing about it made sense. "Like I said, the day had gone badly . . . I didn't want to go for the drink, I just wanted to go home."

"Why did you accept?"

He looked at her. She knew the answer for God's sake. It was so ordinary. The only ordinary part of the whole thing. "I felt obligated to my friend. I guess . . . Anyway, Treadwell's always makes me uncomfortable. It's so . . . stiff."

"Stiff . . . is that the best word to describe it?"

Her question angered him. Why was she picking this way at what he was telling her? It made him want to shake her, upset her cool detachment, make her feel what he was feeling . . . "No, 'fartsy' is a better word." She didn't react. "It's one of those places you almost have to shop at if you're in my business . . . The thing that bothers me most about it is the fitting room. Having to stand there while they adjust you and touch you, it makes my skin crawl. It makes me feel like

... I don't know," he said, not wanting even to think about how he felt violated whenever someone even touched him.

"Do you always feel this way when you go there, or was it something that made this particular time different?"

He watched her put her cigarette to her lips. There was a beauty to her actions ... at the same time they were almost a torment for him. She knew. His doctor *must* have told her. Why was she doing this to him? Another base thought came to mind, of them alone together—he pushed it back, didn't want to think of her that way. The thought of doing it to another person was repulsive ... Concentrate, he ordered himself. If you don't finish now you'll never be able to ... "I never like to be touched, I admit it. But this time was worse, much worse. There was something there ... something in the air ... I can't describe it. All I remember is that when I tried on the second suit my heart started to race and I knew ... well, I didn't know, but I *thought* I was ... this sounds so crazy ... I thought I was shrinking. That's when I left and went to my doctor."

"Has anything like this happened to you since?" Her face showed no reaction to what he had just said, and that infuriated him. She was stripping him, laughing to herself. A tease, like girls his classmates had talked about long ago... Only this was worse. They just teased with the flesh. She teased with something deeper ...

There was more but he wouldn't tell her. She'd laughed enough. She didn't need to know how he'd felt afterward, or how he woke up in his leather chair not knowing how the hell he'd gotten there. Wondering how he'd gotten from his bed to there. Or about the dreams ...

When he didn't answer she said, "You mentioned that your day had been bad from start to finish. What made it bad?"

Hearing her voice, he felt alone, more alone than in a long time. He didn't like the feeling. Sitting across from her he had felt a closeness, now it was gone. There was no future in answering. He already knew that. Still, there was the moment, maybe that would be enough . . .

He wet his lips with the tip of his tongue. "My sister called . . . to invite me to her wedding, and my mother and her . . . husband were on the extension."

The memory of the conversation made his stomach knot. The pain he felt was the drawing kind, like thin lines of wire coming out weblike, reeling him in, wanting to bow his back and fold him like an old pocketknife. He pushed against the chair to keep himself straight.

"Your mother's husband is not your father . . . ?"

"No," he said, trying to will away the pain. "My father died when I was young . . . in an accident. My mother married his business partner . . . afterward."

She stubbed out her cigarette. She'd taken him far enough for now. Reliving the episode had made him afraid again, and it was clear he was emotionally exhausted. So, she realized, was she. But they'd been good together, she felt. They had chemistry. His problem was an interesting one. He'd fought, held back, but had also revealed. To get at the source would take time and work, but she believed she could at least help him. It was too early to tell for sure, but the episode in the store seemed linked somehow to the phone call and his family. Maybe his sister, maybe his mother's remarriage, maybe marriage period. Time would tell, if he gave her the chance and she was good enough . . .

"I think we've covered enough ground for our first session." Her words pleased and displeased him. He felt like he was all in pieces, but he knew he also wanted to stay, to look at her beauty, *be* with her. It was a new sensation.

"What do I call you?" he heard himself say. "I'm not too comfortable calling you Dr. Priest."

She sat, weighing whether it was wise to risk closeness with a patient so new. But she also felt he needed to leave with something, some small triumph. "My given name is Margaret."

He stood up to go. As he walked toward the door he turned and stopped. "Wasn't Margaret the name of the woman Faust sold his soul for . . . ?"

"I'm sure I don't know," she said. And *she* felt a chill.

CHAPTER 4

NATE MERCANTO pulled his old Camaro to the curb and stopped in front of the warehouse on American Street near Third and Spring Garden. Huddled in the passenger seat, an Irish walking-hat covering his now total baldness, was his brother Frank. This was the day each week Mercanto hated the most.

As he reached for the door handle his brother raised a hand to stop him. "You stay. I'm fine. Besides, you have to get to the stationhouse or you'll be late for your shift."

Mercanto wanted to protest, but Frank was right. The captain had ordered him to report at four, and it was already a quarter past three. Still, he didn't like being forced to choose, or even hurry, not with Frank so sick.

Frank fumbled with the door handle and pushed it open. It was a scene they had played weekly for the past three months as they made the trip home from the hospital, only each week the door seemed to get heavier. Frank slowly swung his feet out and looked back. "Call me." There was pain in his face when he said it. The man who spoke bore little resemblance to the older brother Mercanto had idolized all his life—the one in the picture in his wallet of the two of them on the fishing boat out of Atlantic City laughing, carefree, but that's how he tried to think of him.

"You know I will, and I'll stop by during the week," Mercanto said. He hadn't mentioned finding the body. Frank already had enough on his mind. He watched as his brother started toward the warehouse.

The first floor housed a garage specializing in repairs to foreign cars: Jags, Porsches, Ferraris, Mercedes. The second floor was Frank's living quarters and studio where for years he'd tried so hard to get his thoughts and feelings on canvas.

The garage was closed now, had been since the cancer and treatments had weakened him too much to work. He could still drive and care for himself, but not on the day each week when he went for chemotherapy; the treatment made him too sick. At the sound of the car door a young black man dressed in work clothes and wearing a cap advertising Colt .45 malt liquor appeared from inside and hurried up to help.

Mercanto watched them step-by-step as they started up the stairs to the second floor, put the Camaro in gear and started for the stationhouse in lousy spirits. Frank was all the family he had left.

60

○

The Park Squad's headquarters was on Henry Avenue near the Valley Green section. In the twilight, as Mercanto pulled into the parking lot, it looked like a small-town city hall with its stone front, double glass doors and a bit of green on either side of the walk. He parked and started in to change into uniform.

The desk sergeant looked up as he came in. "The captain wants to see you."

Mercanto nodded and walked toward the rear of the first floor. The building had two floors and a basement, the first was reception and administration, the second was lockers, squad room and a small room with a microwave, Mr. Coffee, and three vending machines, designated on the fire map of the building as the "Cafeteria." The holding cells and interrogation rooms were in the basement.

He stopped in front of a frosted glass door and knocked. Behind the desk was Captain Mabel Zinkowsky, a black woman of about fifty. She had joined the force during the Rizzo years as part of an affirmative action program, but it wasn't her sex or her race that had brought her to a captaincy, it was the desire to carry on for her patrolman-husband, killed in the line of duty. Now, because of her age and the way the force was changing, all that was behind her and what was left for her, like for him, was the Park Squad. Unlike him she never let her disappointments show.

Seated in front of her desk was Detective George Sloan from homicide. She motioned to the empty chair beside him. "Sit down, officer."

"What now?" Mercanto had given them everything in his report. As far as he was concerned his business with Sloan was finished.

"You two know each other," the captain said. Both nodded, neither looked at the other. If the captain noticed the hostility between them she did not acknowledge it. In her blunt way she came right to the point. "George, I'm glad you asked for this meeting because it gives me a chance to let everybody know my decision. I'm assigning Officer Mercanto to work with you until we solve the murder in the park."

Mercanto couldn't believe it. It could be a big step toward putting his career back together. On the other hand it meant working with George Sloan.

"Over my dead body," Sloan said. "Homicide rules the roost on murder cases. When I asked for help on this case I didn't mean *him*."

"George, you're wrong on this one. The Gunther situation was unfortunate, but it doesn't alter the fact that Officer Mercanto is a good cop—"

"He's not going to work on this case—"

"Don't get premenstrual on me, George. I've been trying to be nice and act like everyone's mama lately, so don't force me to remind you that captains still outrank lieutenants—and while you are in charge of the case, since it happened in my precinct I can make any administrative decisions I like. What I've decided is to assign Officer Mercanto to the case."

"I can go over your head."

"I don't think so. You're a good cop, too."

Sloan chewed on it for a moment, nodded. Nothing else to do . . .

Mercanto settled back in his chair. The thought of doing some real police work for a change felt good. The closest he'd come lately was investigating some missing rabbits from a pen behind a house on the West Mt. Airy side of the Wissahickon and keeping an eye out for something, probably a stray dog that had killed some ducks near Devil's Pool.

"You understand he's going to have to carry the ball a lot," Sloan said. "Our people are jammed up with that house of death in North Philly. This morning the mayor gave it top priority, and we can't be two places at once."

"He can handle it. He has more experience in plainclothes than anyone in my command. That's why I picked him," the captain said. She took off her bifocals and rubbed the bridge of her nose. "I can appreciate the mayor's priorities but I have mine, too . . . the Valley Green section is a nice little cabbage patch and I don't want it dirtied up. I want the son of a bitch who did this. I want this murder solved . . ."

Mercanto wanted to say amen.

Sloan got down to business. "Here's what we have. The victim's name was Stanley Hightower . . ."

Mercanto frowned. The name meant something to him but he couldn't place it until Sloan said, "He was a Center City optometrist. There was a piece about him in the Sunday paper. He's the guy near Rittenhouse Square who makes the glasses for all the stars . . ."

"You remember?" the captain said.

Mercanto nodded. "Yeah, I saw the piece. He makes stuff like prescription diving-masks and ski-goggles. I think it said he even replaced the windshield in a Porsche with prescription glass for some Hollywood hotshot who didn't want to be seen wearing glasses."

Sloan took it up again. "He's divorced and lived in a condo on Washington Square. Before that he was married to a French clothes designer . . . Dominique's her name."

Mercanto let out a soft whistle. Stanley Hightower was a high-profile citizen. That's why Sloan was willing to let him in on it. Even short-handed this was a case that had to be solved.

Sloan consulted a file in his lap. "The Medical Examiner's

report is in. Death was caused by one shot to the right temple from a .22 caliber gun. The bullet was a hollow point. The impact splattered it too much for it to be of any use ballistically—"

"A pro's gun . . ." Mercanto said.

"Maybe. Death occurred between three and three-thirty a.m. Just before you found the body," Sloan said, glancing in Mercanto's direction.

"What about the mutilation, his hand?" Mercanto asked.

"According to the M.E. that happened after death. He said he could tell by the destruction of the arteries and the coagulation of the blood."

Mercanto nodded, remembering the peaceful look on the victim's face. That's what he'd thought, too. "How was it done?"

"The M.E. identified bite marks on the hand . . . *human* bite marks . . ."

"Human?" There was shock in the captain's voice.

"Yes," said Sloan, keeping it clinical as he could. "The M.E. couldn't make a cast of them because of the destruction to the hand, but he says they were definitely human bites."

Nobody said anything, and after a moment Sloan continued. "Robbery was the apparent motive. The victim's wallet was gone. We made the identification through motor vehicles."

"No, definitely not robbery," the captain said. "Nobody does something like *this* for a robbery. There's a helluva lot more here than that. Any ideas?"

Sloan closed the file. "We've some possibilities. The simplest first—it *could* have been a robbery, a sex-related one. He was divorced. Maybe he picked up the wrong person, a prostitute, took her out there to park and she killed him."

The captain nodded. "It's true, the sex-related ones are always the most gruesome. What do you think, Mercanto?"

"I wouldn't rule it out, still with AIDS everywhere why

would a guy like him risk going to a prostitute? He'd have no trouble getting girls. Of course he could have been kinky, or maybe it wasn't a prostitute. Maybe it was just someone he picked up. Or maybe he was gay and picked up a basher. Is there anything in the M.E.'s report about it?"

"They ran an AIDS test and he was clean. There were no traces of semen, so he hadn't come before he died, which doesn't prove anything one way or the other. If it was like we just said, it would have happened before he had a chance to." Sloan paused. "Another possibility is his ex-wife. Maybe she did it, maybe she hired it done, or had a boyfriend do it and was there for it. Next to sex crimes, domestic murders are the roughest." He paused again. "When she came to identify the body we showed her everything, including the mutilation, and she didn't bat an eyelash."

"She either hated him, or that's one tough woman," said the captain.

Nobody disputed it. "Our third possibility is drugs. The M.E. found traces of cocaine in Hightower's body. We have the pro-type hit. Maybe he was a white-collar dealer who got out of line, and his wallet was taken to confirm the hit. The mutilation could have been to put the fear of God into others involved, or it may even have been part of some damn ritual. He wouldn't be the first. You know how the Jamaicans have been raising hell around town lately. Remember what they did to those kids—"

"That was in the section of the park near the zoo. We haven't had that problem up here," the captain said quickly.

"There's always a first time . . ."

Mercanto had to agree with him. Drugs were big business, crossed all ethnic and social lines, and the Jamaicans had been responsible for a number of recent murders, each more sensational than the last.

"Well, that's what we have so far," Sloan said. "We released Hightower's death to the newspapers this morning. There's no way we could keep it out. But we held back the mutilation angle."

"Good, that's not the sort of thing we want the public to hear about," the captain said.

Sloan turned to Mercanto. "The ball, like they say, is in your court now. You think you can handle it?"

Mercanto just looked at him.

"Do you have any thoughts on it? Something we might have missed. After all, you found the body," the captain said.

He looked at her, then at Sloan. "You left out one possibility."

"What's that?" Sloan said.

"That it was a random killing, and we have a psycho loose in the park."

CHAPTER 5

L ORING WEATHERBY ignored the view from his corner
table at Moselle's. Outside, students from Taft and Penn,
bundled against the chill in the best from Goldberg's and Eddie
Bauer, bustled up and down the University City section of
Walnut Street, but he did not give them a second glance. He
sat staring at the piece of paper he was holding.

A waiter appeared, menu in hand, and stood in front of his
table. Loring looked up. "No, I'm waiting for someone," he said.
As the waiter turned to go Loring stopped him. "On second
thought, would you bring a Bombay martini on the rocks with
a twist?"

The waiter nodded and for a moment Loring felt compelled to explain himself. To say it was after two. That he wasn't going back to the office. That the stock market had already done all the damage it could to him for one more day.

He looked back at the paper in his hand. On it was written the name Margaret Priest and two phone numbers. Her office number and her home, the latter of which he had gotten from the phone book, although it was listed as "M. Priest." In one corner of the paper was written the word "Margaret" three times. It didn't look like his handwriting, but he knew he must have done it, doodling absent-mindedly as he sometimes did.

A busboy filled two water glasses and brought bread. As Loring watched him he could hear the words she had spoken to him at the close of their first session . . . "My given name is Margaret . . ." Now she called him by his given name, too. At first she had been reluctant, but when she saw that it was important to him she gave in. Good . . .

He looked around and wondered what he was doing here. The thought of another business lunch sent his stomach into a spasm of pain. He breathed deeply and pressed his diaphragm down, willing the pain to go away. Sometimes that helped. This time it didn't, but it didn't frighten him either. The pain was only tension, the doctor said. However, if he didn't do something for it he knew he would not be able to eat. He reached into his jacket pocket and brought out a small bottle with a medicine dropper. The label read: "Belladonna, ten drops in water, three times per day." He never traveled without it. Deadly nightshade, the only thing that would relieve the pain, and later the only thing that would bring sleep. He reached for his water and counted the drops of the brownish liquid, barely stopping at twenty-five.

Good for what ails you, he thought, as he raised the glass to his lips, tasting the familiar bitter metallic taste. Almost instantly he felt his stomach begin to relax, and with it a sense

68

of peace began to return. A peace he knew would be short-lived, but one which he was thankfully able to give himself five or six times a day, sometimes more.

He picked up the paper and looked at it again. To hear her voice would make things better, and the warmth of the belladonna seemed to ease the way. "Why not?" he said half-aloud, and pushed back his chair.

The phone was located in the hallway leading to the rest-rooms. Loring picked up the receiver, deposited a coin and dialed. As he heard the phone begin to ring at the other end, a man entered the hallway and began to drop coins into the cigarette machine beside the phone. Loring wanted to hang up. This was one call he did not want anyone to overhear, but a voice answered before he could.

It was her voice. In his annoyance he didn't catch what she said, but he did hear her soft, sure tone.

The man beside him seemed to be having trouble with the cigarette machine. Loring glanced at him out of the corner of his eye . . .

He heard her voice again and wanted to say, "Hello, Margaret, it's me. I just called to say hello." Of course he didn't, it would be too stupid. Instead he listened, silent, until she hung up.

As he walked back to his table he thought of her . . . the rustle of her clothes when she walked, her hair over her shoulders, the blueness of her eyes, yes, and the way she held her cigarette . . .

At his table he was startled to find his lunch date had arrived.

He pushed his blond hair back on his forehead, took a deep breath.

She stood up and held out her hand. "Hello, I'm Erin Fraser. You're Loring Weatherby."

"Yes, right." Her grip was strong, solid yet feminine.

69

He sat down across from her, forcing himself to smile. She was early, he was sure without looking at his watch. A time slave, he thought with a sudden combination of anger and weariness. Right now he needed to be alone for a few minutes. He could feel his stomach beginning to tighten again. Why couldn't she have been late?

"Is anything wrong?" he heard her ask.

Her words jerked him back to the present. He didn't want her to see his displeasure . . . "I was just thinking how times change. That you stood up when I approached the table. Usually it's the other way around. Or at least used to be."

As soon as he said it he knew it was all wrong. Unnecessary. There was more than a hint of coldness in her reply. "I open car doors and light cigarettes for men, too. Does that bother you?"

"No . . . well, yes it does . . . sometimes," he said, unsure of the right answer. For him, this was the hardest part of the investment business. Something he could do but didn't like. Deal with the clients and potential clients face to face. Except for a very few, namely the ones he hoped to go sailing with, he almost never did it, choosing instead to let the profits he generated speak for him.

"Why's that?" she asked.

He answered truthfully. "Because then I don't know how to treat you. It makes something simple like helping you on with your coat or holding your chair seem like . . . well, taking personal liberties with you."

"Sometimes it is," she said, "but it's an interesting question," she added, softening some.

He sat there trying to figure out how he could end this lunch as quickly as possible, potential client or not. He was already feeling the first touches of panic begin to return. The belladonna wasn't doing its job. What he needed was to go home and shut the door on the world, the noise, the people, the aggravation . . . He needed peace, time to think.

Erin shook her head. "I'm sorry," she said, feeling the awkwardness of the moment. "I didn't mean to sound strident. Something that happened this morning got to me, I guess . . ."

"I'm sorry, too," he heard himself say. "Let's start over. How about a drink and then you tell me what happened."

"I'd like that."

When the waiter came and went, Loring sat quietly looking at her. Erin Fraser was around thirty and very pretty. Her dark hair was pulled back and tied, showing off the leanness of her face; long bangs kept the style from being too severe. Her tortoise-shell schoolboy glasses combined with her large round white rhinestone earrings to give her a look of seriousness and sophistication. She was wearing a white suit that was almost a pale gray. The jacket was loose, padded shoulders and notched lapels. Under the jacket was a navy pullover, and she wore a multi-colored scarf looped around her neck and tied in front.

"You know I'm the curator for the upcoming Caribbean exhibit at Taft University's Braddon Museum . . ."

"Yes, Wiladene told me," he said, a mental picture coming to mind of the wife of Cornell Jenkins, star forward for the Sixers and one of his best clients. Wiladene had set up the lunch, telling him in the process about Erin and the large amount of money she had recently inherited from her aunt that she wanted to invest.

"Wiladene's a volunteer at the museum, along with a thousand other charities," Erin said. "That's how we became friends. This is a big exhibit, set to run for two years with over five thousand items . . ." She stopped herself. "I'm not really telling this very well. What I'm trying to say is that there are a lot of people involved in this exhibit, but there are a couple of Taft students, roommates who are like younger sisters to me. This morning I found that one of them is having an affair with a married man. A professor in his forties, a poet," she added with a grimace.

"And you disapprove," said Loring, suddenly wary. What was she trying to say, why tell him, a stranger, at lunch?

"Yes, I disapprove. I mean I'm as liberal as the next person. Nothing wrong with sex. I believe people have to learn about life and love and so forth. But all this man is going to do is use her and toss her away. Not fair. She should learn from someone her own age, that way she'll be less likely to get hurt."

"Sex is like that . . . hurtful, even tragic . . ." he heard himself say. God, he hadn't intended to say *that*.

Erin stared at him. "What an odd thing for a man to say. Do you really think that?"

How could he answer her when he couldn't even begin to answer himself . . . "Sorry," he said, "just thinking aloud about a friend . . . tell me about being an anthropologist."

The waiter came back with her drink and menus, but Erin paid little attention. She was impressed by the way her story had seemed to affect this man. He wasn't at all what she'd expected. With a name like Loring Weatherby she had come braced for Mr. Cool, probably pompous. He was neither. With his good looks he could have fitted the stereotype . . . everything was there for it. But his eyes gave him away. A softness there. A vulnerability? Whatever, she felt like reaching across and touching his hand, to reassure him. Strange role reversal going on . . .

"There's really not much to tell," she said. "Shamanism is my specialty. I've studied it in Jamaica and Haiti."

"Voodoo?" he said, glad for a change. Something abstract to talk about.

"Sort of, but most Caribbean religions are a mixture of African religions with an overlay of Christianity, especially Catholicism," she said, pleased with his interest.

Loring reached for his drink and noticed that he felt no chill in his fingertips as he picked it up. This was something that had been happening lately. The sensation of touch seemed diminished, but of course he'd had problems with his hands ever since that bicycle accident when he was twelve and had broken both collarbones . . .

He set his glass down untasted and put his hand under the table to flex his fingers a few times. It seemed to help. He rubbed his fingertips along his trousers, trying to feel the texture and scratch of the wool.

He picked up his drink, sipped but tasted none of the familiar juniperberry taste of the gin, only a vague taste of alcohol and lemon. He shook his head. The waiter must have brought him a vodka martini by mistake.

He looked across at Erin, sitting quietly, looking at him with a slight smile on her face. Between her thumb and forefinger she was rolling the swizzle stick from her drink. Why was she doing that? Her smile made him feel like he was under a microscope. He looked at his watch. "I have to get back to the office soon, do you mind if we order?"

"No, of course not," Erin said, puzzled at his abrupt change. Was she boring him? He seemed a nice man, she didn't want that.

As they studied their menus his eyes automatically went to the filet mignon with tarragon sauce. By nature he was a beef eater and it was his favorite item on the menu. But today he passed over it.

Since the episode in the fitting room he had found himself unable to eat meat. In fact, every time he tried he became violently sick. One of the many strange unexplained things happening to him lately, and that he tried to write off to tension. After all, with his stomach ...

He scanned the menu for alternatives. For some reason the descriptions of the food made no sense. He tried to visualize the food, ingredient by ingredient, found it all too complex, the shapes, the colors ... Finally his eye stopped on something that did make sense—potato and leek soup. That he felt he could eat.

After the waiter had gone Erin said, "Do you really think this is a good time to invest in the stock market?"

"If you have courage," he replied, watching her closely. She was still twirling the sizzle stick between her thumb and forefinger. He wondered why she had put the question that way. Time wasn't a factor. Time wasn't going to run out. Not until you were dead.

"What would you recommend that I invest in?"

"There are many things ..." he said, feeling strangely unsure of his judgment. "Blue chips, growth stocks, bonds, funds, commodities ..."

"Tell me your favorites."

She was smiling. Why?

"Right now I'm fond of a Japanese company. An electronics firm," he said slowly, choosing his words carefully.

"What do they do?"

"The usual—televisions, stereos, tape recorders, office machines. They also have a computer department ..."

"Maybe I'm being naive, correct me if I'm wrong, but they sound like a lot of other companies. I mean, doesn't everyone make those things?"

The waiter returned with their orders. Loring turned his attention to his soup to give himself a moment to decide how much to tell her. As he brought the first spoonful to his lips he was assaulted by a smell so putrid he almost gagged. He tried not to show his surprise. This just didn't happen, not in one of his favorite restaurants. A bad dish never came out of their kitchen. He stared down. The soup looked innocent enough, creamy white with flecks of green that should have been parsley.

He lowered his spoon and began to talk to cover his feelings. "What you say is true, very perceptive. But I think there's going to be a takeover attempt."

"Could you explain that a little more?"

. . . Maybe I'm imagining again, there's nothing wrong with the soup. He lifted a fresh spoonful to his lips. Again the awful smell, and this time he could identify it. It was the smell of rotten, decaying meat. They must have used a stock as a base in the soup and the stock was obviously spoiled. That had to be it . . .

"Is there something wrong with your soup?" he heard her say.

Don't make a fuss, not now. He pushed the soup away and reached in his pocket for the belladonna bottle.

"No, no, sorry, it's not the soup, it's me, I'm afraid. The old gut, goes with the territory, brokerage business . . . sorry . . ." He counted the droplets as he squeezed the medicine dropper into a glass of water. "Like I said, it's an occupational hazard. Nervous stomach, most brokers have it. The strain of dealing with the market . . ."

A good way to handle it, he decided. But on the way out he would have a quiet word with the manager, be sure they threw out the soup before some less understanding customer tried it and suffered the consequences . . .

"As I was saying, I think there's going to be a takeover attempt by another company—a credit-card company. One of the real giants. I don't know if you're aware of it, but a couple of the international credit-card companies are so strong that they've virtually created a private, world-wide currency."

"Really? That seems incredible—"

"Are you familiar with the Japanese word *honko*? It's a small seal issued to each citizen, and it's used instead of a signature on many official documents."

"Like a Chinese *chop*?"

"I guess . . . Anyway, what this company is doing is researching something that will replace the signature, the *honko* or *chop*, and ultimately maybe even currency. It's a magnetic implant with a code similar to the bar code, the ISBN number you see on packages. When it's perfected it will be implanted under the skin on a person's hand at birth and all he'll have to do is pass his hand by a scanner to record whatever his activity. This isn't public knowledge, which is why I'm pretty excited about it."

"It all sounds very futuristic to me," she said. "Almost ominous, something like the mark of the beast. Isn't that what they used to say?"

Her choice of words startled him, to put it mildly.

CHAPTER 6

MERCANTO PICKED up the keys to Stanley Hightower's apartment from police headquarters on Race and drove to nearby Washington Square. From the file he could see that homicide had not had a chance to go over it yet.

As he drove he thought about how good it felt to be back in plainclothes again. He parked in front of the Athenaeum and walked across the square to the highrise on the South Side near the Hopkinson House. The desk clerk directed him to the thirtieth floor.

He stopped in front of the door and took a deep breath. Even though he had plenty of experience working undercover this was the first time he had ever investigated a murder, and a great deal was riding on it, especially for him. He had no illusions about Sloan. One false step, one missed clue and Detective Sloan would be on his back.

He put the key in the lock and turned it. The door came open with a soft click. For a moment he wanted to call out, announce himself, but he felt foolish. No one, of course, was there. He pushed the door and it swung back, coming to rest against the stop. Down the hall a woman with a load of dry cleaning got off the elevator. Somehow her presence made him feel like an invader. He moved inside and closed the door behind him.

A few steps brought him from the foyer to the living room, which had floor to ceiling windows on two sides. One side faced south, the other east toward the Delaware River. The floors were a blue black tile in four-foot squares whose mirrorlike shine reflected the furniture on it and the sky and buildings outside, giving everything a ballroom's shadow-depth. In the center was a black-and-beige Oriental rug with a busy design that resembled a maze of flowers and plants. Sofa and chairs were like he imagined people in California would have, snow white in color. At each end of the sofa was a large pillow covered in the same fabric. Facing them were two uncomfortable looking chairs with dark wood frames and seat cushions. The coffee table was a polished dark square with books and magazines underneath. In the east windows was a ficus tree . . . he recognized it from the time he had dated a woman who owned a plant store. A black grand piano filled most of the southern windows. The room, in a word, looked like something out of a glossy magazine.

He took off his trenchcoat and began to walk through the

apartment. The blue black tile floors were throughout. The kitchen was small, functional, with white cabinets and counters. He opened the refrigerator. On the top shelf was Beck's beer and Perrier. On the bottom several bottles of white wine. Between were appetizers like cheese, pâté, even caviar. He picked up the caviar and took off the top. The fish eggs were a golden translucence, not black or red like the ones he occasionally bought himself for a treat. He put the tip of his finger to them and touched it to his tongue.

"Stanley Hightower, you sure knew how to live," he said, as he put the caviar back in the refrigerator.

The dining room was as spectacular as the living room, with a chandelier and a round table for six made of the same blue black tile as the floor. The bedroom was in white too, a sofa against one window and a king-size bed. The second bedroom looked like an office. The tour did not give him much of a feeling for the man who had lived there. The apartment was too impersonal, too professionally decorated for that. It was like a mask. "Stanley, who are you? Were you?"

He went back to the kitchen and opened the cabinets. They were mostly bare except for nuts, chips and the like to go with the appetizers in the refrigerator. He looked in the coffee, sugar and flour cans. Nothing hidden there. He checked the freezer and gave everything in the refrigerator a going-over. Under the stove he found a copper-bottom set of pots and pans, but from the shine of the copper he could tell they had never been used.

"Stanley, why do you have all this stuff, that dining room, if you're not going to use it?"

In the living room he looked at the magazines under the coffee table. Architectural Digest, Vanity Fair, Philadelphia Magazine, and stuck among them he also found a two-month-old copy of the National Enquirer.

He smiled. "See, there is a human side to you after all

. . ." he said, trying to picture Hightower reaching out for a magazine at the checkout line, but when he did he thought of the mutilated hand.

He walked down the hall to the bedroom. The closet was filled with suits and sports coats. He took his time going through the pockets. Most were in bags from the cleaners, others yielding nothing. The same was true of the shoes lined up on the closet floor . . . until he got to the black pair of cowboy boots. Inside one he found a plastic bag, and in the bag was a small silver spoon and a quantity of white powder.

"What have we here . . . ?" Mercanto wet the tip of his index finger, touched it to the powder in the bag, then to his tongue. The bitter taste was unmistakable. Almost immediately he felt a tingling numbness in the tip of his tongue. "Cocaine, and high-grade, too." He held the bag up to the light. "At least an eighth of an ounce . . . this good, probably worth nine hundred, a thousand dollars . . . well, well, well."

He remembered the file . . . the Medical Examiner had said there were traces of cocaine found in the body. He turned back to the closet and gave it a more thorough search, checking the walls, the floor, the ceiling, but found nothing. Next he tried the bureau. First he looked through the drawers, then he took them out to see if there was anything taped behind them. Nothing.

In the bedside table he found a bottle of capsules labeled Seconal, the label from a nearby pharmacy. He tossed them on the bed alongside the cocaine. "Helps to have something to get you back down, put you to sleep . . ." There was a second bottle in the bedside table, this one also half-filled with capsules but the label read Amyl nitrate." He poured a few into his hand and looked at them. "Poppers, eh? Stanley, were you gay or just a swinger . . . ?"

From there he searched the bathroom. He took the lid off the toilet and looked in the tank, then checked the medicine cabinet, where he found more prescriptions, all from the same pharmacy. Valium, Darvon, Percodan. He took these with him too as he moved to the office.

He sat in the white chair behind the desk and started to go through the drawers. In one he found an address book filled with names and flipped through it. At first glance none of the names meant anything to him, but there were too many to tell for sure. He put it aside to go over later.

In the middle drawer he found Hightower's checkbook. As he took it out, the phone rang, startling him. He did not answer it. Whoever was calling hadn't seen the paper. It stopped after the sixth ring, but the thought of it left a nagging doubt. Why would someone be calling Hightower at home in the middle of a workday? You would expect a businessman to be at his business. When he thought of that he wished he'd answered the call. This was the sort of slip-up that Sloan would jump on.

As he went through the checkbook he saw something that made him sit up straighter . . . starting about four months before, Stanley Hightower had begun making large cash withdrawals. He hurriedly went through the checkbook, then started over again. No mistaking it, four months ago something had changed in Stanley Hightower's life. The first withdrawal was for five thousand dollars, the check made out to cash. After that there was a similar withdrawal every ten days or two weeks. The total came to forty-five thousand dollars. "Why did you need so much cash?" In the bottom drawer he found a file marked "bank statements." He took it out and began to go through the canceled checks. In a few minutes he had found seven of the canceled checks. The other two had not come back yet.

He laid the checks out on the desk in order. All were the same, made out to cash. The endorsement on each was the same—Stanley Hightower, in a barely legible scrawl that matched the signature on the front. He'd cashed them all at the bank himself.

Mercanto walked back into the living room and stood by the grand piano, from where he could see the Walt Whitman Bridge in the distance. The afternoon light was beginning to fade, but there were no lights in South Philly yet. His own apartment was on Catherine Street a few blocks from here, but it might as well have been worlds away.

"What does all this money mean?" Two answers came to mind: blackmail or drugs. If it was blackmail, it had to be something pretty heavy to leverage so much money in such a short time. Something that would ruin Hightower if it was known . . .

With his right hand he idly plinked a chord on the piano, then sat down on the sofa. Sloan's speculations about it being a sex-related crime came back . . . that he'd picked up someone and taken them there. But it didn't fit. He thought about the parking lot and the car. Maybe it started there. That could account for the place, but once the blackmail began, whatever the sexual reason would have certainly stopped. It would not have been ongoing, only the blackmail would.

He thought about the amyl nitrates. If it was sexual it would probably be kinky. Maybe statutory rape, or young boys. Maybe he was being blackmailed by a pimp. A sum that large would indicate adult involvement. Kids wouldn't think that high. Would they?

The image of the mutilated dead man came to mind and he shook his head. This was not like a blackmailer. They didn't kill the golden goose. Even if he threatened to stop paying, all the blackmailer would have to do was expose him. A lot safer than killing him.

He got up from the sofa and walked down the hall to the bedroom. Maybe it wasn't blackmail, maybe Hightower was paying for services rendered. He shook his head again. No kind of sex worth that much money . . . Was there?

As he passed the office he saw the assortment of drugs on the desk where he'd left them. He stopped and stared at them. Drugs . . . made more sense than blackmail. The papers were full of professional people arrested for drug dealing. People who took it up to support their own habit. He knew coke freaks were like evangelists in their zeal to get others hooked. And there was never enough money for the drugs they needed. Maybe he'd had a beef with his supplier. Like they said at the meeting, the Jamaicans were raising hell all over town. A crime like this would not be past them.

He gathered up the checks, the checkbook, the drugs and the address book—at least a beginning, a solid beginning, he thought as he pulled on his coat. At the door he took a last look around.

"I was wrong," he said aloud. "Stanley, you *didn't* know how to live . . ."

Downstairs he showed a new man on the desk his badge. "You know about the Hightower killing?" When the man said yes, Mercanto asked if he was working the desk that night. The man said he was.

"Did you see him come or go that night?"

"It's a big building, but I think I saw him go out, around eight-thirty or nine. I don't think I remember him coming back or going out again, but I can't be sure."

"Was he alone when you saw him?"

"I think so, but like I said, it's a big building. A lot of people come and go around that time. You know, dinner, the movies, things like that . . . Sorry, but I hope you catch whoever did it. He was a nice fellow."

○

Outside, twilight was settling in, and Mercanto decided to pick up something to eat and stop by to see Frank. They could both use the company.

He drove to Chinatown, parked on Arch and drove up Tenth Street to the Imperial. There was a line, but the owner recognized him and waved him inside. Mercanto went to the bar and ordered a Tsing Tao while he looked at the menu. A waiter old enough to have known Confucius as a boy took his order of won ton soup, steamed dumplings, lemon shrimp, kung pao chicken and a six pack of beer.

While he waited for his order he sipped his beer and wondered what Stanley Hightower had done that night between 8:30 and 3:00 a.m. Mercanto figured when he found the answer he would have the killer . . .

The waiter brought his order, Mercanto paid and left. Outside the Trocadero on Arch a long line of kids was waiting to get in. The poster advertised Warren Zevon—one night only.

As Mercanto drove to American Street near Third he turned the radio to WMMR, which was playing Warren Zevon songs in honor of the concert.

○

"Frank, it's me," he called out as he went in. He was not prepared for what he found.

84

Frank's condition had worsened since the chemotherapy, and he found him half-sitting, half-lying on his couch covered by a blanket, a sketch pad on his lap. The room was cold. Under the blanket Mercanto could see Frank was wearing a wool bathrobe over a sweater, and he was shaking.

"Frank, are you crazy? It's like an icebox in here," he said and went to turn up the thermostat, suddenly angry with him for his self-neglect.

Frank's only reply was, "What're you so dressed up for? You going to a wedding?"

Mercanto shook his head, not sure he could trust his voice. The room as much as the way his brother looked told the story. Dishes were in the sink, newspapers on the coffee table, which was not like him at all. Frank was a bug on neatness.

"I brought us dinner," he said as he opened the bags, but Frank shook his head.

"I'm not too hungry right now, I'll have it later...You didn't answer my question, why are you all dressed up?"

All he said was that he was temporarily back in plain-clothes. He didn't go into any details. Frank knew about Sloan from the Rudy Gunther investigation, and he didn't want to upset him with the news that they'd been thrown together again.

This seemed to cheer Frank some but Mercanto had only one thought, that he was losing him. When he couldn't take any more he pulled on his coat and said goodbye, angry at himself for not being able to help more, do more.

On the way out he ran into DeBray, the black man who worked for Frank, whom Frank trusted to take care of him. He took hold of DeBray by the lapels, pushing him into the side of the building. "You clean that place up. Don't let him get like that."

DeBray didn't push back, but hurt came in his eyes. "You know him, you know how he is."

"I know," he said, releasing him. "But do what you can. He needs us. You know that."

DeBray nodded.

Mercanto drove around for a while. The idea of going home to an empty apartment was depressing. He needed someone to talk to. Maybe he'd drive out to the Valley Green and have a cup of coffee with Catherine Poydras. Someone friendly to pass the time with.

O

Queenie, a duke's mixture of terriers and pet of the McClains on Livesey Street, was making her way toward the Valley Green bridge. She'd been doing this for over a year. No matter how the family tried to keep her in, she would find a way to get out and head for the Maison Catherine, where the kitchen staff would pet her and give her the best leftovers in town. In her mind it was like having her own refrigerator.

Near the bridge, from the woods, she heard a soft whistle. She stopped, perked up her ears, looking around for the source. Finally she spied it, a fair-haired man in darkling clothing at the edge of the woods. The whistle came again, and playfully she headed over to investigate . . .

The man turned and went deeper into the woods, Queenie following. Out of sight of the road, the sound of a loud crack rang out, like a stick breaking, then agonized whimpering, then silence as Queenie's blood seeped into the leaves from the gaping, ragged hole in her throat.

Satisfied, the shadowy figure rose to his feet, dusted off his knees, and moved deeper into the darkness of the woods.

CHAPTER 7

MARGARET PRIEST was aware of Loring's eyes on her as he followed her into the office. She didn't have to turn, she could feel it. An unspoken communication, intimate, and forbidden. The feeling bothered her.

Even though they had not talked openly about his sex life, from the way he said things she knew he had had little experience with women, and the way he looked at her had an innocence about it. Unlikely as it was in this day and time, she felt it a distinct possibility he was a virgin. Not a homosexual. Asexual was more like it. A sublimation of his sexuality. Why, she didn't know but she hoped to find out. Needed to.

They took their respective seats and he said, "You look . . . lovely today." The sincerity of it touched her, and for a moment she almost admitted to herself that he had been somewhere in her thoughts when she had chosen the Calvin Klein blouse and pleated, gabardine trousers to wear today. Certainly Adam hadn't been, not now that she was certain of his affair with his student. The nightly anonymous phone calls had cleared up any doubt about *that*.

For the first time in her life she really hated someone. You couldn't always be a professional. A nameless, faceless, nineteen-year-old who she was sure had better breasts and a tighter body than hers. When she looked in the mirror she could see herself beginning to lose it . . . her skin, her hair, her juices, it made her want to scream. Only then did she allow herself to think of Loring and the way *he* looked at her. No harm in it, she told herself. They weren't together. He would never know. It was just a moment of innocent solace for her. Call it harmless compensation.

She looked across her desk now at Loring. "Today I want to begin a little differently. With an exercise. I'd like you to describe yourself physically."

The word "physically" obviously embarrassed him. He laughed nervously. "You make it sound like an obscene phone call."

She didn't reply, and Loring felt his stomach begin to tighten. Although he looked forward to these moments with her, each session was more difficult for him than the last. Several times she had assured him they were making progress. He took that to mean he was getting better. Except from what?

She refused to name it, other than to refer to it as his "conflict." Well, he didn't feel better. Just the opposite.

Right now the last thing he wanted was to *describe* himself. He could refuse, of course, or try to steer the conversation onto things like art, music, man's fall from grace, but he knew it wouldn't do any good. He'd tried it in their second session. All she did was *sit* there, silent, staring, smoking until he gave in.

"I'm lean, small-boned, blond ... I look like my mother," he said, thinking there was more she wouldn't hear. He was also an inkwell, an aging brandy, the eye of a gnat, a pinprick of darkness in the light ...

Margaret nodded. There it was again, the family reference. It kept coming up over and over in different ways. Today she was not going to let him dodge it.

"You hesitated before you said you looked like your mother. Would you rather look like your father?"

Pain crossed his face. Look like ... what difference does that make, he thought, allowing himself for once to consider his mother, father, stepfather together. The question is, which one do I act like ... the good, the bad, or the ugly ... or even which is which. His sister didn't enter his mind. He knew she was immune. It was a plague visited on the eldest.

"I guess most men would rather look like their father, but it's okay. My mother is a fine woman ... Besides, looks aren't something you have a choice about anyway ..."

"Tell me about your mother."

He crossed his legs and picked at the crease of his trousers, ingoring the tingling of his fingers. He tried not to think about how his hands had been getting worse. Now most of the time they were almost numb. They still worked. He'd lost none of his grip, only the sensation. That's why he hadn't been to the doctor. There was nothing a doctor could do. He was sure it was just the cold weather irritating the damaged nerves from the bicycle wreck when he was young. Usually the belladonna helped, if he took enough. Several times he had thought of mentioning it in one of the sessions but hadn't because he didn't want to ... to worry Margaret pointlessly.

"Tell me about your mother," she repeated. At the sound of her words he looked up but did not meet her gaze. Why did she always try to do this to him? The question made him resentful but he pushed back the feeling. He couldn't be that way with her.

"I'd rather not. I want to concentrate on my own problems."

Margaret pursed her lips slightly, deciding what to say next. Should she go to "my own problems"? The word *own* showed he felt his problems weren't the only ones in his family. She decided not to. To zero in on a word or two like that at this early stage would only make him more guarded. Instead she chose to go abstract, give him some breathing room.

Over their sessions she'd tended to speak clinically to him, he seemed to take comfort from that, find it reassuring. In any event, the depersonalizing of it tended to make him more responsive. As for herself, it was important she admitted to herself that their use of given names and their exchanges did draw her to him more as a patient, as a human being. Nothing wrong with that. He was *highly* intelligent. Sensitive. Decent and very troubled.

"Most everything begins in childhood, as I'm sure you've heard. Experiences then tend to shape us ..."

"I *do* know all that," he snapped. "Do you think I've been living in a vacuum? I took psychology courses. I've gone to the library and read since I've been coming here. I can quote you chapter and verse on all the disgusting stuff like the Oedipus complex. You're not fooling me, I know where all this is leading. You're trying to say the episode in the fitting room when I thought I was shrinking was caused by a desire on my part to return to my childhood—"

"Or a fear of it . . . ?"

His anger made her feel she'd done something. She knew he'd been researching. His responses in earlier sessions had told her that. She also knew it was because he wanted her to think well of him, to hide what he thought were the bad parts from her. A lot of patients did that. Early sessions were often a game of hide and seek, but *this* was an honest emotional response. She was at least beginning to be able to draw him out. It was a good feeling to be able to help him do that.

Loring stared at her. His anger seemed to make everything crystal clear . . . "Fear is a conch shell. You hold it to your ear and think you hear the sea."

She prompted him. "But it's only an illusion . . ."

Her response pleased him. At last she was beginning to understand. "Yes, but it's a universal one. You put a gun to the head of a Frenchman and he'll feel the same thing as an American."

Margaret paused to light a cigarette. He was trying to slip away again, but she wasn't going to let him. They needed to make progress together. So far their sessions had led her to believe that his episode in the fitting room was an hysterical one, not psychotic. His high anxiety level, his stomach trouble, his inability to sleep all went with it. A retreat from the unpleasant through illness or illusion. A statement of vulnerability, as Jung might say.

Even though the fitting room episode was more severe, she was sure he had had similar episodes in the past, and that this one had been triggered by the invitation to his sister's wedding.

But why?

"We were talking about your mother . . ."

Loring stared at her for a moment. Maybe she can understand, he thought.

"You're much younger, much prettier, much smarter, but sometimes you remind me of her when you do that . . . smoke, I mean. The way you look at me when you do that. It's as if you know a secret. There's a cool elegance . . . a sensual—sorry, shouldn't have used that word. It's unprofessional here."

He was still not accepting his role of patient. "You mean the word 'sensual'? It's okay if you find something about me sensual."

By the book, she told herself, but in spite of her words Margaret was now self-consciously aware of her cigarette. He had boxed her into a corner. If she continued to smoke after what he'd just said he might well interpret it the wrong way, as sexual interest on her part. But if she stopped he would certainly interpret it as rejection. She took a drag on her cigarette, trying to keep her movement as natural as possible while watching him watch her.

Of the two possibilities rejection was the more serious. Patients often developed crushes on the analyst. She could handle that, but if he felt rejection all their work, the trust would come undone. She blew out the smoke and tried to think of it as building a working bond between them rather than a submission on her part.

From the first, if someone had given her a pencil and told her to draw an *emotional* portrait of him she figured it would be a hunchback, body bent, twisted, handsome features filled with pain. Not a cripple. He wasn't that. She was adamant with herself about that. In time he would straighten, realize his worth, but the pain of the process would be his. Her role was to have the guts and skill to help him face that pain.

As he watched her he felt something that he had never felt before. He knew it was not another of the things that happened nightly since the episode. Things he hoped were dreams but feared were not.

What he felt now was not of the darkness but of light, and he wanted it to fill him, he wanted to revel in it, to nurture it, to call it ... love. It must be, he told himself. See, she feels it, too. She gives herself to me. We are no longer faces on playing cards that rub against each other in the deck. We are one, like Lancelot and Queen "G" ... The desire teared his eyes.

From a distance he heard her say, "Why haven't you seen your parents since you graduated from college," and the mood was broken. He felt a bubble of anger release and before he could stop it, rise to the surface.

The explosiveness of it startled Margaret.

"Don't call them my parents. Parentology should be the name of a religion. A California church that sells vitamins. You sound like my sister. They are *not* my parents. She is my mother, an accident of birth ... he is her husband. My father is dead. Do you hear that ... my father is dead ..." His voice rising.

Margaret sat very straight in her chair. What was happening was important, their first breakthrough. It was so sudden, so powerful. She continued to smoke with deliberate movements, wanting him to feel the bond between them, mentally urging him on, thinking the words "Come on. Let it out. Come on," over and over.

He turned away from her in his chair, feeling ashamed. Like a night long ago with his mother. The femininity of tears made him embarrassed and he didn't want Margaret to see him.

"Don't you understand?" It was as if he was feeling one

language but speaking in another, unable to link them.

"Look at me. Help me to," she said quietly, feeling something of his pain, wanting for a moment to touch him, to reassure him.

He turned to her. "He . . . he killed himself . . . when I was eight . . ."

The past, that part of it, came rushing at him in a jumble. It was on his lips before he could think. Stop, he told himself. You'll lose her. Don't say a word. You'll lose her if you say any more.

Margaret waited. When he shut up she knew that the door that had opened so abruptly had closed again. She was, of course, curious about his father's suicide, but only as it related to Loring. It wasn't her immediate concern. They could go back to his father's death later. She was more interested in his feelings about his mother. Clearly his outburst was linked to her, provoked by talk about her.

"After your father's death she remarried . . ."

"He was my father's business partner. They were manufac- turers' representatives," he said, holding himself tight in check.

The way he answered bothered her. His tone was flat, empty of emotion, each word getting a too measured beat with no emphasis. The flatness could mean he was trying to tell her his displeasure that he was unable to express in words.

"How long was it before she remarried?"

He shook his head. Why this? Why did she go out of her way to hurt him? Didn't she understand that painful as these sessions were, being here with her was the only thing in his life that he looked forward to? Maybe if he explained it in his own way she would understand . . . "A few months," he finally said. He knew Margaret wanted more, but there were things about those years he would not even let himself remember, much less speak about.

"Even though she's artistic, structure is very important to my mother. At first you wouldn't think the two would go together, but they do. She weaves these incredible tapestries from scratch. They're like nothing you've ever seen, not colors or flowers, human figures, I mean whole scenes. They sell for thousands and thousands. Museums buy them, collectors, she's booked up years in advance. Always has been . . .

"Once after she remarried I drew a picture like one of her tapestries and gave it to my sister. It was of a picnic. In it was my mother, my sister, Wolf my German shepherd, and me. When my mother saw it she was angry." His tone was still flat.

Margaret was delighted. The door hadn't closed after all. So far he had refused to discuss his dreams, but at least here, fertile for interpretation, was his subconscious at work. Freud had said dream-thinking and wish-thinking were the same thing, central to the resolution of the conflict, bypassing the repressions of the conscious mind. Well, they were getting closer. she liked the feeling, the bond between them. Her patients were *people*, not modules of neuroses, she reassured herself. They were important to her, but because of the intricacies of his particular conflict, and perhaps his newness, she admitted that sometimes he seemed more so than some others.

"Why was she angry?"

"She said it was a bad picture. The structure was all wrong, that I'd made Wolf too large in relation to the other family members, but I knew the reason was really because I hadn't included her husband. You see, she'd made her choice . . ."

"And you weren't too happy with her choice . . ."

95

"Happy or not happy . . . it was her life," he said.

"It was your life, your sister's life, too," she said, wanting him to confront his anger about her choice.

"My sister is happy, always has been."

"Then you . . ."

"There were times . . . it was okay with me. I was happy . . ." Suddenly defensive.

She lit another cigarette. "Do you remember actually drawing the picture?"

"Vaguely. It was a long time ago."

"When you drew Wolf larger than the people, what were you thinking."

Her question brought back memories of Wolf. Of his room and Wolf sleeping at the foot of his bed, protecting him. Of them together, exploring the world, their fort, their playtime. Finally he said, "That was the only real friend I had."

"What about the other people in the picture. Weren't they your friends, too?"

He shook his head. "Maybe when my father was alive . . ."

Margaret took a drag on her cigarette. He was no longer watching her when she did, his attention seemed on the far away, as if he was watching scenes from long ago. The look on his face was so unhappy that she wished she could be in those scenes with him to help him through.

"Do you miss your father?"

He looked around the room. It's cool softness reminded him of a cave. He tried to think of it that way. Their fort, his and Margaret's. It could be.

"A day never goes by that I don't think of him," he answered truthfully.

The *aloneness* in his reply had to move her, and she remembered her own father's death.

He focused on her. "They're wrong, you know, when they say the body can't remember pain ..."

Her eyes momentarily widened. It was the exact thought she was thinking at that moment.

CHAPTER 8

SLOAN LOOKED at the findings from the Hightower apartment and listened to Mercanto's theories without interruption. When he finished there was a look of some respect on Sloan's face that Mercanto had not seen before.

"I have to agree with you. It looks like you're on to something. Of your two theories you're probably right, drugs look like the more likely. His lifestyle fits it. The park fits it, but I wouldn't rule out the blackmail theory, either."

"You have something in mind?"

"The ex-wife . . . remember how I told you she acted when

99

she came to identify the body? Seeing him mutilated like that didn't faze her. Could be something sexual . . ." Sloan said, picking up the amyl nitrates, "something that started when they were married, and she hated him for it. Maybe it wrecked their marriage and the blackmail was a way to get even. Maybe he decided he'd had enough. That's why they met, for him to tell her he wasn't going to pay her any more and she flipped out."

Mercanto nodded. "Makes sense . . . in a sick sort of way."

"It's a sick business. Keep at it."

Mercanto drove from the Roundhouse on Race to Locust Street near Rittenhouse Square. He parked and walked down the block to Hightower Opticals. The business occupied an entire brownstone.

The first floor reception area was more like an art gallery than a place that made and sold glasses. Scattered on the polished pine floors were low square chairs covered in black, glass tables with magazines on them, and green plants. Soothing music was piped in. Mercanto recognized it as New Age by a Japanese musician named Kitaro. He'd heard it before from friends in his Aikido dojo.

He went up to the receptionist, a young blonde with long hair seated behind a white desk, and showed her his badge.

"I'm here about Mr. Hightower's murder. Could I see whoever's in charge?"

The sight of the badge seemed to make her nervous. "That would be Cheryl Goldman, the manager," she said.

While she made the call Mercanto strolled over and looked at one of the large paintings on the wall. It was done in blues, greens, and reds, all blending together in a soft harmony without any discernible lines. A brass plaque at the bottom of the frame said: "Seafire by Murray Dessner." He knew Frank would admire the way it seemed to capture from the inside the essence of its subject.

The receptionist hung up the phone. "She'll be right down ... God, the place has been in a upheaval since ... you know. We were all so shocked. He was such a nice man. Who would do such a thing?"

"That's what I'm trying to find out."

A tall, dark-haired woman in a close-fitting black dress entered the room. "I'm Cheryl Goldman," she said.

Mercanto showed his badge again and followed her to an office on the second floor. She sat behind the desk, he in front.

"This seems like a pretty big operation here ..." he said.

"It is," she said proudly. "We have a staff of twelve. For an optometry practice that's an incredible size."

"What makes this one so special? Chestnut Street is loaded with them," he said.

"You may have seen some of the articles. We cater to difficult needs in glasses ... Are you the man who's heading up the investigation into Stanley's death?"

"That's right. I'll try not to take too much of your time, but there are a few points I need to clear up." He consulted his notebook. "Right now we're trying to piece together what happened the night he was killed. Do you have any idea what he was doing that evening from, say, eight-thirty on?"

"Well, when he left here he was going home to change, then he was going to have dinner at Lagniappe with John and Elizabeth Cohen. They're old friends who own Interiors, the decorating place on Walnut near Le Bec Fin. We used to have dinner with them at least once a week."

"You say we, were you there?"

She hesitated. "Usually the answer would be yes, but that night he didn't invite me."

"Did he give you any reason?"

"No, he just said he wanted to see them alone."

"... And that was unusual?"

An angry look. "What are you driving at?"

"I'm just trying to figure out what happened. Let's backtrack. I never met him. Tell me what he was like."

Her eyes began to tear. "I met him when I was in optometry school, four years ago. I worked for him part-time then. He was the nicest man I ever met. A caring man. My last year of school I ran out of money and he paid for it. When I graduated I came into the practice full time ... he had terrific enthusiasm, it just bubbled over. Everyone around him felt it. That's really the secret to the practice ... his enthusiasm. People were drawn to him. I can't imagine what life's going to be like without him."

"Now about that day, what was his mood like?"

She thought for a moment. "I guess if I had to put it in a word I'd say preoccupied. He wasn't himself. He seemed very distant. I thought afterwards he even seemed sad."

"Was this a new side of him?"

Again she thought before she spoke. When she did she chose her words carefully. "No, for the past three or four months he'd had days like that. Several times I asked him about it, but he would just shake his head. I didn't press too hard. Stanley was a private person. When he didn't want to talk he wouldn't."

"What about dinner that night? Do you know if he had any other plans?"

She shook her head. "I don't know of any. Stanley did like to party. Often when we went out we would close things and even wind up at an after-hours place like the Black Banana. In fact, the last few months it seemed like whenever we went out we did that."

Her answer didn't surprise him. Not with all the drugs he'd found.

"When you did stay out late was there anyone in particular you ran into on a regular basis?"

"No, he knew lots of people. We'd run into one and then another. Why do you ask that?"

Sex or drugs. Mercanto chose sex. "What I'm getting at is his personal life. Aside from yourself, did he see anyone else?"

"He didn't *see* me, either. Not the way you're implying. Stanley didn't believe in getting involved with people he worked with, but I'll tell you, all he had to do was say the word and I would have. I don't know of any *partners.* Satisfied?"

"What about his ex-wife? Did you know her?"

"To know Dominique is to loath her. I knew her. She was the most mercenary two-faced bitch I ever met. All she ever cared about was what she could get out of him. She didn't care about Stanley. Their divorce was the best thing that ever happened to him."

"When were they divorced?"

"Less than a year ago, and he had to force it then. Otherwise she would have hung on to the bitter end."

"Financially how were things for him?"

"The divorce cost a lot. She got plenty of cash. He had to buy a condo, have it decorated, but he was still all right. Like I said, the practice is lucrative. When you do the kind of things we do, you can charge a lot for it."

"Still, there's no such thing as too much money, is there?" Mercanto said, thinking about the withdrawals from Hightower's checkbook.

"No, I guess not."

"You mentioned that he helped you out with your last year of school. Was he doing anything like that for someone else?"

"Not that I know of."

Should he mention the drugs? If she was involved it would tip his hand. He looked at her. The look of sadness on her face was too real. She was genuinely upset or a hell of an actress. He didn't think she was involved but he didn't want to take the chance of ruling her out yet.

"Do you have any idea who could have done it?"

She shook her head. "No, not at all. Everyone loved him."

""I guess that's all I have, although I might need to talk to you again." He reached for a pad on her desk and wrote down his number. "If you think of anything give me a call ... Now, if you don't mind, I'd like to spend a few minutes with each of the staff, one at a time. I won't keep them long, I promise."

"Will you tell me one thing . . . when will the body be released?" She paused. "I want to make the funeral arrangements. I know what he would want."

"I can't answer that, except to say it will be as soon as we've completed our investigation."

She stood up. "Thank you. Why don't you use my office. I'll send in the staff like you want."

Mercanto spent the rest of the day questioning the other employees. They all said more or less the same things, but by the end of the day one thing had clearly emerged ... for the past few months Stanley Hightower had shown a marked change in personality from a bubbling, enthusiastic person to one who was distant, preoccupied, some even said gloomy.

On the way home Mercanto again took dinner to Frank, but this time he didn't stay because all Frank wanted to talk about were plans for his own funeral. He couldn't sit there and listen to that.

At his apartment on Catherine Street he changed clothes and lit a fire in his small fireplace. While he was at Frank's he had not eaten, and for a few minutes he toyed with the idea of making dinner but settled for a Rolling Rock instead. In the living room he put on a tape of Michael Feinstein at the Algonquin and settled himself in front of the fire. As the music played he tried to relax and not think about the case. He had three more beers while the fire burned down, using the case to keep his mind off Frank. About ten he went to bed but could not sleep. His mind was in a jumble.

Lying there he kept wondering what had caused the personality change in Stanley Hightower, and what the hell was he doing in the park at three in the morning?

After an hour he gave up on sleep, dressed, slipped on his shoulder holster, picked up his coat and left the apartment.

He drove across town, up the parkway and past the art museum. Traffic was light on Kelly Drive, the river shimmering darkly beside it.

As he turned into the parking lot near Forbidden Drive he tried to imagine Stanley Hightower doing the same thing. Was he alone when he came here?

There were two cars in the parking lot ... an old Ford station wagon and a Toyota sedan, parked near the steps leading up to the Maison Catherine on the hill. He recognized them. The Ford belonged to Catherine Poydras, the owner of the restaurant, and the Toyota belonged to her chef, Wilson.

Still trying to picture Stanley Hightower he drove slowly across the lot and parked in the place where he'd found the black BMW.

"What were you doing here? What brought you here at that time of night? You'd had dinner and you came out here to meet someone ... who?"

Wait a minute. Why was he thinking Hightower had come here alone? What about Sloan's theory that he had picked up someone and driven them here? Maybe, but sitting here now,

the only way he could imagine him was alone and waiting
. . .

That night came back to him . . . the rain, the cold. He
remembered getting out of the blue-and-white and walking
toward the BMW. There were stains on the ground. Oil stains,
he'd thought at the time . . . then he remembered the sounds
he'd heard by the garbage can and later in the woods. At first
he'd thought it was a dog. After finding the body he wasn't
sure . . . he still wasn't . . .

A knock at his window startled him. He turned and in the
darkness could just make out a teen-ager on a bicycle. He
rolled down the window. "Yeah."

"Mister, I thought you'd like to know your rear tire is going
flat."

Mercanto got out to look. There was nothing wrong with
the tire. When he turned back the teen-ager had a gun in his
hand.

"Hand over your wallet, motherfucker."

Anger boiled. At himself for being stupid enough to get
suckered this way. At the teen-ager for trying it.

"Look, why don't you forget it and take off—"

The teen-ager cocked the pistol. Was this how it happened
to Hightower? he thought. He shook his head. It didn't feel
right, didn't answer the question what he was doing here at
three a.m.

The teen-ager took his words and the shake of his head to
be a refusal. "I'm going to count three and blow your fucking
head off if I don't have that wallet."

Mercanto had seen street violence too often not to be afraid.
It was surely drug money the kid was after. A kid like that
would do anything. In the faint light his gun looked like an
old Western Colt .45, an unlikely gun for him to be carrying.
It could be a fake, one of those replicas. He hoped it was. If

it wasn't . . . He thought for a second about announcing he was a cop, decided against it. Play for time.

"Put the gun away, let's talk about this . . . I think we can straighten everything out," he said, feeling like an amateur snake-charmer with a cobra in front of him.

"One."

Mercanto wanted to reach for his own gun but pushed back the thought. It was almost like one part of him had stepped out of his body and was watching from the sidelines. The night of Rudy Gunther's death replayed itself. Stay cool. Be persuasive. His career couldn't stand another incident like that, especially not involving a teen-ager.

"You're making a mistake, son. I've only got ten bucks on me. Why don't we forget about it? If I see you around sometime I'll buy you a beer and we'll maybe laugh about it. Believe me, I was your age once—"

"Two."

Mercanto looked at him closely, trying to fix him in his mind. About six feet, dark hair, no scars or marks. Clothing dark, hair cut short, like a prep school kid from the West Mt. Airy side of the park. Could this possibly be Hightower's killer? If he was, he had to bring him in . . . hopefully alive.

"Tell me one thing, why are you doing this?"

"What's it to you?"

He wanted to shout out because I'm a cop. But unless he had the drop on the kid, all an anouncement like that would do was scare him into the act, and Mercanto didn't want to feel a .45 slug tear into his body.

"I just thought maybe I could help. Sometimes stuff gets out of hand, it's good to talk about it. We've got time," he said, knowing it sounded foolish but not able to think of anything better. Step back and contain, that's what he should have done they said after Rudy Gunther. Easier said than done—

"Maybe you've got all night, I don't. Give me that wallet."

Mercanto had to recognize the finality in the tone. He'd heard the same thing on the street too many times before.

"All right, you win."

He moved his hand slowly inside his coat like he was reaching for his wallet. His hand closed around the butt of his revolver. God, please don't let this kid make me shoot him. He pulled the gun free of the holster, letting a little of his breath out as he dropped into a combat stance. "Get your hands up. I'm a police officer."

The teen-ager fired. Mercanto felt the slug tear into him, and he began to fall. His last thought was, it's true . . . you do feel it before you hear the sound.

CHAPTER 9

L ORING SAT huddled on the rocks at Cape May, the waves of the Atlantic crashing around him with the bubbling hawk-and-spit of an old man expectorating. He'd been there alone on the beach all night. The cold wind from the east had leeched its way inside his parka hours ago, and he was chilled to the bone. With the dawn, sky and sea separated until one was gray, the other oily black trimmed with whitecaps. In his mind he heard the sounds of the Passion of St. Matthew with its complimenting strength and delicacy matching the growl of the sea.

The music had begun last evening after the call from Wiladene Jenkins and had continued in his mind all night with symphonic clarity. Unexplained as it was, he marveled at how it seemed a part of him rather than a memory. At times through the night its beauty had moved him close to tears.

He pulled his knees tighter to his chest and tried to focus on what she had said. That she wanted him to ask Erin Fraser to the opening party for the exhibit at the museum. He appreciated Erin's aloneness in her moment of triumph, but he had still refused. There was only one woman in his life . . . Margaret. But Wiladene was adamant. No one could say no to her, and in the end he relented.

He called Margaret at home immediately after to explain what he'd done, but when she answered, like always when he called, he couldn't make himself speak. All he did was listen until she hung up, feeling that he had betrayed her by giving in to Wiladene.

After that the walls of his house seemed to close in on him. He tried to think of other things, to read or relax somehow, his stomach a bundle of nerves that even belladonna would not loosen. He paced, he cursed, he hated himself. A pawn to other people's desires, a piece to be moved around, that's what he was, what he'd always been. He was not a man, at least not his own man. Otherwise he would not have betrayed Margaret like that.

He sat at his desk. If he couldn't bring himself to speak to her on the phone at least he could write to her. He picked up his pen. The words flowed like acrylic paint onto the paper. The beauty of the contrast between the black ink and the white paper was hypnotic. This was right, he felt it. Margaret had to know. There was too much not to pass it on. Essential information. Not the present, that was only confusion, bad dreams, chaos, except for her, but the past. She had to understand heroics were not important, only survival. Concentration camp lessons from legions of the undead. Nazi lessons. He decorated the margin of one sheet with swastikas to illustrate, knowing she would understand when she saw them.

On the third page he redrew the picnic picture they'd spoken about in therapy, only this time he included his stepfather with Hitler's features and gave his mother huge breasts. Above her picture he wrote the words "Eva Braun." It was all clear to him now and would be to Margaret.

Sometime during the letter he heard the music in his mind. He wasn't aware of the exact moment it started because once he realized it was there it seemed like it had been there forever.

The letter went to sixteen pages before everything was said. All the answers to all the questions. All the knowledge that the terror of his history had given him. His sin, his years of punishment.

When he finished he felt closer to Margaret than ever before. Her face was with him as he got in his car and started to drive. He imagined her sitting next to him as the Jersey shore towns rolled by, her knees tucked under, coolly smoking, watching him.

He thought of her breasts as his free hand strayed to his own nipples, and he began to caress them through his shirt, feeling a pleasant sensation that moved over his body. This wasn't sin. It wasn't dirty. It was pleasure. This was how Margaret would feel, he thought. It would feel good like this if he touched hers, or she touched his. He knew the sensation would be the same because he was her, she was him. Not peas of the pod, but one, free to use this oneness to bring goodness, not pain or humiliation like others did.

Now on the rocks hours later he was alone again. Just

himself and the sea. His body was shivering as he looked east toward the horizon, the letter tucked safely in his pocket.

The words of the book of Genesis came to mind. First there was the darkness, then the waters, then the light. The sea was where it all began. Life as we know it, he thought. Sea creatures to land creatures. Out there somewhere off shore it's still happening. A wave is born, moving slow and small, gaining momentum, maturity on its way to shore. Each one separate and distinct from all that have come before it. Each one powerless to change its course or to stop itself from dying in white water on the beach, he thought. Like me . . .

He got up and started for his car, the music no longer playing in his mind.

Erin and Wiladene were in one of the upper rooms at the Braddon laying out items for a Channel 12 telecast on the exhibit when he arrived.

They both looked up as he came in, and Wiladene smiled. She should, he thought. I'm here like one of the waves.

"Aren't you working today? I'm not used to seeing you without a suit," Wiladene said.

"I'm taking the day off."

"That's not like you. Don't you feel well?"

"I feel fine."

Erin didn't believe him. He looked haggard, worn, like he hadn't slept all night. She hoped he wasn't coming down with something.

Wiladene looked at her watch. "Gosh, I just realized I've got to run out for a few minutes. I'll be back in a little while," she said, gathering up her coat and purse.

They watched her go. Erin knew it was a ploy to leave them alone. Wiladene had told her Loring was going to invite her to the party but that he was shy about such things.

112

He moved around the room, looking at some of the items, lightly touching others. "All these things are from the Caribbean . . ."

"That's right. Mainly from Haiti and Jamaica. They have the richest cultures, but there are items from most of the other islands as well."

Shyness was a quality she could appreciate since her own relationships with the opposite sex were marked by an awkwardness she found impossible to control.

"Do you ever want to go back to the islands?" he said, thinking of how life had been so simple when he was planning his own trip to Barbados. It seemed like he'd grown old in the short time since his sister's call about her wedding had ruined those plans.

"Sure, all the time. Especially when the weather's like this. Doesn't everyone?"

"I guess."

She had to admit she liked him better in a parka and jeans than in a suit. He seemed more real. She'd already made up her mind to accept if he asked her. Wiladene had seen to that, singing his praises every time they were together, but he seemed so uncomfortable. Maybe if she helped him a little . . .

"What brings you to the museum today?"

Her question brought Wiladene's call back to mind. "Ask Erin to the party," she'd demanded, as if the decision was *hers* to make, *his* to obey. Like his mother . . . If you love me, you'll do what I want . . . The times he had bitten his tongue to keep from telling her the truth . . . that he did not love her . . . never *had.* She wouldn't have understood. To her, love was a capitulation. That's how she measured her own, how much she gave up. His, too. The greater the cost, the greater the love.

It was the only possible explanation for what he'd seen her do with him ... her husband, long ago.

"I dropped by because I ... wanted to ask if I could take you to the opening party for the exhibit," he said. "I know with you being the director it's not exactly right for me to ask. I don't mean to intrude but I thought ..."

"I'd like that very much. Thank you."

In a way he felt relieved when she accepted. It made his surrender easier. Like all the other times, he told himself. Don't think about it, just do it and it'll be over with.

Erin saw the look on his face and was glad she'd helped him. She would have preferred a bolder approach, but there was something charming about him.

He picked up a mask from one of the tables. "What's this?"

She went to stand nearer him. "It's a Haitian voodoo mask. The reason it's here is because of its unusual design," she said, thinking of the circumstances in which she'd first seen it worn.

He turned it over in his hands. It was plain like a death mask, following the imprint of the face closely. There were no feathers or decorations except for a trickle of rhinestone tears leading downward from the corners of the eyes. The top half was violet, coming to a point at the tip of the nose, making it seem elongated, animal like. The bottom half was the red pink of torn flesh.

As he looked at it he heard the music again in his mind. The sacrificial mass. The music seemed to make it clear to him, and he understood the mask. It was the inner face of the damned, the soul of the one who made it and wore it.

The feeling scared him. What if they were kindred spirits?

The feeling of doom he'd felt in the fitting room came back. He knew that had been caused by overwork, but there was still the feeling ... the same feeling so plain to him in the mask. Then there'd been his lunch with Erin, something he'd dismissed as just bad food, but now he wasn't so sure. What if it had been an episode, too, or even worse . . . a sign. Of what? Movement toward the same knowledge the maker of the mask had had?

Something started to form. A memory he didn't know was there. One that was worse still because of its newness. He tried to push it back, out of his consciousness. It's just a fantasy, he told himself, but the harder he tried, the more clearly he remembered. His chair . . . his cleric's chair . . . waking up there, not knowing how he'd gotten from his bed . . .

He put the mask down and walked over to a tapestry on another table, trying to focus on it. It was red with gold, woven, blocky figures of three stubby-legged men and a dog. The dog was out of proportion, like Wolf in his own picnic picture.

From a distance he heard Erin say, "That's a Mayan tapestry from the ruins near Cozumel."

"My mother makes tapestries," he said.

Erin watched the way he touched it, traced the figures with his fingertips as if they were Braille. He was experiencing them through touch. "It's very old, over three hundred years," she said.

He heard her words but they didn't register. When he turned to ask her to repeat it he saw the mask again. It's position on the table caught the light and made the rhinestone tears look wet. The anguish of it drew him, unlocked the scene in his mind he knew he didn't want to remember. Get a grip on yourself, he told himself, you're not a character from Shakespeare. You're Loring Weatherby, stockbroker.

As he thought this, he remembered getting up from his chair and looking in the mirror. Like the mask, the lower part of his face was covered in blood, too . . .

Then he knew—what he was remembering didn't happen.

115

He was remembering a dream, a nightmare. It had to be. Wasn't Margaret always talking about dreams, wanting him to tell her his . . . That's what it was . . . a nightmare. More than a nightmare . . . the granddaddy of nightmares. I'll go to her now and tell her. She'll be glad, finally one of my dreams to interpret.

The thought of being with Margaret made him smile. He looked at Erin. On some level she reminded him of his sister. Going out with his sister was no betrayal of Margaret. That thought made him feel much better than he had since Wiladene's call. He reached out and touched her arm. "Thanks for accepting. I'll call you later to go over the details. Now I have to run."

He took Market Street from West Philly back into Center City, weaving in and out of the heavy traffic. He wasn't due to see Margaret today but he knew she'd understand, be glad to see him. At Nineteenth he took a right, crossed Chestnut and Walnut and circled Rittenhouse Square. He parked illegally near the Warwick and hurried to her office.

He felt buoyant, like bringing home a good report card. His troubles were over. She'd led him to the key in her soft womanly way. He wasn't going crazy. All these things were just dreams. Super realistic dreams. If he talked about them they would go away.

The waiting room was empty. He crossed it in two strides and opened the door to her inner office. The sight inside shocked him. Margaret was not alone. There was a man with her.

She looked up in surprise when he burst into the room. "Loring . . . Mr. Weatherby, what are you doing here?" he heard her say.

The man was lying on the couch, his jacket off. Margaret was sitting in a chair near the head of it. She seemed to be writing something on a pad, but the look on her face gave her away. It was guilt, he decided. The same look he'd seen on his mother's face that night long ago when he'd come into the den and found her on her knees with *him* mounting her.

She stood and smoothed her skirt. "I'm very sorry about this. Please excuse me for a moment," she said to the man.

As she crossed the room to him, he saw the anger on her face and now he was embarrassed. If only he could turn the clock back five minutes he could undo it, but like that night, the damage was done.

"Step outside, please," she said.

He stumbled backward through the door and she followed him into the outer office, closing the door behind her.

"I'm with a patient . . ."

"But I need to see you."

"Right now that's not possible. Your appointment is to-morrow . . . if you feel it's so urgent you can't wait, then I can refer you to someone—"

"Please, this is important . . ."

She could see he was telling the truth. He did need her Worse, when she looked at him she knew the way he was seeing her now . . . the unfaithful one, he had caught her with another man. Seeing them like that was to him like seeing her in bed with someone . . . the physical act was not what hurt so much as the shared intimacies, and the idea that Loring, her patient, could see her in that way hurt her more than it should have. It was hard to do the right thing, but she had no choice. He needed her too much. She had to be strong . . . even if it meant hurting him.

"You cannot come here on a whim. I have other patients, Mr. Weatherby." It was like a slap when she didn't call him Loring. Had he done something *that* wrong . . . He hardly heard her when she said, "If you feel you need to see me more often we'll talk about it tomorrow. Perhaps we can arrange something, but you may not just break in on me whenever you feel like it. Do you understand?"

Only too well. His mother had said it that night. Yes, he understood. Why didn't *she*? Didn't his needs count? He felt something building in him that he'd never felt before. Because of its unfamiliarity he couldn't put a name to it. It was rage.

It filled his chest, expanded it until he felt it would burst. His heart was beating with the strength of someone pounding on a door.

"Now you really must go," he heard her say. "I'll see you tomorrow at our regular time..."

What she saw on his face made her reach out and touch his arm to reassure him. It was the first time she had ever touched him, and it calmed him. What was she saying to him? What did she want from him? Did she really want him to go, or did she want him to protect her? To drive the man on the couch away and take his place at her side. All she had to do was to say it and he would move mountains for her.

They walked to the door and she turned, leaving him alone in the hall. As she crossed the office she felt his eyes on her, and she wanted to turn and look at him but she didn't ... she didn't know if she could handle the look on his face. She would make it up to him, give him extra time and attention...

He heard more than saw the door close, and knew she was gone from him, back to the man on the couch. He crept back into the office. There had to be something here to help sort out the confusion. A sign. Something to begin again with.

He saw the closet. He opened the door. Inside was her coat and scarf. He touched the scarf. It had her scent. A lady's token, like Lancelot and Queen "G." He took it and left.

CHAPTER 10

MERCANTO WOKE up to find himself in strange sur-roundings. He was groggy and in bed, that much he knew. The room was bright, and he could hear noises in the background, but he didn't know where he was or how he got there. All he knew was he felt like he'd been on a long drunk. When he tried to move a sharp pain in his chest stopped him. He raised his hand to his face and found a small tube taped to his cheek and running under his nose. Air from it was blowing up his nostrils.

He wanted to say, "Where am I?" but the words came out, "What day is it" and he heard someone laugh.

He raised his head painfully. At the foot of the bed were four people . . . a nurse, Captain Zinkowsky, Sloan and Catherine Poydras. All except the nurse had worried looks on their faces.

"You're awake, good," said the nurse. She took his pulse in a businesslike manner. Satisfied with the results, she turned to the others. "You can talk to him now, but because of the anaesthetic he probably won't make much sense."

The nurse left, and the captain and Sloan came and stood beside him. Catherine Poydras hung back.

"You were shot . . . Catherine found you," the captain said.

Mercanto raised his hand. Catherine, a petite woman in her forties with hennaed hair, came forward and took it. "Thanks," he said.

"When I closed the restaurant, I saw you in the parking lot. *Mon dieu*, I thought you were dead."

He managed a laugh, and the physical act of it sent spasms of pain through the chest. "That would never do. It would be bad for business. Two in such a short time," he said, trying to make her smile.

His little joke made an angry look cross her face. She pulled away from his hand. "Men," she said, but she looked more like her old self as she said it.

"Can you tell me what happened?" Sloan asked.

Mercanto tried to sort out his thoughts. "I went to the park . . . while I was sitting there a kid came up to the car . . . tried to rob me." Mercanto raised his head, trying to get his eyes to focus. "Did he get my wallet and gun . . . ?"

"No."

"Good," he said, and let his head sink back on the pillow.

"You should have given them to him," Sloan said.

Mercanto smiled. "And have you ream me out?"

"The doctor fished the slug out. It hit a rib, broke it. If it wasn't from a .22, like the one that killed Hightower, you'd be dead. Looks like you found our man," Sloan said.

Mercanto thought back to the parking lot. He shook his head. The movement sent the pain through him again. "It was an old Western Colt he had. I thought it was a .45."

"They make them in .22, too," Sloan said.

"Thank God," Mercanto said, and meant it.

"Can you describe him?" said the captain.

Mercanto stared at the ceiling for a minute. "A teen-ager .. about sixteen. White, six feet, dark hair and clothes . . . on a bike."

"From the neighborhood," said Sloan. "What'd he say to you?"

"He said I had a flat . . . like a damn fool I got out to see .. He pulled the gun . . . I tried to talk him out of it."

"Why didn't you shoot?" asked the captain.

"Rudy Gunther . . ."

"This time you should have," Sloan said.

"Maybe next time I'll get it right," Mercanto said.

The captain said, "You're tired. Time to talk later. We'll send someone around for the details when you've had some sleep. You'll be on leave, six weeks convalescence."

An alarm bell went off in his mind. "My brother . . . you didn't tell him about this, did you? He's sick. It would only worry him."

The captain said, "No, we didn't notify him. We were waiting to see if you were okay."

"Don't . . ."

"Whatever you say."

As they turned to go, he said, "What about the case . . . ?"

"We'll take it from here. Don't worry," said Sloan.

The next morning he was released. An officer from the district drove him home in a blue-and-white. They'd already brought his car, it was parked in front of his building.

The stairs to his apartment seemed to take forever. His chest was taped tight, each breath sent a sharp pain from the broken rib. He downed two of the painkillers they'd given him and sank into bed.

His sleep was of drugged dreams of the shooting. First he was himself, then he was Hightower, staring at the teen-ager. The muzzle of the gun looked like a cannon, and each time he saw the shot fired it was trailed by flames like a rocket. He woke drenched in sweat, again not knowing where he was. The day had passed, the room was dark. In his confusion he wondered what woke him, then he heard the sound. Someone was knocking on the door. He struggled to his feet and made his way to the living room.

"Just a minute." His voice was hoarse. His head was pounding.

He fumbled with the door, then realized he hadn't locked it when he came in. "Some cop you are . . ." he said. He opened it and saw Sloan standing there.

"How are you feeling?"

"Like hell."

Sloan followed him in and turned on the lights. "I was shot once."

Mercanto lowered himself into a chair while Sloan stood watching. Sloan opened a bag and pulled out two Budweisers. He popped the top on one and handed it to him. Mercanto took a sip while Sloan took off his coat. The cold bitterness helped, and his head began to ease. They sat quietly. Midway through the second beer Sloan said, "Feel like talking?"

"Not much to tell. I said it all in the hospital."

"I'm not talking about that. When a guy gets shot it does things to him."

"It hurts. Period."

Sloan accepted it. "What were you doing there, anyway?"

"I couldn't sleep. The case was on my mind so I went out there to see if I could piece anything together. I spent the day talking to Hightower's employees, especially a woman he saw on the side. She said he'd been distant, gloomy for the past few months."

"What do you make of it?"

"The more I think about it, the more I think drugs. The cash withdrawals, and you know how coke changes a person. That would explain his moods, coming down after a big night."

"I agree. If he was dealing that would explain how he and the kid were in the park at the same time." Sloan took a sip of his beer. "We've got everybody out looking for the kid. When we find him we should be close to solving the case." He stood up to go. "Meanwhile, enjoy your vacation."

"One thing . . . what's going to happen to me? I mean, I don't want to go back into uniform again."

Sloan pulled on his coat. "We'll discuss it later."

The next morning Mercanto forced himself out of bed. In the mirror his swarthy looks were sallow, his eyes sunken and bright, but he managed to shower and dress. Something in the night made him decide not to give up on the case. As he tossed and turned, replaying the shooting in his mind, he remembered what the captain had said . . . The kid did not take his wallet. That meant he panicked and ran, not exactly the killer who had coolly shot Hightower and mutilated the body afterward . . .

He made coffee and sat down at the table. The bottle of

painkillers was in front of him, he thought about taking some but didn't. The pain was less sharp. If it got worse he could take them later. Right now he needed a clear head.

The window at Interiors was filled with a small sofa and two end tables, the bases of which were china elephants. Looked expensive.

Inside he was greeted by a man in his forties, dressed in a crew neck sweater and chinos. Mercanto showed him his badge and said that he was looking for John and Elizabeth Cohen. The man led him to an office in the rear where a woman with a mane of blonde hair was working at a drafting table.

"Now, what can we do for you?" the man asked. The woman came over to join them. When he said he was investigating the Hightower murder they looked real sad.

"We had dinner with him the night it happened," the man said. "At Lagniappe..." the woman added. "We were so shocked to hear what had happened. Stanley was one of our best friends. He and John have known each other for over twenty years."

"That's why I'm here, I'm trying to reconstruct what happened that night."

"We always had dinner once a week, sometimes twice. Usually it would be the four of us ... Dominique, when they were married, and Cheryl Goldman, since the divorce," Elizabeth said. "That night, for some reason, it was just three of us. Lagniappe was Stanley's idea. It was his favorite restaurant."

"Why just the three of you?"

"I guess that's how he wanted it," John said.

"What was his mood like?"

They looked at each other. Elizabeth said, "He wasn't himself. You'd have to know Stanley to understand it. The

124

evening started okay. He was lively. We had a couple of bottles of champagne, but I noticed there was an edge to him, like he was forcing himself to have a good time. Almost manic. When the conversation would let up a look would come over him like he was ready to . . . to cry or something."

"What do you think was behind it?"

"I don't know. Once, when John was in the men's room I asked what was wrong. He said nothing, but he squeezed my hand and held it like he didn't want to let go."

"Like she said, you had to know Stanley," added John. "That was unusual. He wasn't the type to start touching."

"How had his mood been over, say, the last three or four months?"

"Odd you should ask, because we talked about it afterward. We'd both noticed a big mood change in him lately. He'd been distant, sad, but he'd never confided in us why," John said.

"To be truthful, his mood started to change around the time of the divorce," Elizabeth said. "When he said they were splitting up, we were shocked. Oh, Dominique could be difficult, but that was her way, and they had always seemed so happy together. Then one day, out of the blue . . . After that he seemed like a kid again, he was so happy. I told John he's got a girlfriend. Probably a young one . . ."

"Cheryl Goldman, the girl from his office?"

"At first we thought so," Elizabeth said. "The way he started bringing her to dinner almost immediately, but then I decided not. It was the way he treated her, like a friend, not a lover."

"Do you know who it was?"

"No. We teased him about it but he never said. Then when his mood changed for the worse three or four months ago we assumed it was over."

"Did he try for a reconciliation?"

John shook his head.

Mercanto's chest was hurting with each breath. He wished now that he'd taken the painkillers.

"Going through his papers we found he'd been making large cash withdrawals from his checking account for the past few months. They total almost fifty thousand dollars. Do you have any idea what they might be for?"

The Cohens looked at each other. "No," John said. "We don't."

"We also found drugs. Cocaine and prescription drugs . . ."

"You think drugs might be tied in to his murder," Elizabeth said. Mercanto noticed that there was no surprise in her voice. "It's possible."

"Nonsense," said John. "Stanley liked to do a line or two...I guess we all do, but he wasn't that deep into them."

"John, that's not true. How many times did you tell me you were worried about how much he was doing...and his moods. That could have been caused by drugs."

John gave her a look. "It wasn't that bad. What he's saying is that Stanley was in over his head. That wasn't so."

Mercanto shifted, trying to ease the pain. John knew more than he was saying, at least that much was obvious.

"Look, sir, we need all the help we can get. I'm not a reporter, I'm a cop. I need the help. One of the things I haven't been able to find out is who he was buying drugs from . . ."

Silence for a few moments. Finally John spoke. "We don't know his name, but Stanley mentioned he'd been dealing with a Jamaican."

"Do you know where they met? Was it the park?" Mercanto asked.

John shook his head. "I don't know. It was something we really didn't want to know too much about, if you see what I'm saying."

"Let's get back to that night. What time was dinner over?"

"We finished around eleven but stayed on for a few drinks. I think we closed the place," John said.

Elizabeth added, "That's because John's not sure. He had a few too many. We did close the place. After that we said goodnight and went home. That's the last time we saw Stanley."

"Think back. Did anything unusual occur while you were having dinner?"

"No," John said.

Elizabeth looked thoughtful. "There was one thing...about, oh, one forty-five he got up and made a phone call. He was only gone a couple of minutes but that did seem odd. I mean, who do you call that late?"

Mercanto's heart picked up its beat. "Did he say who he was calling?"

"No. In fact, I think he said he was going to get cigarettes. The only reason I know he made a call was that from where I was sitting I could see him," she said.

"Nothing, not a clue . . . ?"

She shook her head, and Mercanto was, once again, stopped cold.

CHAPTER 11

MACE'S CROSSING was busy with late lunch customers when Margaret arrived. The Valium she had taken before leaving the office had calmed her, and she waved hello to Mace, who was at the bar talking with the Campbell brothers and John Sgarlat, businessmen she knew slightly from Racquet Club dinners with Adam. Mace waved back and pointed to a table near the window. Waiting for her there was Charles Foster, her own analyst, and friend.

Charles was a slight man in his mid-sixties, shrewd eyes and a face that radiated warmth and interest toward everything around him.

She tossed her coat on one of the extra chairs and sat down. While she fished her cigarettes from her purse, Keith, the bartender, brought her a glass of white wine. She and Charles had been meeting here for lunch for years. It was the personal touch that kept them coming back.

"I was pleased when you called," Charles said. "It does my image a world of good to be seen with a beautiful woman."

She was glad to see he wasn't really angry with her. Since her father's death years ago while she was in graduate school, Charles had been her mentor, her stability, and she didn't want anything to disturb that.

Through the years he had gone from being one of her professors to her personal and training analyst to her friend. They chitchatted for a few minutes, then Charles said, "Now, what's on your mind . . . ?"

"What makes you think there's something on my mind? We're friends, can't we just have lunch together?"

"Your smoking. You don't normally chain-smoke unless something's bothering you."

She looked at her cigarette. He was so right. "Why's everyone suddenly picking on me about my smoking?" she said, remembering Loring's words from one of their sessions. When he didn't answer, she went on, "I don't now how to begin . . . God, I sound like one of my patients."

"Why don't you start by satisfying my curiosity. Who else has been commenting on your smoking?"

She took a sip of her wine. "Charles, you're good, do you know that? One of my patients said it. He said I was sensual when I smoked." She felt herself blush when she said it. Jesus, some analyst. Well, now she was the patient . . .

He noticed her reaction. "How did it make you feel?"

130

"Good and bad. I'm still a woman, and a woman likes compliments, but he said it in a transference situation—"

"Transference with whom? Another woman, I assume . . . his mother, his wife?"

"He's single. It was his mother . . . I guess I'd better start at the beginning."

She detailed her sessions with Loring, careful never to mention his name. She told of the episode in the fitting room, his conflicts, his statements, her theories.

Charles listened. When she was finished he said, "What an interesting case. Complex, intelligent, responsive. What's bothering you?"

"What he's not telling," she said.

"Nothing unusual about that, especially with symptoms this complex. Besides, it's early, you've only touched the surface. You know that." He stopped for a moment. "But then you're not talking about his past, are you? You're talking about the present."

She lit another cigarette. "He broke in on one of my sessions today . . ." She considered telling him that Loring had stolen her scarf afterward but didn't, even though it was what had led her to call Charles for lunch. The scarf was such a bare statement of Loring's need. To discuss symptoms with another professional was one thing, but to tell about the scarf would, somehow, be a sort of betrayal on her part . . .

Charles's eyebrows raised at this information. "I see, and what did you do?"

Margaret turned and looked out the window. In the near distance she could see the Cathedral of Sts. Peter and Paul. "I sent him away."

"And . . . ?"

"I didn't want to, he was in a bad way. He needed me—"

"Needed you . . . or needed to see you?"

She took a drag on her cigarette. "Same thing—"

"No, it's not, you know that . . . is he attractive?"

"*That's* inappropriate. You wouldn't ask a man that. This is a professional situation we're talking about."

"That's true, it is a professional situation we're talking about, but I think it's a valid question. And one that I most certainly *would* ask a man describing a similar situation with a female patient."

"I just don't much like the way you're putting it. You make me sound like a so-called typical female. Is that how you really think of me?"

"No, of course not, and I'd think after all these years you'd know that. Let's table the question."

"Let's not. Yes, he is attractive. One of the handsomest men I've ever laid eyes on. Satisfied?"

Charles nodded, continued in a soft voice as if her outburst never happened. "Is he the first patient who has ever broken in on one of your sessions?"

"There have been others."

". . . And you sent them away, too," he said. When she said yes, he said, "But something made this one different. What was it? Was he suicidal? Did he threaten you or appear violent when you told him to go?"

She shook her head. "He would never hurt me." She realized she'd better explain that, even if she wasn't being entirely honest. "He's not that kind of man, he's very gentle, he could never hurt anyone. That's what makes it so bad. When I sent him away I really hurt him, I know I did. He thinks I rejected him . . ."

Damn it, this wasn't how she planned it. Everything she was saying was coming out wrong. Charles was being argumentative. She looked away. God, was she going to *cry?*

He put a hand on her arm. "What you're telling me is

dangerous ground. You did the right thing to send him away. If you're going to help him you've got to maintain control, and from what you're saying he *does* need your help."

"That's what I'm trying to tell you," she said.

"Margaret, what you're going through happens to every analyst at some point in his career. He meets a patient who gets around his reserve. Not as often as the public thinks, but it happens. Patients can be very seductive. You're alone with them for long periods of time. They expose themselves to you. A special closeness develops. It's almost sexual by definition. Sex is, after all, the physical communication of unspoken needs."

"It's not like *that*, Charles. I'm not going to go to bed with him, for God's sake."

"But you're thinking about it."

Instead of denying it, she straightened and asked him why he said that.

"We're discussing distance. If we look at ourselves as the center, and the people of our lives as concentric circles around us, like rings on a tree, the most distant circle is our enemies. The closer in we get, the more intimate the relationship, until we reach the center, which is symbolized by the sex act, when the statement of closeness is made by one partner actually being inside the body of the other."

He paused to light a pipe. "Your exact words a moment ago were—'I'm not going to go to bed with him.' You didn't say, 'I'm not *thinking about* going to bed with him.' Which indicates to me that you've moved him one concentric circle closer to the center. More important, you've gone from a passive, romantic speculation to an active denial, which, as you well know, means that in your own subconscious you've accepted the possibility as reality."

"No Charles, you're wrong. What I'm telling you is that

. . . what I'm telling you is that this is a patient I'm *very* concerned about. Period."

"No," he said gently, "you're telling me that you're human, that you're afraid you're about to make a mistake, that *you* need help."

She looked at him. "What you're saying doesn't make me sound very professional, does it?"

"Bullshit. I'm not Bill Buckley. Your libidinal considerations aside, what we're talking about here is plain wrong from every standpoint. Sheer folly, as they would have said in the nineteenth century. There are no grounds on which you can justify it. Patients are like your children. They *trust* you. You can't betray a trust."

"Charles, you're way out in left field. What I want to talk about is the best way to help him."

"That's what I'm talking about, too . . . Look, satisfy an old man's curiosity. Tell me your dreams."

She looked at him for a long moment. It was a mistake to come here, but if I don't answer him he'll think something worse anyway. "All right. I dreamed about him twice. Each time we were in a house. He was in the kitchen making dinner. I came and stood in the doorway—"

"I won't insult your intelligence by interpreting *that* one for you . . . What about your waking hours? Your wish-thinking?"

"Can I have another glass of wine . . . no, make it a Perrier," she said, remembering the Valium.

He caught Keith's eye and ordered.

"I think Adam is having an affair . . . with one of his students. She's nineteen. A friend told me about them. At first I didn't believe it, hated her for telling me. You know . . . kill the messenger, but after a while I couldn't deny it any more. Oh, he has an excuse every time he's late or goes out at night but . . ." She turned to look out the window again. Damn it, *she* needed someone to care about her for a change. "Charles, nineteen-year-olds can be very indiscreet, and heartless. Every night she calls. If I answer she just listens, doesn't say a damn word. Adam calls it a prank caller, but I know it's her." She paused. "But there have been times when I pretended to myself it was my patient, not her."

"Is this a what's-fair-for-the-goose deal?"

She whipped around to look at him, her eyes angry. "Don't humiliate me. We've been friends too long. I didn't come here for that."

He was silent for a moment, then: "I'm sorry for what's happening between you and Adam. I don't want to see you hurt, but—"

She shook her head. "I know what you're going to say—but you're not listening to me, you're projecting—"

"*I'm* projecting? Talk about transference. Margaret, face it, you're becoming emotionally involved with a patient who has a very complex psychological disorder. Run-of-the-mill neurotics don't go around having psychotic episodes in men's stores."

Loring's face came to her mind. Charles was no god. Loring was *her* patient. Charles didn't know him. "It wasn't psychotic. It was hysteric. There's a big difference, I believe."

"I'm aware of it, I only hope you are. From the way you described him, he could also be schizophrenic. The symptoms are often similar, but they're worlds apart in what could happen."

"He's not schizophrenic."

"How do you know? Have you given him a Minnesota Multiphase or done any other testing?"

"No, it's too early. His therapy is just getting underway."

"Then I'm going to keep the book open on whether he's schizophrenic, and so should you. But that doesn't change things, you're upset yourself, and you're letting a very disturbed person become obsessed with you. Sleeping with him is not the question, we both know that the wish can have the effect of the deed. The absence of the physical can be just a salve for conscience. What I'm saying is that you're endangering both of you by continuing with him under the present circumstances. I think you should withdraw and refer him to another analyst."

She reached for her cigarettes. "That's not what Freud would say. He would say the solution to the conflict is through catharsis—"

"Screw Freud," Charles said, "and don't try to cite Jung's affairs with his patients, either. I'm talking about what's right and wrong for you and for this patient. I'm not talking about a relative situation. With the present stress in your own life, you just cannot help him."

"Charles, please believe me. This time the wish is not the deed. I'm not going to sleep with him. I want to help him."

He looked at her for a moment. Finally he said, "I believe you . . . on both counts, but the best way you can help him is to cut him loose. Don't endanger yourself and your patient, too," he repeated.

She shook her head. This time this wise man was plain wrong. There was no danger. She was grateful to Charles for the past, but she'd been wrong to involve him in this situation. It wasn't something even Charles could take in second-hand. She would help Loring herself. "I'm sorry. I can't," she said. "To withdraw would be the real danger." She honestly believed that.

CHAPTER 12

BRIAN COLLINS quietly slipped on his dark jacket and left by the back door of the West Mt. Airy twin. His mother had gone to bed early. She was a sound sleeper and wouldn't miss him. The night was his, he thought as he stretched in the cold air, looking up at the sky. There were clouds. It might rain before morning, but the moon still shone brightly. A bomber's moon was what it was called in the novel he was reading. That's all he needed, just enough light to see by. He headed for the garage where he kept his bicycle.

He hadn't been back to the park since the night he encountered the man with the gun. It was the first time he'd ever shot anyone. Always before they handed over their money without a fight.

Inside the garage he didn't turn on the light. He didn't need it, the garage was his domain, he knew every inch of it by heart. His workshop was there, his chemistry lab from years ago, even a couple of well-worn copies of Playboy and Penthouse.

He went to an old sofa in the corner and lifted one of the cushions. Wedged there was the gun. He picked it up and twirled it on his finger cowboy-style. The weight felt good in his hand. The gun was his proudest possession, even though he couldn't show it to anyone. It was exactly like an old West Colt .45 except it was a .22. He'd taken it and a box of shells from a house on Livesey Street in his second burglary. That was over a year ago. So much had happened since then.

Also wedged among the cushions was a pint of Gordon's vodka. In the faint light he could see there wasn't much left. He took off the top and drank from it, grimacing from the sterile non-taste. If he had his choice it would be bourbon, he liked the brown color and its sweet richness better, but it left a strong odor his mother could smell on his breath. He replaced the top and wedged it back among the cushions. What he really wanted was a line or two of coke, but he'd been out for over a week. Maybe tonight would change all that, he thought as he jammed the gun into the waistband of his trousers and zipped his jacket again.

The vodka bottle had been full his last time in the park, but the shooting left him so shaky he drank almost all of it as soon as he got back to the safety of the garage, and then paid the price by being sick and throwing up twice during the night. Fortunately his mother thought it was a stomach virus and let him stay home from school the next day. Otherwise he didn't know what he would have done.

He pushed his bicycle outside and got on, wishing it was a car. Someday . . . he thought, as he started to pedal. Right now things were too tight. He knew the worried look on his mother's face, and he wouldn't add to it by asking. The only reason he was able to go to prep school was because of his father's checks. A couple of times when the checks were late he told himself it didn't matter, but he knew it did. That's why he studied so hard.

As he pedaled toward Emlen he thought about the chemistry he was studying earlier. It was all math, nothing like his old lab in the garage, and no matter how hard he tried he couldn't seem to make heads or tails of it. The only reason he continued to take it was because it would be helpful later when he tried to get into college.

When he reached Emlen he paused to consider his best approach to the park. He didn't really think the man he'd shot was a cop. Every day since he had poured over the papers. There was nothing in them about it, only about the Hightower killing, and they always wrote up every cop shooting. But if he was a cop it could mean trouble in the Valley Green section. They might have it staked out, so he decided to go to Hortter instead. There was always someone parking near where it dead-ended at the stables. Maybe one car would be enough to get him a gram later. That would take about a hundred, which was reasonable to expect from two people parking. He started to pedal again.

He was fifteen when he burgled his first home, a colonial on Allen's Lane that belonged to friends of his father who were away on vacation at the time. It was a disappointing experience. He had no way to dispose of televisions or stereos so he had to settle for the less than thirty-five dollars he found in a kitchen drawer. Nowhere near enough to get the Jamaicans to sell him some. It made him so angry that he poured a gallon of bleach onto the Oriental rug in their living room.

Several cars passed him before he reached Hortter. Each time he kept his head down so they wouldn't see his face. All together he'd burgled about fifteen homes before he got up his nerve to use the gun to hold up people.

Since then things were much more profitable. Now he could afford cocaine on a regular basis with even a little extra to share. No doubt about it, he thought, his life had taken a turn for the better. Gone was that feeling he wasn't good enough. He was king of the hill whenever he wanted to be. Who cared if he didn't play football. He had plenty of friends, people at school who eighteen months ago wouldn't give him the time of day.

He even had a girlfriend . . . blonde, sophisticated, good-looking. Traci was her name. On Saturdays she would take him to the Germantown Cricket Club or to parties, not that any of that mattered much to him. Not when compared with the pleasure of getting high. That was what really counted, getting to the edge and holding it. A little coke, when that started to get out of hand, a mouthful of vodka or a toke or two on a joint, then a little more coke. Fine tuning, that's what it is, he thought, and the world's a better place for it.

At Hortter he turned right. What he was doing wasn't wrong. If those fatheads in Washington would wake up and legalize marijuana and cocaine, it wouldn't be so expensive. Everyone knew the stuff wouldn't hurt you. Hell, half of the people in Congress used it. It was just their hypocrisy that kept them from doing the right thing.

He crossed Wissahickon Avenue and slowed down. It was only a few hundred yards to what he thought of as his private "fishing hole." He stopped and hid his bicycle up the hill in the woods where no one would see it and went along on foot. In a few moments he saw that fish were present this evening in the form of a station wagon with imitation wood paneling, the kind a family would use. He was sure they had no business here.

Over the year most of the cars he held up had no business here. Many of them were gays, which pleased him. They were never any trouble. It was almost like they enjoyed it. Not like the tough-looking guy with the gun. Cop or no cop, his car should have been a tip-off, an old beat-up Camaro. Only a hard ass would drive a car like that. It was a mistake he would not let himself repeat in the future.

He thought about the shooting. It was the most exciting thing he'd ever done, even though in his panic he'd run off without the loot. The fact that there was no mention of it in the papers showed him that the man wasn't dead, but he didn't care either way. Not any more. Pulling the trigger was easy, and it was fun. He would do it again without hesitation.

His watch said midnight. He wondered what they were doing now in the car. Timing was so important. The part he liked best was jerking open the car door and seeing the look on their faces. He smiled at the thought of it. Tomorrow night at the basketball game he would have a gram, maybe two, and everyone would get well. Even Traci, if she was especially nice.

He pulled the gun from his waistband and spun the cylinder, making sure it was loaded. With a nod to himself he started for the car, thinking he was just keeping with tradition like Billy the Kid or Jesse James, or the guy he'd been reading about lately . . . Charles Manson. All the people who saw society for the crock of shit it was.

Crouching slightly, he moved closer, being careful where he stepped. Surprise was the key to the whole thing, that and the gun. A few more steps brought him to the rear fender on the driver's side. He was almost trembling with excitement. This was the part he really dug.

The light came on inside the car when he jerked open the door, and he got a good look at the two people in the front seat. A man and a woman. The woman's blouse was open and her pants were down. The man's fly was open, and they were kissing and touching each other all over.

The woman let out a little scream when she saw the gun. The man turned around, angry and scared at the same time. "What the hell—" Then he saw the gun, too.

Brian smashed the man's ear with the gun, and the fight went out of him. Brian smiled at how ridiculous the man looked, all exposed like that.

"Don't hurt us, please," the woman said, trying to cover her breasts.

He grabbed the man's hair and pulled him out of the car. His experience with the tough-looking man had taught him one thing . . . don't be so easy with them. He made the man lie down on the road beside the car.

"Please stop. We'll do whatever you want," the woman said.

He looked at her in the light. The frightened look on her face turned him on. "Move your hands, I want to see you," he said.

The man on the ground tried to get up. Brian kicked him in the face.

"No, stop. I'll do it." She moved her hands and sat there for him. Her body wasn't as good as he'd thought.

"Give me your purse."

She slid it across the seat. He took it and pulled the keys from the ignition, tossed them on the road somewhere ahead, then he took her wallet out of her purse and turned to the man on the ground. "I'll take yours now, Slim."

The man reached into his back pocket without trying to get up again. Brian took it from him. It was one of those nylon wallets with a Velcro flap. He hated that kind of wallet and thought about kicking the man again but didn't. Instead, he pointed the gun at him and cocked it. The sound of the cylinder turning was sweet. The man lay still at his feet. Brian wondered what he was thinking.

The woman leaned across the seat, her breasts swaying. "Please ... I'll do anything you want ..." Tears were streaming down her face.

Brian smiled. "This is just to let you know that now I know where you live. If you tell anyone about this, I'll come for you and I'll kill you."

"We won't ... I promise ... we won't ... Dear God, just go ..."

He thought about staying around and toying with them a little longer but knew it was a risky idea. He turned and started up the road, glancing back at them as he went. The woman was out of the car and on her knees trying to help the man. He knew she was telling the truth. They would be no trouble.

A few hundred yards into the darkness he turned and climbed the hill into the woods where his bicycle was hidden. It had been a good night. He paused long enough to take the money from the wallets, then throw them away. With the moonlight only filtering through the trees he couldn't see how much he'd gotten, but time enough for that later.

He pushed the bicycle, moving deeper into the woods. There was a path nearby that he knew would take him back to Wissahickon Avenue without meeting up with his victims again. It was one of the things he liked best about this spot.

As the wheels of the bicycle turned they made a soft, clicking sound, not unlike the cylinder of his revolver. The clicking sounded out of place in the woods. He paused for a second to listen for the sound of the car engine that would mean his victims were on their way. He heard nothing.

"Probably still too scared," he said aloud, thinking of the

143

woman's breasts as she leaned across the seat toward him. "I should have played with them . . ." he muttered.

Then he heard another sound. A faint, rustling near him. The wind's beginning to pick up, he thought. He felt the first drop of rain. "Better get home," he said. "Wouldn't want to have to explain a bunch of wet clothes to mom."

He pushed the bicycle on, wishing it didn't make the clicking sound it did. The rustling stopped, then started again. His thoughts went back to the woman. Yes, he should at least have touched her breasts. Tomorrow that's what he would do with Traci after the basketball game . . . make her sit there with her clothes open before he'd give her any coke. She would do anything for a line or two.

A branch snapped nearby, like someone stepped on it? He stopped, listened. He looked to where he thought the sound came from but saw nothing except the outlines of the trees and brush, just shadows in the faint moonlight.

More drops of rain hit him. He turned up his collar to keep their stinging coldness from his neck. The path was near, then a short distance to Wissahickon Avenue and the ride home, but now something about the woods had changed. He couldn't tell what, only that he felt uneasy, a light prickling along the back of his neck.

He tried to dismiss it. For years he'd played in these woods . . . but the feeling didn't go away. His hand went to his waistband to check his gun. It was gone. He patted himself down but it was no use, he'd dropped it somewhere along the way. He had to find it.

Leaving his bicycle behind he started to retrace his steps. A flashlight would make the job easier, he thought, but he hoped the metal would gleam in the moonlight. He stepped carefully on the carpet of dead leaves, trying not to move around and possibly cover it up. He would not go home without it.

His concentration was so great that at first he didn't hear the rustling when it started again. When he did it was closer and slightly behind him, distinctly different now from the wind in the trees or the falling rain. It was the sound of something moving in the brush.

"Probably just a dog," he said aloud. "Nothing to worry about . . ."

He continued his search, but moving more quickly. The shuffling noises continued with him, seemed closer now.

He didn't actually think it, but he felt something new to him . . . he was no longer the predator, pursuer. He was the intended victim, the pursued.

He hated the feeling. Now he *had* to find that gun.

The noises were louder now. He could hear a grunting, animal-noise with the shuffling. It had to be a dog. Sure. He picked up a rock and threw it in the direction of the sounds. It bounced harmlessly off the trees. He threw another, and heard the noises retreat.

"Good," he said, "that'll show you."

He listened for a moment. The woods were quiet again except for the wind in the trees and the rain falling harder. He was almost back to Hortter Street. Only a couple hundred more yards. The gun had to be here somewhere. Then by God he'd show that dog—

Almost at his elbow he heard a low growl. The dog had not gone away, it had moved ahead of him in the woods. Jesus, what if it was rabid . . . He looked around for another rock. As he bent to pick one up he heard a snarl and was knocked flat by a heavy weight on his back.

His face was buried in the wet leves. He felt hot breath on his neck, and tried to fight back, to get free. Over and over they rolled, this crazy dog growling and snarling like no dog he'd ever heard. In the faint light he caught a glimpse of feverish eyes, lips pulled back from teeth. It was no dog that

145

was attacking him, it was a *man*. He tried to hit out with his fists but was overpowered.

He managed to roll to his stomach, trying to protect himself. As he did he raised his head. Just out of reach he saw the gun in the leaves. He swung his elbows hard as he could, trying to break free. No use. He tried to crawl, the man still on his back, his legs almost around him.

Now pain sharper, more intense than anything he'd ever felt as teeth ripped the side of his neck. He screamed a silent scream, his face buried in the wet leaves. Warm blood began to cover his neck and face from his torn carotid artery.

He barely raised his head again as he tried to reach the gun. It was the last thing he saw before the clawlike fingers dug into his eye sockets.

CHAPTER 13

A T STANLEY Hightower's office Cheryl Goldman and Mercanto were again sitting opposite each other. There was a puzzled look on Cheryl's face. "When I called your office to see if there was any news about when Stanley's body would be released I was told you were no longer on the case."

Mercanto adjusted his coat to ease the pressure on his rib. This time he'd brought the painkillers with him. If he needed a couple he was going to take them.

"That's right," he said. "I'm officially on sick leave. I was shot the other night."

"Oh . . . I'm sorry. How did it happen?"

Even with the painkillers he was having trouble sleeping. Every time he moved, the pain woke him, and the two together were taking their toll on him.

He shrugged. "I got to thinking about the case the night after I was there and drove out to the park where he was killed. A kid held me up. When I tried to arrest him, he shot me."

"God, how awful . . . Do you think he might be the one that killed Stanley?"

"It's a possibility . . . the place was the same, and the gun was the same type . . . There are a few more questions I'd like to ask you . . ."

"Fire away," she said, then she laughed. "Sorry, that didn't come out like I meant it."

Mercanto smiled. It eased the way for his questioning. "When we talked last time I didn't mention that we found drugs in Stanley's apartment. Can you tell me anything about them?"

"Why no, of course not . . . Why is this important anyway? It sounds like you know who did it and all you have to do is catch him."

"Maybe," Mercanto said, "but I'm not sold on the idea that this kid's the killer. Certain things were different about the two incidents . . ."

"Like what?"

"I can't go into that right now, but trust me, if you knew you'd agree."

She looked skeptical. "The last time someone said 'trust me' he . . . never mind."

"If it will make it any easier for you, I've talked to John and Elizabeth Cohen. They've confirmed that for the past few months he was using a large amount of drugs. Approximately the same period as the withdrawals from his bank account, and his depression."

She thought about it for a moment. Mercanto sat waiting. Waiting was what a cop did most of the time.

Finally she said, "It's true, he was doing a lot of drugs the past few months . . . I guess by our association it means I was doing a lot, too."

He liked her honesty. He also liked the way she stood by Hightower. Loyalty and honesty didn't come along much in his line of work.

"That's not what I'm here for," he said. "My job is to see his killer brought in. When I was talking with the Cohens they mentioned that Stanley bought his drugs from Jamaicans, but they didn't know who. Do you?"

She nodded. "His name was Rashid, that's all I know. I never saw him, but Stanley mentioned him a couple of times."

At least he had a name. That could account for the call Elizabeth Cohen saw Stanley make from Lagniappe. With so much in his apartment it wasn't likely he was buying that night, but maybe he was going to pay somebody off. Drug dealers didn't usually give credit, but when you're talking about big withdrawals, a new set of rules could apply.

"Where would they usually meet?"

"I don't know," she said. "All he ever told me was the man's name . . . I can't help you any more than that."

As he stood up to go he said, "Did he call you between one-thirty and two the night he was killed?"

When he heard her say no he had to smile. Now he was sure that call was made to the killer . . .

From Hightower's office he drove to a loft building at Eighteenth and Callowhill. Stenciled on the heavy steel door was the word "Dominique." He pressed the buzzer under the intercom. After a moment a voice asked who it was. The intercom had so much static he couldn't tell if the voice was male or female. He identified himself, and the voice said, "Just a minute."

The minute stretched to five before the door opened. Standing in front of him was a young man with a spiky two-toned crewcut, blond and green.

"Sorry, I couldn't hear you too well upstairs."

Mercanto showed his badge. "I'm here to see Mrs. Hightower."

The young man led him to a freight elevator that they took to the third floor. The elevator opened into a large room that took up the whole floor. People were working at cutting tables, sewing machines or drawing boards. In the center of the room, on a small platform, a man and a woman were fitting and pinning a dress to a mannequin while a small dark-haired woman dressed in jeans and a black turtleneck stood off to one side watching.

The man with the crewcut pointed. "That's her."

"Mrs. Hightower..."

She turned, eyes flashing. "My name is not Hightower. It's Bouquet...Dominique Bouquet," she said with a heavy French accent.

He showed her his badge. "Sorry, I'll remember next time ...is there somewhere we can talk?"

"Come with me."

He followed her to the elevator and the fourth floor. Like the third it was also one large room, but it was broken up with free-standing black-and-white partitions cordoning it off into different sections. The one they were in was dominated by a large sectional sofa in black suede with a gold standing lamp at each end.

"Your living quarters?" he said, looking around. She sat down on the sofa, tucking one leg under her. "Yes," she said. "Now I know who decorated your husband's offices."

A look of interest crossed her face. "Ex-husband," she said. "How do you know that?"

He sat down beside her. As he sank into the cushions he could feel the pain begin again in his chest, and he had to sit forward.

"I've seen his apartment and his offices. This looks more like his offices than his apartment. I like it better," he said.

"I take that as a compliment. Now what can I do for you?"

"I'm investigating Mr. Hightower's murder. I need to ask a few questions. Had you any regular contact with your ex-husband since the divorce?"

She picked up a pack of cigarettes from the coffee table and lit one. "I'm not sure what you mean . . . regular contact. We spoke, yes. I told the other officers that when they made me look at his body. We had drinks together once or twice, that's it. I loved him very much. The divorce hurt me. It was better that I forget him. Why do you ask?"

"Would you mind telling me why you were divorced?"

"He fell out of love with me."

"Are you also saying that he fell in love with someone else?" he asked, remembering his conversation with the Cohens. Elizabeth had mentioned she thought he was involved with someone else but didn't know who, that his good spirits ended and she assumed the relationship was over.

"If you like," she said. Mercanto looked at her closely. She was very pretty.

"Who was it?"

"I don't know . . . he wouldn't say . . . This has been hard for me. After a divorce a woman still feels things . . . you wouldn't understand."

"Try me."

"She wonders if maybe it was her fault. What did she do that was wrong, then to see him like that . . . dead, and hurt like that . . ." She shook her head.

Mercanto said, "Right now we're trying to find a man named Rashid . . ."

She raised her eyebrows. "So you think it had something to do with drugs?"

"It's possible. We found a large amount in his apartment and for the last few months he'd been taking a lot of money out of his checking account."

She drew on her cigarette. "Stanley liked many things . . . wine, cocaine, sex. He was a hedonist, but not to the excess you're thinking. I do not say he couldn't have been killed by someone involved in drugs, but I know him, he did not spend the money on drugs."

She seemed so sure. "What then?"

"He was a generous man. He put the girl in his office through school. He set up my business. Perhaps he just gave it to someone . . ."

"What about Rashid? What can you tell me about him?"

"He is a Jamaican, that's all I know. I never met him, only heard Stanley speak of him."

"Do you know where I can find him?"

"All I know is somewhere on Germantown Avenue."

Outside, he sat in the car for a few minutes. At least Rashid felt more right to him for the murder than the kid, no matter what Sloan thought. The kid, he reviewed, panicked and ran after shooting him without even getting his wallet, which was what the holdup was about. That wasn't how it happened with Hightower. Whoever shot him was first of all *inside* the car, not outside like the kid. Second, after he shot him he took the wallet, and then proceeded to mutilate the body.

Teeth marks, that's what the Medical Examiner said. And

152

a word came to his mind, one no one ever wanted to use...
cannibalism.

No question, someone who would do something like that
was out of control, over the edge. Not true with the kid. He
was a street punk, that's all. Otherwise Mrs. Mercanto's boy
would have wound up like Hightower. Was this Rashid that
much out of control . . . or could it have been some sort of
ritual? A message to others? Rashid was Jamaican. Maybe it
was something like voodoo or that movie he'd seen about
Haitian zombies. It was a possibility to consider . . . Or was
it just the work of a certifiable madman? Stories like it were
already leaking out about the house of death in North Philly
that Sloan was investigating.

His chest was starting to hurt again. He started the car and
headed for home. At the rate he was recovering it was going
to take the whole six weeks of convalescent leave before he
was normal again.

Inside his apartment he put on a tape of Miles Davis' softer
stuff like *My Funny Valentine* and *Flamenco Sketches* and
went to make a fire only to discover he was out of wood. All
he had was one of those damned chemical logs.

"Better than nothing," he muttered as he placed it in the
fireplace and lit the paper it was covered in. He took two
painkillers and stretched out on the sofa but couldn't sleep.
He was too worn down from the pain and too keyed up by
the case.

He got up and went to the kitchen table. Stanley Hightower's checkbook and address book were there. He went through
the checks again, wishing they could somehow tell him more
than they had so far. They must have been for Rashid, there
was no other explanation. No one gives away fifty thousand
dollars, even generous Stanley Hightower.

He went to the address book. What if Rashid's phone

number was there? He turned pages. Nothing under "R," maybe it was by his last name with a first initial. He started at the beginning, went through it page by page. Nothing—until in the M's he stopped cold. *Frank's* phone number was there. He looked at it for a long moment, shook his head, went to the phone.

Frank answered on the fifth ring. His voice sounded weaker than last time. "Feel up to some Italian? You always liked that?"

"Yeah, sure," Frank said. "What have you been up to lately? I haven't seen you."

"Working on a case . . . Listen, Frank, how do you know Stanley Hightower? Your name's in his phone book."

"That the case you're working on? I've been reading about it. Sounds like a rough one. Yeah, I used to work on his car . . . a black BMW. I tinted the windows for him. Remember he wanted them real dark. Seemed like a nice guy."

Mercanto pulled on his coat and walked to Mama Yolanda's on Eighth Street. It wasn't five yet and the place was empty except for Dee, who was setting up tables, and John, the owner.

When John saw him he smiled broadly. "Hey Nate, what'd you say? Come on in here, have a beer . . . on me."

Mercanto followed him into the bar. John opened a bottle of Moretti and put it in front of him, opened a bottle of Lite for himself. When he saw Mercanto looking at it he patted his stomach. "Gotta watch my weight. Guess what, pasta'll put it on you."

Mercanto smiled, and John leaned across the bar. "I hear you got shot. Something to do with that case in the park . . ."

"Where'd you hear that?" Mercanto said, taking a sip of his beer.

"Well, you know, people talk. How's Frank?"

"He's in a pretty bad way . . . That's why I'm here. He isn't eating. Thought some of your good chow might cheer him up."

"Know what you mean, my uncle had the same thing. Tell you what. We'll make him some nice Zuppa Pavese with a little cheese, some poached eggs, chicken broth. Good for the stomach. Then a little Penne all'arrabbiata with some bacon and tomatoes. He doesn't need a cream sauce. It won't hold up, you'll see. A little red sauce will be better. It's hardier, stay with him. We'll make enough for you, too."

He called Dee and gave her the order. When she'd gone he leaved across the bar. "That fellow who was killed . . . used to be a customer here. Nice guy, fixed my glasses for me once . . . Understood whoever did it did him up pretty badly."

"People talking again . . ." Mercanto said. There were no secrets in the Italian community. Everyone you went to school with was either a restaurant owner, a cop, a judge, a contractor, a Mafioso or a doctor, and they all kept in touch.

Mercanto filled him in, including the mutilation John had heard about.

"So what do you think?"

"Right now, I don't know," Mercanto said. "It's the mutilation that makes it so tough. I keep coming back to it. Either it's crazy, or some sort of ritual . . ."

John took off his glasses and wiped them on a towel. "Ritual . . . you mean like in that movie *Serpent and the Rainbow* . . . God, that picture made me want to throw up."

"That was Haitian. I'm thinking more in the neighborhood of Jamaica, but you've got the general idea."

"Jamaican, Haitian, it's all the same to me. I've been to Puerto Rico and the Bahamas, that's all I know. Maybe you ought to check it out."

Mercanto took a pull on his beer. "I am, but it's going to be tough. I'm no longer officially on the case, I'm on sick leave so I have to be sort of careful. And anyway, this isn't the sort of thing I can waltz into headquarters and start mouthing off about. People are sensitive these days."

John nodded his head and reached for his cigarettes. He started to put one in his mouth, then stopped. "That's the Caribbean, right . . ." When Mercanto said it was, he snapped his fingers. "Maybe I can help you. Bing, bing, bing . . . that museum, you know . . . the Braddon, they've got a big exhibit on the Caribbean. We're doing the food for a party they're having. They love us. The whole schmear . . . clams, mussels, maybe four or five kinds of pasta, antipasto, the works . . . I was talking to the director the other day . . ." He rummaged around behind the bar until he found a business card. "Real nice woman. An expert on the Caribbean, I understand."

"Oh . . . ?" Mercanto took the card from him.

"People talk . . . what can I say?"

Mercanto looked at the card. On it was the name Erin Fraser.

CHAPTER 14

SOMEHOW MARGARET made it through the rest of the afternoon after her lunch with Charles, delaying going home as long as possible, and then finding the house dark when she got there. Adam no doubt was "out" for the evening with his Twinkie.

As she went from room to room turning on lights, the emptiness of the house spoke more tellingly than anything they could say to each other. She poured herself a brandy and went to change. Slipped on a long nightgown with an Empire line, but when she saw herself in the mirror the sight repulsed her. The soft material and lace covering her heavy breasts were too sexy. That sure wasn't how she felt. Charles and Adam had seen to that. Tears began, she wiped them away angrily. She chose a shapeless sweatsuit and pinned up her hair.

She made scrambled eggs, something her mother always fixed for her when she was sick as a child, then went to a corner of the sofa in the study where she spent the rest of the evening, a blanket over her lap. Vivaldi played on the stereo. About eight the phone rang. When she answered no one was there. The same thing happened a half-hour later. When it happened a third time she turned the bell off.

It occurred to her that her life was like one of those tapestries Loring had described, only in her case a key thread had come undone and the whole thing was unraveling around her. It hurt like hell.

Could it be *that* good for Adam with his nineteen-year-old? She had never denied him anything sexually. What could this girl do that was so different, so much better? (Besides being younger, she thought, and dismissed it.)

And how could Charles so cavalierly dismiss her relationship with him, or at least seem to ... didn't the years count for anything there either? Or was he like Adam, looking for new, more desirable subjects ...

Several times during the evening she had looked at the phone, sure that it had rung again and again, even though the bell was off. Was it a crank call, as Adam claimed? Was it the girl—but Adam was with her, wasn't he? Was it Loring, was he trying to tell her that she had somehow failed him, too? Had she, in fact?

Around midnight she gave up and went to bed but she couldn't sleep. Much later Adam came home. She was still awake but pretended sleep. He got into bed, and she waited, hoping that he was drunk, that that was why he was out. If

158

he'd only touch her, even roughly, that would be fine, just as long as he touched her. He didn't.

○

In her office next morning she heard the bell announcing the next patient. Loring. She touched her hair, adjusted the collar of her blouse, annoyed that she looked like she felt, exhausted. When she opened the door Loring looked exhausted too. Strangely, it made her feel better.

Loring caught her half-smile. Just like his mother when she'd come to his bedroom that night to try to explain what he'd seen her doing—an it's-our-secret kind of smile. "Sometimes men need to . . ." she'd said as she sat on the edge of his bed. He remembered her smell. He thought he smelled it now as he went past Margaret.

His coldness didn't surprise Margaret. After that scene when she sent him away she expected it. What surprised her was its intensity, almost like an aura around him.

She followed him into the office and sat down behind her desk, automatically reaching for her cigarettes, lighting one as sort of an unspoken communication between them. As usual, his eyes followed her movements.

He said, "It's Marguerite, not Margaret."

Puzzled, she knew better than to ask. Wait, she instructed herself.

He looked at her like he was seeing her for the first time. Today her hair cascading down onto her shoulders, her gold hoop earrings, the blueness of her eyes did not move him. "Marguerite was the woman Faust sold his soul to the devil for . . . not Margaret."

At least his words didn't signify outright rejection, as in "I-don't-like-you-anymore,-I-don't-want-to-see-you-again." A more subtle shift was going on, more like she wasn't worth what he had thought. And had betrayed him ...

She tried to accept it professionally. It was altogether natural after what had happened. "I understand that you're angry with me for sending you away. Shall we talk about that?"

Loring looked around the room. It felt hostile to him. No longer were the blues and grays their cave, their fort together. "What's to talk about?"

"How did you feel when I told you I couldn't see you?" When he didn't reply, she said, "Were you angry, hurt?"

When he looked at her he drew back slightly like he was farsighted and trying to get her into focus. "I don't get angry. I don't make scenes. I just get things done."

She drew on her cigarette. An interesting response. His denial of his anger again confirmed it, though he wasn't unwilling to acknowledge it openly. "By getting things done, you mean get even?"

He shook his head. Sometimes talking to her was like talking to a child. "No, that's *not* what I mean. Getting even is living in the past. By definition the best you can expect is to regain status quo, but in so doing you waste a lot of time and energy that could be directed elsewhere, so you never get even, you're always behind."

He was enjoying the lecture, she thought. Reversing roles. "Go on," she said.

"What I'm saying is that life is made up of self-contained incidents, like a fight. When one incident is over you add up whether you won or lost and move on to the next thing. The key is to not look back."

She'd never heard a patient give a more telling definition of sublimation. "Is that what you intend to do now ... move on, pretend that what happened between us never really happened?"

160

He looked at the couch, again seeing her there with that look on her face when he opened the door. "It happened," he said through clenched teeth.

"That's right, it did. What's important is how you felt when it did."

He turned to look at her. "You're starting to sound like a nag. I'm trying to explain things to you. One intelligent person to another. Why do you always insist on trying to personalize things when there's really nothing between us to personalize?"

His words had an effect. She understood at least some of his anger, but she needed a moment to regain control. "What happens here between us is not clinical. You can't progress by denying it. Life isn't a series of small compartments. Sometimes they spill over, sometimes it's messy. That's what we're here to deal with. Now tell me how you felt."

"There's nothing to talk about."

God, like Adam and Charles to her. "Yes, there is. You're angry you're trying to shut me out. This is not something that happened fifteen or twenty years ago, this is fresh, and we are going to talk about it." She paused, needing to get her own emotions under control. "Now once again, what did you feel when I told you I couldn't see you?"

The way she said it, the tone, had the crack of a whip in it.

He gripped the arm of the chair. White showed around the center of his eyes. His heart was pounding. It wasn't Margaret in front of him, it was his mother sitting there. *"That you were a whore . . . satisfied!"*

"Why?" she asked, although it didn't surprise her. What he was saying fitted with his earlier remarks about women. Two categories—madonnas and whores. No middle ground where most real women lived . . .

Mother was still in front of him, smoking, that knowing

look on her face. "No . . . that's not right, I didn't mean that."

"I think you did. What makes me a whore . . . that you saw me with another patient . . . that I was rejecting you . . . or that I had the capacity to care about more than one person?"

He looked at the couch again. "You enjoyed it . . ." he blurted out, thinking how his mother wallowed in the excitement of it, hating her for it, wanting to be part of it.

"And I betrayed you by enjoying it," she said. "Would you have felt differently if the patient you saw me with was another woman instead of a man?"

"I don't know. How should I know?" It was less a challenge than a cry for help, for an ally.

Margaret sensed this and moved to reassure him. "What you felt is normal. What happens here, the feelings we share and explore, it's natural to feel jealousy or anger or both at the sight of me with another patient. There's nothing wrong with that. All I wanted you to do was to express those feelings. Being angry doesn't make me think less of you. On the other hand, I have a full practice. There are others who have a claim on me and my help. That's why I couldn't allow you to interrupt, and intrude on one of those patients' time."

He turned and looked at her. His mother wasn't there. How could he even have thought that? It was Margaret, and she looked tired. Wrong to think badly of her. Margaret was beautiful, the way her hair caught the light, the way it lay on her shoulders, her only jewelry the wide gold hoop earrings he'd seen her wear before. Her blouse was open at the throat. He let his eyes travel down to her breasts. His own nipples began to tingle as he looked at the outline of her breasts under her blouse. He knew how he would touch them. Gently, softly, stroking them, letting the warm good feeling take her over . . . He thought about her husband. Even though she'd never talked about him, he was sure she had one. He thought about what she felt when he made her do it . . . hoped it wasn't the same as with his stepfather . . . that he was gentle and respectful. Never mind, even if he was, Loring knew he hated him.

Through his thoughts he heard her say, "When you came, there was something you wanted to talk to me about. What was it?"

Her words drew him back to the present. "My dream . . . I came to tell you about it." When she didn't speak, he quickly added, "You always want to know about them."

"Yes, tell me about it."

"It was one of those dreams that was so real you thought it was actually happening. You know how sometimes you have nightmares like that. That's how this one was . . ."

What was the best way to tell it? "I have a chair in my house, a club chair, and I dreamed I woke up in it . . . I often take naps in it . . . but this time I didn't know how I got there. When I looked down my hands were covered in blood. I stood up and looked in a mirror. My face was covered with blood, but I wasn't cut anywhere. No signs of violence. Nothing was out of place. Just me, covered in blood." He waited.

"How many times have you had this dream?"

"Three. Once after that day in the fitting room, and twice since then."

"Did anything out of the ordinary happen to you during the last few days?"

He didn't answer immediately. He didn't want to tell her about Wiladene forcing him to take Erin to the party. He knew there was nothing wrong with it, still he didn't want her to know. "Nothing except what happened between us," he finally said.

"Think back. What else did you do in the dream? Did you walk around, go outside, shower . . . what?"

He shook his head. "No, that's all. I just got up and looked in the mirror."

"In the dream what were your feelings when you saw yourself like that . . . covered with blood?"

"I don't know . . . I guess afraid . . . afraid I'd done something wrong . . . the blood, I mean. Yes, that was it . . . fear. I was more afraid than I can ever remember, and I kept wondering what was happening to me."

"I don't think you need to worry. Was that the only reason you came?"

He was silent for a moment. Should he tell what else? About how he felt about her? "It was the dream . . . and to see you." There, he'd done it. He'd made the crossover. He'd given himself to her.

Clinically, of course, it was transference. But still, his admission touched her. She knew how hard it was for him to make, a man who trusted so little.

"Thank you," she said, and he promptly took it as a sign. He watched her draw on her cigarette and exhale. Her movements pleased him. He could feel the burn of the smoke in his own lungs.

"Now about your dream," she was saying, now talking to him as an equal, a colleague. "Jung described man as a symbol-making animal. The blood in your dream, being covered with it, could mean several things. For instance, blood symbolizes family unity. We are blood-related, as people like to say. Blood covering you could mean that because of your sister's wedding you are being drawn back into an unpleasant family situation, forced to be a part of things you don't like . . . the way, for instance, you didn't like what you saw when you opened my

164

office door. The fear you described came when you woke up in your dream and imagined some terrible deed was done."

She paused again to draw on her cigarette, giving him time for what she said to sink in.

When he said nothing, she went on. "Blood also can symbolize conflict. A fight for control, against losing control. Which can be very scary. The issue of control is one of the most difficult a therapist deals with. Its counterpart is trust. For therapy to work, a patient needs to trust the therapist enough to give up some of that control. And as I've said, that can be terrifying to some people."

He said nothing.

"You're my last patient today, so I have a little extra time. I'd like to go back to the moment you opened the office door and saw me with the other patient. Try now to tell me everything you felt about it. Remember about trust. And that I'm not your adversary. I care about you. I'm the person you can say anything to."

"I can't."

"Is it because I'm looking at you?" she said. He started at her words. Her perception startled him. The blue of her eyes told it all. She knew everything he was thinking. They were transmitting feelings through the air. "Yes," he admitted.

"I want you to lie down on the couch. That way we won't be facing each other, and it will relax you—"

"But I want to see you."

"This time it would be better if you didn't. I want you to be able to clear your mind and let everything come out, without distractions."

The soft voice was caressing, it was like she was hyp- notizing him. In her power, that's how she wants you. It frightened him until it dawned on him that he didn't care. The idea of giving up control, of her making the decisions, of him doing whatever she wanted seemed suddenly appealing.

He went over to the couch and stretched out on it. Immediately his senses seemed heightened. Through his clothes he imagined he could feel the man he had seen on it, like sweat through the fabric.

Behind him he heard the rustle of Margaret's nylons as she came near and sat down just out of sight. The sound of her gave him goose bumps.

"Are you comfortable on the couch? Tell me how you feel now?" she said softly.

He smiled. "Like the fucking Rose of Shannon," he heard himself say, and was astonished. He couldn't *believe* he had said that word in front of her. But it felt delicious when he did.

"Good," she said, and he was sure she meant it, that she was smiling too. "Now start at the beginning and tell me everything you felt."

"When I opened the door and saw you sitting there . . . you looked guilty . . . like I'd just caught you doing . . . something."

"Doing what?"

He hesitated, then let go . . . "Going to bed with him . . ."

"How did that make you feel?"

"I don't know . . . angry, I guess . . . ashamed . . . it's confusing. I mean, there was no reason for you to do it. You didn't have to, I didn't mean to embarrass you . . ." Speaking to his mother, but did he realize it at all?

"What about the man? What did you feel about him?"

He shifted on the couch. "I didn't like him. I didn't want him to do that with you," he said, seeing too vividly that night.

"Tell me what you saw."

He felt something deep down inside him, a stab of pain, and

before he could stop himself he began to cry. He put his hands to his face, partly to keep her from seeing him and partly to block out the memory.

"Tell me," she repeated.

"I saw you with him," he said ... saw his mother sitting on the edge of the bed ... "I got up to get a drink of water and saw you on the couch with no clothes on. He was behind you doing it ..."

Margaret had no doubt he was describing, reliving, the scene as a boy seeing his mother with a man. But which man? "Your stepfather?" she said quietly. He didn't deny it. "How did you feel when you saw them?"

"Awful, I didn't want him to do it. God, how I hate him. I despise him. I wish he was dead," his voice rising.

And now he sat up on the couch, staring straight ahead. "The best day of my life," he said, his voice low, strong, "was the day Wolf bit him."

There seemed no fear in him now. Only in her.

CHAPTER 15

ERIN WAS just leaving the museum when her phone rang and the receptionist downstairs announced that there was a policeman to see her.

It startled her. She didn't even owe any parking tickets. She looked at her watch. With the opening party for the exhibit staring her in the face she didn't have much time . . .

"All right, I'll be down."

In the lobby the receptionist pointed to a dark-haired man in a trenchcoat. His hair had a bit of a widow's peak in front, which with his dark complexion gave him, she thought, a rakish look.

"Miss Fraser?" Mercanto showed her his badge. "I'm with homicide. Don't get worried, it doesn't have anything to do with you. I understand you're an expert on the Caribbean and this case seems to have a Caribbean connection, that's all. It won't take long."

"I was just going out, but okay."

Mercanto was surprised at the way she looked—in jeans with her hair pulled back and big schoolboy glasses. Not what he expected a curator to look like. "Maybe we could get some lunch."

"I'm really pressed for time, but if you'll take a hot dog from the campus bus, we could talk and eat," she said.

"Sounds good. Cops love hot dogs." They started toward the museum's entrance. "Do they have chili?" he asked, holding the door for her.

"No, but they have sauerkraut and onions."

"Just as good."

Outside, she said, "How did you get my name?"

"From John at Mama Yolanda's."

"Well, in my book, John's name is a pretty high recommendation. Known him long?"

"With a name like Natale Mercanto, yeah, I've known John a long time. We're from the same neighborhood."

"You live near his restaurant . . . ?"

"My apartment's around the corner. I usually stop in once, twice a week."

As they walked toward Thirty-fourth where the bus was always parked she wondered for a moment if Mercanto was married. The way he mentioned his apartment made her think not.

The pace got to be too much for him, and sharp pain filled his chest. He stopped for a second to lean against a building.

"Wait up," he said, breathing shallow as possible to minimize the pain. He patted his pockets. Naturally he'd forgotten his painkillers again.

When he told her to wait, she started to make a remark about the police department needed more exercise, then she saw his face. "Are you okay?"

"Yeah," he said, feeling the pain lessen slightly. "I've got a broken rib, and sometimes it gets a little uncomfortable."

"How did it happen?"

"I got shot."

Mercanto took her arm and they started again. There was a certain naturalness in his touch, the gesture seemed complete in itself, not a prelude to anything.

They slowed down, Erin figuring her schedule would survive a little interruption. At a bench near the bus she made Mercanto sit down while she went for the hot dogs and soda. He tried to pay but she wouldn't hear of it.

Once seated beside him, she said, "It must be tough on your family, you being in such a dangerous occupation."

"Well, all I have is my brother Frank, and he's not doing too well . . ."

"Does your shooting have anything to do with the case you want to talk to me about?"

"Yes, but before we start let me say there's no danger in this for you. I've been investigating the murder of a Center City optometrist named Stanley Hightower. You may have seen something about it in the papers. It happened in Fairmount Park. The other night I went up to look it over again, a kid tried to hold me up while I was there. When I went to arrest him he shot me."

"I don't quite see how this ties into me," said Erin. "I'm an anthropologist who studies the Caribbean. My specialty is shamanism. Any help there?"

"What exactly is shamanism? Any relation to Shamus? Sorry."

"Essentially it's a study of primitive religions. We call them primitive because their history is a spoken rather than a recorded one, and they have little or no established hierarchy above the local level. A shaman is a priest of one of these religions."

"Like voodoo . . . ?" Mercanto asked hopefully.

"Yes. Why do you ask?" When he didn't answer she said, "I think you owe me that much if you expect me to help you."

"You're right. At the moment everyone's thinking the kid who shot me is Stanley Hightower's killer. Could be. But it seemed to me a couple of things need to be checked out from another angle, say, a Jamaican one. Understand, I know nothing about this stuff. Does Jamaica even have voodoo?"

"Yes, most Caribbean countries have some form of voodoo. The word 'voodoo' comes from vodun, the religion of Haiti, which is a mix of West African religions with an overlay of Christianity, especially Catholicism. In Cuba it's called Santeria, in Brazil it's Candomble, in Jamaica it's obeah."

"And *this* is your specialty?"

"That's right. The shaman is a leader of a cult. He differs from our notion of a priest. He doesn't interpret any body of law, history, dogma or whatever you want to call it. He teaches from a personal basis, from within. He's almost always someone who's had some powerful emotional experience that becomes the basis of his teaching. In this country I suspect many shamans would be considered schizophrenics. In their cultures they're revered."

172

"You've seen their ceremonies . . . ?" When she nodded, he said, "Tell me about them, their sacrifices, for example."

"If you want my help you'll have to be more . . . more forthcoming."

Mercanto sighed. "Okay, we know that Stanley Hightower was involved with some very rough Jamaicans. His murder had a professional look to it, with one add-on . . . the body was mutilated afterward in a damned strange way. I was wondering if it might be some sort of ceremonial thing."

"How do you mean strange . . . the mutilations, I mean?"

He shifted slightly on the bench. Their knees came in contact. Erin could feel it through her whole body. She knew she should move to break the contact. After all, she'd just met him, but she didn't.

"Cannibalism," he said finally. He turned his hand over and showed her his right palm. "When we found him, this whole part of his hand had been ripped away," he said, tracing the area of damage with the index finger of his other hand. "According to the medical examiner it was done by teeth, human teeth."

"And you think this type of mutilation might be part of a ceremony or some sort of voodoo sign . . . like no trespassing, or death to outsiders. Something like that?"

At first her reaction, or lack of it, to the cannibalism surprised him, then he realized she'd probably seen a lot of things equally gruesome in her studies. It was like being a cop. It went with the territory.

"That's what I was hoping you could tell me."

"There are a lot of misconceptions about voodoo," she said, settling back on the bench and crossing her legs. "Like I said, it's a primitive religion. God, as we know him, is worshipped, but they also worship other gods. Not multi-armed deities like we associate with Middle Eastern religions but more like a hunter society in which animals are worshipped for their special traits. For instance, the wolf because of his bravery, cunning, hunting ability . . ."

She paused. "Along with this is the concept of reincarnation. They worship the dead, figures from the darkness. The purpose is appeasement. This idea of reincarnation, or transportation between the real world and the underworld is at the root of Haitian zombies. By drugs, hypnosis, or whatever they reach a state that's between life and death, one foot in each camp. This is probably as extreme as it gets."

"But they do have sacrifices, things like that . . ."

"Yes, they do. Most times a chicken, sometimes a goat. They're the most common animals around. You just go out in the backyard and get one. Sacrificing an eagle or a leopard would be tough. You have to understand, *most* religions have live sacrifices.

"In other religions certain rituals are often mistaken for sacrifices. In Tibet, for instance, the dead are often taken to a hillside and chopped up, their meat left for the birds. It's called a sky burial but it's not a sacrifice. Or in Africa there are different pubertal rites like circumcision, tattooing, various mutilations. In fact, I remember one Haitian shaman— but that was something else entirely. What you're talking about doesn't exist in Jamaican voodoo."

"You're sure?" he said, obviously disappointed.

"Well, I'm not sure it couldn't have been done by Jamaicans, but it is not part of their voodoo."

CHAPTER 16

MARGARET CLIMBED the steps not looking forward to the night ahead. Tonight was the party at the museum, a must for faculty members and their wives to attend, but she was in no party mood.

When she opened the door she heard the sounds of the Rolling Stones' "Brown Sugar" blaring on the stereo. Adam was home. She dropped her coat and purse and went into the study, feeling shot.

Adam was at the window staring out, a pitcher of martinis and two glasses on the coffee table, waiting. He turned and came toward her, his biggest smile in place, his eyes unnaturally bright. He had on jeans and a heavy sweater. His curly hair was matted and oily, and he hadn't shaved. When he bent to kiss her she could tell he hadn't bathed either.

"Hi," she said, making no effort to return his kiss.

"Come on in, sit down. I've been waiting for you," he said, leading her to the sofa. She sat down, looking at him like he was a stranger while he poured their martinis.

"What are we celebrating?" she asked over the din of the music.

"My poetry," he said exuberantly, taking no notice of her distance. "The whole volume of *Vietnam Nights* is finally finished, put to rest, the whole thing." He went to the stereo and turned it off. "I thought we might have a couple of martinis to put the cap on it."

In spite of herself, she was pleased for him. "I know it's been giving you a lot of trouble."

"It's been a bitch . . . reliving those experiences has been the most painful thing I've ever done. Sometimes I think it was worse than being there. You know how things are when you get older. People say they don't affect you like when you're young, but they're wrong. They affect you more. When you're young you're too busy to feel anything, not so when you're older, you're more vulnerable to the emotion . . ."

She took a sip of her drink. "You make it sound like we're ready for the old-age home." Which tonight is how she felt.

"Not by a long shot, but you know what I mean . . . God, it feels good to be through with it."

She watched him drain his glass with a gulp and move to pour himself another. It was like watching the Adam of ten years ago, the part of him she had loved best, the zest for life that wouldn't be contained by anything.

"I wouldn't have too many of those. We still have to go to the party at the museum tonight," she said, deliberately holding back, afraid to let her mood rise to meet his, knowing he was right . . . when you were older you sure were more vulnerable.

"The way I feel tonight I could drink a gallon of these and they wouldn't affect me at all," he said.

At least half-true. Adam did have a tolerance for booze that defied belief. He continued his pacing, almost boyish with his enthusiasm.

"Now that it's over we can get back to being ourselves," he said, taking hold of her hands. "I know I've been . . . distant lately but I'll make it up to you."

If a patient had recreated this scene for her, she would have tried to make her see the reality of it. But now she was no analyst—she was a woman wanting badly to believe . . . "Right now we have to get ready for the party."

"Yeah, I guess so." He finished his martini and poured another. "I'm not looking forward to it."

She kissed him on the cheek as she got up to go change. "Me either," she said.

As she applied her makeup she could hear Adam singing in the shower. His cheerfulness seemed to point up the loneliness that had become so much a part of her life. It seemed her whole life consisted of being there for others but having no one for herself. A lousy imbalance, as she might suggest to a patient.

In the mirror she could see their bed, and remembered how she felt when Adam crawled in and went to sleep without touching her. The major continuity in her life was her practice, and, she had to admit, especially tracking Loring's case—

Adam's booming voice broke through her thoughts, singing the Beatles' "Yellow Submarine." His off-key gusto made her smile, such a silly song but it made her think about their better years of marriage.

This wasn't the first time he'd withdrawn, she had to admit. Whenever he was working he was always distant. And at the best of times he was too mercurial ever to take for granted, to predict.

But of course what made *this* time different from the others was his affair. That's where the loneliness came in. She wasn't even forty yet. She wasn't ready for the scrap heap. Giving and receiving pleasure with a man was still important to her, damn important.

She took off her housecoat and inspected herself in the mirror. The martini's glow helped. Adam took her for granted but someone else—lord, what was she thinking? *Who* was she thinking of? Like a reluctant patient, recognizing and not acepting the unacceptable, she pushed away the object of her thought . . .

She turned abruptly and went to her closet, where she chose a floor-length sarong-type evening dress by Carolyne Roehm.

Behind her she heard Adam's voice. It startled her. She hadn't heard the shower stop. She turned to see him standing in the doorway in his terrycloth robe. "Remember that French film we saw . . . the one where the guy said it's sexier to watch a woman dress than undress . . . it's like seeing her prepare for another lover?"

The guilt she felt made her angry. "Adam, please not now." He shrugged and left.

Charles' words about wish-thinking came back to her . . . the wish is the deed. Pure theory, she thought impatiently as she slipped the dress over her head.

Adam was in the study when she came downstairs. He had

178

switched from martinis to beer and was standing there in his tux with a Heineken bottle in hand.

"I'm sorry, I'm just a little edgy tonight," she said. She went to him and straightened his tie like she did whenever they went to something formal.

"You look very nice," he said as he helped her with her coat. Which was what he always said when they got dressed up. The familiarity of it made her teary.

O

The Braddon was lighted like a Hollywood premiere. People were milling around in evening dress.

Adam took her arm. "Let's see if we can find the bar."

They started down the hall to the main room. Exhibit cases on both sides were filled with colorful tapestries. A beautiful way to open the exhibit, she thought. She resolved to wander through the whole exhibit before the evening was over. In the distance she heard the sounds of an orchestra playing. A night of dancing—suddenly she stopped. On a pedestal in the center of the hall was a small glass case, and in it was a single item—a mask. She went for a closer look. It was simple in design, like the mold of a face. The top half was violet, the bottom half a fleshy pink that somehow seemed to convey . . . what? Agony? The only decorations were tracks of rhinestone tears from the eyes.

"That really stops you short after those tapestries, doesn't it?" said Adam. "It's like what you'd find underneath if you pulled the skin off a person's face." He read the card at the bottom of the case. "Haitian voodoo mask. Some kinds of knowledge you're better off without."

Her eyes were still fixed on it. Something about it . . . like she'd seen it before but couldn't say where, when.

179

Adam took her arm. "Now about the bar . . ."

She allowed him to lead her away, searching for perspective, for what it reminded her of.

The music was louder, the crowd thicker as they neared the museum's main room. The band was playing "Bad Bad Leroy Brown."

"There must be five hundred, a thousand people here. What would you like?" Adam asked.

"White wine," she said, and waited as he pushed on the final few feet to the bar. While she stood there the head of Adam's department and his wife stopped to say hello. They exchanged small talk until Adam returned with their drinks.

His face betrayed him at the sight of the department head. Theirs was a strained relationship. He was an old-line English professor, a tweedy appreciator of Hardy and Conrad, while Adam was more avant garde, preferring the works of people like Bukowski and Crews.

"Erin Fraser's done a grand job with the exhibit, the party, the whole works. Do you know her?" the department head said.

"I don't believe so," said Adam.

"Come on, we'll introduce you to her. We're damn lucky to have her. A remarkable young woman. Tops in her field," he said as he began to lead the way.

"Duty calls," Adam mouthed, and they followed the department head and his wife across the dance floor to the far corner where another bar was located.

There, talking with a small group, Margaret saw a young woman dressed in an evening gown with a strapless shirred bodice and a gently gathered skirt. In one hand she held a small evening bag and a pair of schoolboy glasses. She turned toward them now at the sound of the department head's voice as he said, "Erin, here are a couple of people I'd like you to meet."

The man beside her also turned, and the rest of the department head's words were lost on Margaret.

The man with Erin was Loring.

The shock of it made her heart race. She almost said, "What are you doing here?"

Seeing Margaret stunned Loring. But his immediate reaction was guilt. After all, he didn't want her to think he had betrayed her by going out with another woman. It was all Wiladene's fault. If she hadn't meddled in his life . . .

As the introductions were made Margaret delayed shaking hands with him, going first to Wiladene Jenkins, a beautiful black woman in a Georgio Armani outfit, then to her husband Cornell, the star of the Sixers, and finally to two teen-agers with the group—one named Traci, with dark curly hair; the other a short-haired blonde named Jennifer who was dressed in a dinner suit with a rayon piqué jacket and floor-length skirt complete with a *godet* flare. When Loring's turn came he took her hand but gave no sign of recognition. Well, he's in control, Margaret thought.

"You've done a fabulous job with the party," said the department head.

Jennifer took a cigarette from her purse. "Yes, hasn't she. We're all so proud."

Erin seemed to bristle as Adam lighted Jennifer's cigarette. "Thank you," she said coolly. "Excuse me, there are a couple of details I still have to attend to. Wiladene, could you help me?"

"Certainly," she said, and they went off into the crowd.

Loring made no attempt to follow. Let them have their illusion that this party, this exhibit, meant something. Reality was Margaret in front of him dressed in midnight blue.

"I think I need a refill," said Adam, looking at his glass.

Margaret understood that he needed to get away from his department head, and he left. A moment later Jennifer drifted off.

The department head and his wife then saw someone they wanted to talk to, and Margaret was alone with Loring.

"Are you enjoying yourself?" Loring asked.

"Yes, thank you," Margaret replied, thinking they sounded like lovers in a chance meeting. She shook her head to dismiss the thought.

He looked around. "Erin says the food is from Mama Yolanda's. Would you like some?"

She felt his touch on her bare arm as he led her through the crowd. It was a violation of their relationship, but how to free herself from him without drawing undue attention.

Her apparently allowing him an intimacy gave him a feeling of power. He was her protector. She was safe with him. When they were together nothing bad could happen. He knew she understood this.

She looked around for Adam, but when she finally spotted him he was on the dance floor with Jennifer.

Loring followed her gaze to Adam and Jennifer. What a disgusting creature he was, how could she ever have married him. Some evil spell . . .

"Your husband is on the faculty," he said.

"Yes," she said, waiting for the dance to be over, but when it was Adam stayed on the floor.

The band began to play "Shadow of Your Smile," and she felt Loring's hand on her arm. "This is our dance, I believe."

She was furious at Adam for staying with Jennifer, but she also knew this situation with Loring was impossible . . . But she had no way out, or so she told herself as he led her onto the dance floor . . .

When the dance was over Loring stayed at her side, his hand

still on her waist as she looked over the crowd for Adam. But somewhere in the closing moments of "Shadow of Your Smile" he and Jennifer had disappeared from the floor. Well, damn it, she wouldn't make it worse by going to find him. To check up on her husband, for God's sake.

The music began again, she felt Loring's hand rise to touch the bareness of her back. Wrong, but to hell with it. She could manage the situation. She was Margaret, Doctor Margaret ...

Erin, the party, everything and everyone was lost to Loring. All that mattered, existed, was Margaret, their being together. He led her down one of the corridors, she full of thoughts of her dissolving marriage, he full of her. She was hardly aware when he opened a door and led her into an office with a fireplace and closed the door.

When she abruptly realized they were alone she nearly panicked. This had to stop. Now. When he tried to lead her to the sofa she said, "No, Loring ..." and put her hand on his chest to push him, gently, away.

He resisted. Acting out his mother and stepfather. He had her against him, trying to kiss her, reaching for her breasts.

God, Charles was so right. He *is* like a child. This is so crazy.

Somehow she got her hands free and grabbed his hair, pulling his head back. "No, Loring. I mean it. I do not want this."

Slowly his expression changed, like one of those trick cinematic dissolves, changed from lust to a dawning horror. He backed away, like a penitent child.

"Oh, God ... look, I understand," she said. "It wasn't wrong of you to want ... you were showing that you cared ..."

He shook his head. Too late. With this terrible moment he had lost everything. He turned and ran from the room.

CHAPTER 17

MERCANTO HEARD the phone as he opened the door to his apartment, flipped on the light and hurried to answer it. On the other end of the line he heard Sloan's angry voice. "Where the hell have you been? We've been trying to get you for hours."

"My brother's . . . I stopped by to see him."

Silence, then in a quieter voice Sloan said, "Oh, yeah, I forgot about that. How's he doing?"

Mercanto resented Sloan's question. Frank's condition was

none of his business. "So-so," he said, nestling the phone against his cheek as he struggled out of his top coat, the movement making him wince. "What's up?"

"Come out to the park right away. Hortter Street near the stables. We've got another body. Looks like it might be the kid who shot you."

Mercanto was pulling his top coat back on as he headed for the door.

Twenty-five minutes later he turned off Wissahickon Avenue onto Hortter and saw four blue-and-whites, an ambulance, two unmarked cars and a crime lab van parked along the wooded stretch leading to the stables.

A uniformed officer with a flashlight approached to tell him to move on. He shone the light in the window and recognized Mercanto. "Nate, they're looking for you. Better park along the side and go in on foot."

He parked behind the nearest blue-and-white, where uniformed officers were milling around in the glare of the flashing lights.

One of the uniforms said, "Nate, looks like they found your boy..."

Mercanto pulled his coat closer around him against the night chill and walked toward them. "What happened?"

"A couple of kids playing after school found him...it's bad."

"Hope you didn't eat before you came," one of them said. Nobody laughed.

Up the hill and through the trees Mercanto could see the glow of portable lights powered by cables from the crime lab van. There was a special tension, it showed in their faces. Whatever it was had to be real bad. He knew these men, professionals, not a rookie in the bunch. Death was nothing new to them. Normally they took it with a gallows humor. Part of the job. You either accepted it or got out. But not tonight. Each man was quiet, very quiet.

"Might as well go have a look," he said.

As Mercanto started up the hill it occurred to him that there was no good place to die, not even in bed with your woman. But some places, like this one, seemed worse than others.

The climb into the woods made his chest hurt, and twice he stopped to catch his breath. Once the thought crossed his mind of his lunch with Erin. Something in the memory was comforting, made the unknown waiting for him at the top of the hill somehow seem less a threat.

The portable lights lit up the crime scene like a movie set. The Medical Examiner and another man were working on the body. Their backs shielded it from his view. All he could see were the legs. Sloan was off to one side talking to Captain Zinkowsky and a woman in a down parka who would have been pretty except for the hardness in her face. Mercanto saw the badge pinned to her parka and recognized her from the Roundhouse.

She saw him first and pointed. Sloan turned. "You know Mary Kane from Seven Squad," he said. "A couple of kids found the body late this afternoon. They were torn up by it, you'll understand when you see it."

When Mercanto looked around for the kids the woman said, "We sent them home already. No need to keep them."

Sloan produced a plastic evidence bag. Inside was the gun. "Recognize it?"

Mercanto took it, the pistol looked like an old West Colt .45. The sight of it made him remember it in the kid's hand, the feeling of the bullet going into him. He wanted to throw the gun as far as possible into the woods. "Yeah, it looks like the same one."

Sloan took the gun back from him. "We found it a couple of feet from the body. No fingerprints, we've had a lot of rain lately, but we figure the kid must have dropped it in the struggle. You ready to see the body?"

Mercanto steeled himself and walked with Sloan to where the body lay, leaves and twigs rustling underfoot as they moved along. The Medical Examiner and his assistant looked up, then moved away to give them a clear view.

The body was on its back. A teen-age boy dressed in jeans and a dark jacket. Short hair, like prep school kids wore. The front was covered in leaves and dirt. What turned his stomach was the head. Someone, something had torn a gaping hole in the neck. Dried blood from the hole nearly covered the face, staining it dark brown like an old-time minstrel, and in the midst of it, where the eyes should have been, were two empty ragged holes.

Finally the Medical Examiner said, "He was face down when we got here. We turned him over. It looks like he was attacked from behind."

Sloan handed him a photo of the boy standing in front of a Christmas tree. "Is it the kid who shot you?"

Even through the dried blood there was no mistaking that face or the one in the picture. Mercanto nodded.

"Name is Brian Collins," Sloan said. "His mother reported him missing a couple of days ago. Said she woke up and he was gone from the house. We found a bicycle further in the woods. That same night a couple reported being held up while they were parked down here. A lone gunman. The description fits. The man was pistol-whipped and kicked around some. The kid made the woman show herself to him but didn't touch her, just took their wallets. We found them closer to the road. There was about a hundred and twenty-five dollars on the body."

Mercanto knew what the boy was like, he had first-hand experience. That was hardly the issue now. "Yeah, but this ... who ... what did *this* to him?"

The M.E. looked at Sloan before answering. "It was human,"

188

he said. "Damn strange human, but you can see the teeth marks in the neck. We'll try for a mold at the lab. I'm taking odds it's the same one who killed Hightower. Young male, *very* strong, and in some kind of rage . . ."

"How do you know it was a male?"

"Because this one was alive when it happened. You can tell by the blood. He wasn't shot first like Hightower. Whoever did it jumped him from behind and ripped out the carotid artery, plus a chunk of neck muscle. With his teeth. You know the kid had to be fighting like hell while it was happening. Tell me a woman, even a crazy one, who'd have that kind of strength."

"What about his eyes?"

The Medical Examiner knelt beside the body. "Gouged them out with his fingers, most likely."

Mercanto shook his head. Even feeling about the kid like he did . . . nobody could wish that on anybody. He turned away from the body and started back to the edge of the light where Captain Zinkowsky and the woman detective were standing.

"We've got to get this son of a bitch," he said to Sloan.

Sloan just looked at him. "One thing, this blows away our theories about Hightower's death. No kinky sex, no blackmail, no ex-wife. None of that stuff. A new ballgame but an old diamond—the killer is in the park, we've got to find him . . . and before he does it again. Jesus, like a fucking animal . . ."

"Wait a minute before you rule out drugs—"

The three of them looked at Mercanto. "I know, I've been on leave but I've been nosing around and I've got a name . . . Rashid, a Jamaican drug dealer working Germantown Avenue. I've confirmed it from Hightower's ex-wife and a couple of friends. He was the one selling to him. There could be a connection . . ."

Captain Zinkowsky and Sloan just looked at each other, said nothing.

Mercanto hurried on. "I know it's weak . . . a Germantown dealer who's smart enough to sell almost fifty grand worth of stuff to a Center City type like Hightower wouldn't be crazy enough to do something like this himself, but maybe he hired it done. Maybe the kid was somehow into him, too." Here he was going way out on a limb. "Just looking at the Hightower case, I thought it might be some sort of a ritual or a message we didn't understand, something Jamaican like a cult or voodoo or something, so I went to an expert on this stuff at the Braddon Museum—"

"And . . . ?" Zinkowsky said tightly.

Mercanto knew he was running out of steam. "Nothing. She said it wasn't part of any ritual." He took a deep breath. "But at least it's a place to start . . ."

At least Sloan didn't dismiss it. "We can't rule it out, said that all along. Drug people do crazy things." He turned to the captain. "Does the name mean anything to you?"

"No," she said, "but he shouldn't be too hard to find. We'll bring him in."

"Meanwhile," said Sloan, "here's what we do. Until some real evidence, we assume Rashid isn't our man, that this guy is a psycho, a random killer on the loose in the park. Time is everything now. I know you're on leave, Mercanto, but tomorrow morning you be at the Roundhouse. We're going to powwow with the shrink and see if he can develop some sort of profile on this guy. Maybe we can match him up to some weirdo sex offender or someone just out of the funny farm. A guy this sick can't have slipped through all the cracks unnoticed. Someone has got to know something about him . . . After we finish here tonight Captain Zinkowsky and I are going to meet with the Chief and the Mayor. It's already been arranged, they're waiting for us. I'm going to tell 'em we got to put every available man on this. Including a house-to-house canvass of the neighborhood. Somebody must know something, or seen something suspicious . . . Two-man patrols, undercover men and women as parked couples, the works . . . even the granny squad if necessary. But I want this S.O.B. caught. Clear?" He smacked his fist into his other palm in punctuation. "I want him caught *before* he can do it again," his voice rising.

Mercanto did a silent amen to that.

CHAPTER 18

MARGARET HURRIED back to the party to find Loring but he'd vanished. She had to find him, what happened between them had to have precipitated a crisis, at least she was sure of that.

Finally she located Adam still with Jennifer at one of the bars. She ignored his guilty look and took him to one side. "I have a splitting headache. Take me home. *Please.*" She turned and started for the door, and he followed, reluctantly.

On the ride home she sat silent, staring out the window, smoking, thinking what a disaster the evening had turned into. Seeing Adam with Jennifer topped by what had happened between her and Loring. Her problem with Adam had to wait. Right now the priority was to find Loring and deal with their crisis . . . yes, their's . . . before it had time to undo all the work they'd managed together.

At the house she didn't wait for Adam, got out of the car and went in alone. In the bedroom she began to undress. Below she heard the front door open and close.

A moment later Adam was standing in the doorway, his tie undone, a Heineken in his hand. "Look, I'm sorry about tonight . . ."

"Yes, I know," she said as she stripped off her clothes. She was in a hurry but blurted out, "Tonight you put me down in a way you've never done in this marriage. And that's saying something."

"Hey, I know I'm not exactly the ideal husband but—"

"Adam, I've known about you and that girl for some time. I'm not stupid. She can fall for your line of crap, not me. Not anymore."

She turned to the bureau and got out fresh panties. As she pulled them on he said, "It's not what you think, I'm not having an affair with her. She's just one of my students. My God, she's young enough to be my daughter."

She didn't bother with the obvious answer as she turned back to the bureau for a bra—

He had her by the arms, turned her around. "Margaret, believe me, there's no one else, never mind how it looks. God, I know you're not stupid. Neither am I . . . do you think I'd risk losing you for a kid like—"

She pulled free, started to put on her bra. He ripped it out of her hands. "Damn it, I'll show you."

He pushed her down on the bed. She tried to move away but he held her there, jerking her panties down. He pinned

194

her hands above her head, holding them with one hand, forced her legs open with his knees.

In the stillness of the room she heard the sound of his zipper, then felt him against her. When he entered her she stopped struggling, willing it to be over. Her thoughts were not on him, but . . . and it startled her . . . on what she would say to Loring when she got to him.

He was quick, and when she felt him shudder it was as if it was happening to someone else. Then he lay quietly, his weight on her. "There, damn it, that should tell you something."

It does, she thought, as she pushed him off, got up and silently dressed in slacks and a sweater. He watched her closely, and when he saw her pull on boots he said, "Wait a minute, where are you going?"

"Out."

"When will you be back?"

She picked up her purse and started for the door. "*I don't know.*"

He followed her downstairs. "I'll wait up for you, we'll have a drink, listen to some music like old times."

His smile was his most winning. Right now, though, it made her faintly sick to her stomach.

O

On the drive she tried to sort things out. What was it Charles always said . . . that sex was the physical communication of unspoken needs. The kindest interpretation of what Adam had done, but that was for patients. Adam was her *husband.* Loring was the patient, and in effect that was what *he* was doing, or trying to do, at the party . . .

She stopped at her office long enough to get Loring's address from her files. For a moment she thought about calling instead, then decided it was better to see him in person. They had to deal face-to-face with what he had done tonight. Yes, *"they,"* *both* of them.

Admit it, she was angry, he had endangered the therapy. Probably she should terminate his therapy with her, but she was damned if she was going to. Too easy for her. And if she didn't continue to try to help him, no one else would ever be able to. He would never trust anyone again . . .

One good result had come from it. No matter what happened between her and Adam, Loring, she was confident, was no longer going to be a subject of her fantasies. He'd be another patient, like all the others. She'd moved him several concentric circles back from her center, she decided, remembering Charles' words at lunch.

As she passed Wissahickon and Hortter she saw the police cars alongside the road, lights flashing. Whatever had happened, it had to have been something major to involve that many blue-and-whites. God, not another murder, she hoped, like the optometrist she'd read about. The parks were risky enough without having people actually killed there. This was Philadelphia, not New York . . .

After a few minutes she found Loring's cottage on the edge of the woods facing Wissahickon Creek. There was a Mercedes in the driveway. The house was dark but she thought she saw a light in the rear.

No one answered the bell until the third ring. "Yes?"

"Loring, it's me, Dr. Priest. I believe we should talk."

"Go away."

"No, Loring, we have to talk."

A long silence, then she heard the sound of the lock being turned.

The door opened. As soon as she saw him she was even more

certain she'd made the right decision to come now, not to wait or to phone. He still had on his tuxedo, minus the jacket, like he was getting ready to go out, not coming home. But from his red eyes she could tell he had been crying.

"Come in." A defeated voice.

He closed the door behind her and she followed him into the living room. She'd wondered what his home would look like. It was a very masculine room, more so than he projected in his personality, with windows along one side, lots of book-cases and a stone fireplace at one end.

○

He watched her sit down on the couch. The sight of her sent a spasm of pain into his stomach. He had had fantasies of her sitting there, but now that she was here, all he wanted was for her to go, leave him in peace. Too much ...

"I want to talk about what happened tonight," she said, just like he knew she would when he let her in. Pandora. Open the box at all costs, no matter what, damn you ...

"Can I get you a drink?" Changing the subject.

She hesitated, not exactly professional, but this meeting was outside the canons too. "A small brandy, thank you."

In the kitchen he poured two drinks of Rémy Martin, then drew a glass of water for himself, took out the bottle of bella-donna from the cabinet and squeezed the dropper into the glass, counting the drops like he always did, this time not stopping until he reached fifty, five times the prescribed dosage. His need had long ago passed that point. He drank it down in a gulp. The familiar bitter taste of the deadly night-shade sometimes seemed the only thing still real in his life.

Back in the living room he handed her her drink. "Sit down," she said. "What happened tonight was serious, important. So much so that I did not want to let it wait until our next session."

Watching her, he felt it begin to happen, the change, the double-vision of his perception . . . oh yes, he was there and she was there, but she had now assumed with increasing force and sharpness, as it had before, the outlines and then the substance of another, the image of someone so terribly, frighteningly familiar, superimposed on, gradually blotting out, the image of Margaret . . . it couldn't be, he didn't want it to be, even tried to will it away but failed . . . mother . . . it was she and no mistaking, emerging out of the features of what once had been Margaret. The sound of the voice, the tone, were the same. And so was the deceit, but he would defeat it, it would not destroy him . . .

Margaret felt more than saw what was happening. She felt his remoteness, his defensiveness. She tried to apply what she could to relieve him of what she was sure was his guilt over what had happened this evening . . . "Please understand that you are not at fault here. What happened is not all your responsibility. But it is your responsibility to care about your therapy, to understand that it matters more than anything else to you now, but it is *you* that we are working to reveal and understand and so make you well . . . " My God, his pupils, they're so dilated, has he taken something . . . ?

I know you, he thought. I know who you are. And then he was able to give voice to his feelings, now that he had clearly seen who she was, what she was trying to do to him, just like always . . . "*I know you*"—voice rising—"you hurt me before but no more. I will be free of you, I won't be tortured any more to please you . . ."

She looked at him closely. Obviously he was going into another phase, but she was still startled, and not a little frightened by the intensity of him, by what might be coming

198

and wondering whether she would be able to handle it . . . Concentrate, she told herself, on what he is really saying, on those words about being tortured . . . "Tell me who is torturing you," she said.

His voice was near-strangled. "Oh, you know, you damn well know, you've known right along but you pretended like it wasn't happening. I won't be part of it, no more, I'd rather be a speck in space, lost out there, nothing . . ."

Like a schizophrenic, she thought, or an aggravated hysteric—never mind the clinical analysis, she lectured herself, this is a sick man, a patient, a human being. Never mind the label and get back to work . . . "Who is torturing you?"

He was looking beyond her, through the windows and into the darkness and the woods beyond. He knew, of course, that they were being watched. His stepfather, he was out there and he had come with her. A wary half-smile now . . . "You won't get me to say it, I'm too smart for that. I can keep a secret, I have for so long . . ." And the look froze, gradually melted into an expressionless mask.

The clinicians, she knew, would call it transference, to her of what he had seen between his mother and stepfather. She *was* now the mother, and he was talking to her, saying things he may have once said to her, or wanted to say. She must keep it going. For him it was like hypnosis, a self-hypnosis. She watched his eyes watch her, move to follow her movements as she reached for her purse, took out a cigarette, lit it. She knew he liked to watch her smoke, that it reminded him of his mother and reinforced the transference . . . "You can tell me," she said.

"No, I can't, not you . . ."

"Some secrets are better shared. Share yours with me," she said quietly, inhaling and blowing out a plume of smoke.

But he was looking through the windows again. Yes, he was

still out there, he could feel *him* there, and now that he was concentrating, looking closely, he could see the eyes watching in the darkness. Those mean terrible scary eyes . . . It was starting again, all over again . . . "Listen, I'll bet you didn't know that when a person dies, his hair goes right on growing, at least for a while. Do you think that means the soul doesn't leave the body right away, just slowly, in pieces, little pieces that can escape out there . . . ?"

"That's an interesting notion. I didn't know that. But I do know that's not the secret . . ." No question, he had slipped into some form of self-hypnosis, into his own world, with its terrors and traps and escapes. He was reliving the most awful part of his life in the only way his mind could even begin to handle it . . . in a hallucination that nonetheless was bordering on the reality of his affliction.

His eyes seemed to focus more as he looked at her, puzzled and angry all at once. He shook his head. "How could you *like* something like . . . that? *Want* it to happen?"

She held her breath, waited. When he did not go on she said, "I'm sorry, I don't understand—"

"Oh yes, yes, you do." He had gotten up and gone to the fireplace, staring down now at the cold ashes and the burned log. "You let it happen, whatever he wanted, you wanted. He's out there and you're here for him, like always."

"No, I'm not here for him. I'm here for you. I want to see you free of this, but it won't happen unless you tell me about it."

He was fiddling with the picture of the dog on the mantelpiece, turning it one way and then another, then picking it up and holding it ever so gently, like it was delicate china. "That's not true. Wolf was the only one who helped, the only one . . ."

She got up from the couch and went to stand beside him.

"May I see?" And at her tentative gesture toward the picture he froze, then slapped her. "You, don't you *ever* touch him. The only time it ever stopped was when Wolf saw what he was doing to me and bit him. You know that. And you know that when he left me alone it was because he knew Wolf would stop him and protect me . . . and he did, until he was murdered . . . killed . . ."

Her legs were weak, she was still reacting to his slap but forced herself to pull herself together and backed off to the couch. It was a stupid thing to have done, to have approached him and threatened him that way. But maybe not . . . maybe it had provoked him to open up more . . . "Your stepfather, you're talking about your stepfather . . ." At least that much of the secret was out in the open, though it had been there for her to suspect for some time. But now *he* had brought it out. She would risk pushing him another step . . . "He was abusing you—"

"'Abusing' me . . . what a nice proper way to put it. Don't be so delicate. He was doing to me what he did to you. Just like I saw him do to you that night. Never mind, be nice to him, try to love him, he's your father now, that's what you always said. And I tried. I tried . . ."

His face was tight, showing some deep pain, some shameful pain. But at least it was clear now—what lay behind his hatred of his mother, who did nothing to help, nothing to protect him . . . "You never told," she said. "Why?" Knowing even as she asked the reason but wanting to hear it from him, wanting him to hear himself say it.

"Because I knew what he would do—"

And abruptly his expression changed, as though someone had snapped their fingers to bring him out of his depths, out of his hypnotic state. He had to escape to the present, to the unreal world that seemed safer. Mother was gone, Margaret was back, and shame came over him about what he had wanted, what he had felt about her, and wanted and tried to get from her earlier that evening. He had become the kind of man he most loathed . . . the kind of man his stepfather had been. Shame and guilt brought a craving for punishment, any punishment, including the worst that might be waiting for him out there in the darkness. He deserved it.

He turned away to look down at the fireplace again, afraid he could not say what he wanted to if he were looking at her. "Margaret, at least this evening has shown me some things about myself, not pleasant but at least I've seen them . . . I just want you to know that I love you . . . I've never said that to anybody before . . . oh, yes, that's what a lot of men say, but I mean it . . ." He kicked idly at the burned log. "When I tried to show you how I felt, it all was wrong, it got mixed up somehow. Things have always been mixed up for me . . . I've never admitted this even to myself, but there were times when I . . . oh, God . . . when I almost welcomed what was happening to me, when I was old enough . . . by then it didn't hurt so much—this is terrible to say, but what I mean, it wasn't like that about you. I wanted it to be so different, and then I ruined it . . ."

"No, that's not true," she told him. "Your feelings were fine, normal, but they were with the wrong person. Under other circumstances, with another woman, not your therapist, I'm sure your feelings and attentions would have been welcomed. You have it in you to be a fine, sensitive man. A husband, a lover. You have a ways to go, but it is possible, try to believe that . . ." And try to believe it yourself, she added silently.

He was going on in a monotone, as if he hadn't heard her . . . "Margaret, I want you to go now. I am not going to see you again not after what I did tonight . . ."

"And your therapy?" She tried not to show the near-panic she felt.

"That's over too, believe me, I know, I know what is best ... Now go, I can't talk about it anymore. *Go.*"

The tone, the finality in it made it clear to her there was nothing more to be done now. Nothing but to say: "I'll keep your appointment times open. We're so close to your problems. I very much hope you will reconsider."

When he did not reply or look at her, she had no choice but to go to the door, open it slowly, pause, then walk out and close it gently behind her.

○

After she had gone he went to the old leather club chair and curled up in it, the oxblood redness cold at first, then absorbing and reflecting his own heat like a caress. From there he could see the darkness outside the windows. He searched for the glint of the eyes he knew were out there. And then he saw them, gleaming faintly in the trees, staring unblinkingly at him, twin pinpoints of light in the black night. Now as he watched they seemed to move slowly closer, and he looked away, willing them to be gone from his life.

No use. It never was ... He heard the voice, a man's voice, soft and seductive. "You cannot hide from me, Loring. No one can help you. Not her, that's why you sent her away, you knew. You belong to me, Loring, always have."

He shut his eyes tightly. "Who are you?"

"You know who I am. Abbadon, the angel of the bottomless pit, with the power to change men, to make them seek out death."

This was no dream, this was real. But it couldn't be, it was

203

happening to him but it wasn't. Like those other times, beginning in the store with the shrinking, and later, just before the loss of all awareness, and the awful sickness he felt afterward. Afterward . . . ? Was it the belladonna? No, yes, he didn't know. Abruptly he thought of the Bible class at St. Ignatius, and the text from Revelation . . . "And the fifth angel sounded, and I saw a star fall from heaven unto the earth; and to him was given the key of the bottomless pit." No, not the belladonna, it was the voice of truth, telling the damnation he felt but tried not to believe was real, was happening to him. Pray . . . "Holy Michael, the Archangel —" The voice stopped him, reading his thoughts, censuring him . . . "No, Loring. Michael did not help you when I changed you in the store, when I made you shrink. He has not helped you the other times you pretend not to remember. He will not help you now . . ."

So he had not been hallucinating, it had really happened to him in the store . . . "What do you mean 'the other times'?" His voice was below a whisper.

"Come on, Loring, you know. The park, of course. The rabbits, the ducks, the dog, the man in the car, the boy, all as I ordered, and you, good boy, obeyed. You have a convenient memory, Loring. But that must change now. You must pay for your deeds. Remembering them is the beginning . . ."

He tried to clear his mind, to block it all out, but no use, what the voice said was true. And in a terrible flood, everything came back to him, the blood, death. He *saw*, disbelieving, yet knowing, saw himself steal the rabbits from the pen and kill them with his teeth, then later the ducks from the creek . . . and finally the taste for human flesh . . .

His stomach heaved.

When he was finally able to speak again he could only say,

"Please kill me," and meaning it with all his heart. His back was to the window, unable to look into the darkness, at the all-knowing eyes. "I can't live, knowing this . . ."

"After a time," the voice said, "but first there are things you must do for me."

He squeezed into a tight fetal position in the chair. "No, no more. Just let me die, now, *please* . . ."

"'Please,' you say. Like always. Please, mother, please, father, please. Please what, Loring? You fooled Margaret, you were really very good. You even fooled yourself. But you know better, of course. You did not hate your mother because she did not protect you. You hated her because she had another man, because you were so *jealous*. She belonged to you, she had betrayed you, and she and the others would pay. You *liked* what your stepfather did to you. You liked the redemption through his punishment. It felt good, Loring. Remember, remember, it is beginning. And now you are ready to do what I have prepared you for. You are the angel of peace, the savior, the wolf . . . you will cleanse the herd, and only then be able to save yourself. Now stand up, Loring, and see for the first time what you have become."

Resistance was useless. He had no will. He stood and looked in the mirror over the fireplace. At first he felt relief, it seemed nothing had changed, and then he knew he was deceiving himself again . . . because as he stared he saw the eyes staring back at him, eyes not his own, eyes with a dark fire inside. And his lips, it was not so but it was. His lips were pulling back, revealing teeth . . .

And then blackness.

CHAPTER 19

MERCANTO TOOK his seat at the conference table in the fifth-floor room of the Roundhouse. He had stayed at the crime scene late into the night, walking around, trying to get a feel for the killer, but in the end he had come up empty. Even after seeing the results of two killings first-hand, he still had no telling clue. The man was, to put it mildly, an enigma.

Crime was not such a difficult thing for him to understand. Growing up in the inner city he'd seen it all his life. The druggies, the gangs, professional thieves, husbands who battered their families, barroom fights, even rapes made *some* sort of sense to him. He didn't condone any of it but he at least understood where it was coming from. They all had motives, most of which boiled down to love and/or money, with the balance spilling over into injured pride. But this was different. A kind of violence where it seemed the act was the reason rather than the end-result. A perpetrator whose rules were known only to himself.

Seated around the table were Captain Zinkowsky, Mary Kane and three detectives he recognized as Rafferty, Evans and Spivak from Sloan's unit Seven Squad. Sloan was at the head of the table talking with a man Mercanto did not recognize. Everyone in the room was smoking except himself. The air stung his eyes. In the center of the table was coffee in styrofoam cups. He helped himself to a cup as the door opened and the Medical Examiner came in with a file under his arm. He looked beat from his long night of autopsying the body.

Sloan looked over. "We're all here. Let's get started."

The man he was talking to took a seat. Sloan held up a copy of the morning edition of the *Globe*. The headline read: "Cannibal Loose in Fairmount Park." Mercanto had not seen it. Below the headline was a picture of the body bag being unloaded at the morgue.

"I'm not going to ask who leaked this to the press," Sloan said, "but if I find out he's in trouble." His gaze seemed to be more fixed on Mercanto than the others. "We kept this quiet in the Hightower case but whoever did it now has made our job twice as hard as before. The switchboard downstairs has been ringing off the wall since this hit the streets. Not only do we have a weirdo killer to contend with but a frightened public as well."

No one at the table had to be told what that meant. Teenagers would be cruising the park hoping to get a glimpse of him. Citizens would be getting out loaded guns. And worse yet, some other nut might be inspired to imitate.

People shifted uncomfortably. Sloan put down the paper. "Spivak, you're going to be in charge of sorting out this part of the mess. That means fielding the crank calls, reassuring the public, making sure no valid lead from any of them gets by us. Any further statements to the press will be handled by me."

Sloan looked at Captain Zinkowsky. "How we coming on this Rashid character?"

"Nothing yet. I'm meeting with the drug people after we finish here. We'll get him, don't worry," she said.

The name caused looks of interest to be exchanged around the table. "For those of you who don't know," Sloan said, "this Rashid is a lead Mercanto turned up. He's apparently a Jamaican drug dealer working the Germantown Avenue area. Hightower was involved with him. That could explain what Hightower was doing in the park that night. We don't know about the kid yet." He turned to the Medical Examiner. "Any trace of drugs on the kid?"

The Medical Examiner opened the file in front of him. "He wasn't high when he was killed, but we did find traces of cocaine in his system."

Mercanto remembered the look on the kid's face during the holdup. So he was right, the kid was a user.

"We've finished the autopsy," continued the Medical Examiner. "There was nothing that we didn't expect to find. Death was caused by loss of blood from a torn carotid artery in the neck. From traces of saliva we found in the wound, we were able to determine that the killer was a male with blood type 'O.' We also found blond hairs on the body. They were from his head, not from a mustache or beard—under a microscope you can tell the difference. Because of the violence of the killing, specifically the biting aspect of it, I think we can assume that the absence of any facial hairs in the wound or on the victim means that the killer was cleanshaven."

He paused to look at the file again. "Sorry I don't have this on the tip of my tongue but I'm speaking for the lab boys, too, and I want to be sure I'm right," he said. "It rained the night of the murder. I checked the weather report to be sure. We found some footprints at the scene. They came from a man's sneaker, size ten. From the tread we think it might be the Nike brand but can't be sure. There are other models with similar treads. We were able to make a partial mold of the teeth marks from the wound. They seem to match the teeth marks from Hightower's mutilation. But we can't be positive of that either."

"Why not?" asked Mary Kane.

"With wounds of this type it's not like making a mold from a half-eaten candy bar or chunk of cheese where you have a clean bite. Here we have as much tearing as biting, so the impression is distorted, in some places obliterated."

Which brought an uneasy silence even over this table.

"Last night Captain Zinkowsky and I met with the Chief and the Mayor," Sloan said. "They've agreed to clear the decks, give us all the help we need. Temporarily our headquarters will be the park station. Beginning today we're tripling park patrols. That means more cars, more men. We're bringing in the whole mounted patrol. With the terrain, horses may be more useful than cars, but we're going to have both."

He unfolded a map of the park on the table. "As you know, the park is the largest city park in the world. At one point you can ride on horseback for over twenty-five miles without coming out of it. Effectively patrolling the whole thing is out of the question, so we're going to eliminate the area around the zoo, Strawberry Mansion, Robin Hood Dell, Kelly Drive, West River Drive and Lincoln Drive. For now we'll use the two murder sites as our boundaries and concentrate on the area between them.

Mercanto well knew what a big area they were still talking about. The killer had too many places to hide.

Sloan drew an imaginary circle on the map with his forefinger. "Inside this area we're also going to deploy plainclothes people posing as couples parking. Might draw him out. On the West Mt. Airy side we're beginning a house-to-house canvass. Captain Zinkowsky will be heading that up."

It would be the biggest manhunt any of them could remember.

"This is Dr. Charles Foster, a psychiatrist who consults for the department," Sloan went on. "Maybe he can give us some help about the man we're looking for." Sloan nodded toward the man in his mid-sixties who was sitting next to him.

Dr. Foster cleared his throat: "I don't need to tell anyone that the person we're talking about is severely disturbed. From what the Medical Examiner just told us, we know he is male by his saliva and hair. Because of the viciousness of the attacks we can assume he was a young man, somewhere between his late teens and mid-thirties, I'd say. He will be someone who's badly repressed, unable to express his true feelings in any normal fashion. We all know people who are *like* this in one degree or another. In its mildest form it can be the sort of person who is fine when he's sober but becomes an unpleasant drunk. Or in its more serious stages, like now, the sort of person who internalizes things until such a rage builds that he goes on a killing rampage. The kind of man the neighbors invariably describe afterward as being a quiet man who kept to himself and never made any enemies."

"A psycho . . ." ventured Mary Kane.

"Not exactly," Foster said. "The term is often misused. A psychopathic personality is usually a very charismatic one, made up of impulsive, immoral behavior marked by antisocial tendencies. For our purposes a psycho, a psychopath, is a person who has no guilt mechanism or ability to distinguish between right and wrong beyond a very rudimentary level. I doubt that is the sort of man we're looking for. More likely our man will have a very clear-cut idea of right and wrong, at least by his lights, and that may just be the triggering influence of his disturbance."

"Disturbance," Mercanto thought. Some fucking "disturbance."

"What kind of a job will he have?" Spivak asked.

"Difficult to say," said the Holmesian Dr. Foster. "Let's use the word psychosis to describe his illness. In this case the psychosis is in a very advanced stage. If this is something that has been occurring in varying stages throughout his adult life, he is likely to be unemployed or a menial employee. If it is something that has had a long latent period, he may well be anything—a lawyer, a businessman, an accountant—"

"A doctor?" someone muttered.

Foster let it pass. "Whatever stage he is in now, he will have increasing trouble functioning."

"What do you mean?" Sloan said.

"He will have periods in which he seems normal, then periods when he is clearly not. Right now the periods when he is not normal will probably be greater than the periods when he is. Since he has no control over these periods they will naturally affect every aspect of his life, his job, his friends—"

"What about his family life?" asked Mary Kane.

Foster hesitated. "That's a complex matter. In all likelihood he is single with probably no close attachments. His behavior is too bizarre to go unnoticed within a family circle, but that doesn't mean that he wasn't married at one time. Separation could be a triggering influence."

"Sounds like my theory about the drug dealer is kaput!" Mercanto said. "Him being Jamaican, I thought it might be something cultural, like voodoo. I asked an expert at the Braddon—"

"I could be wrong," said a suddenly cautious Foster, "but I don't think the dealer is the answer, at least not without seeing him or the people he employs. It's a question of control. The kind of rage our killer must be feeling is not something that can be turned on and off."

"What do you think's causing this rage?" Spivak asked.

Dr. Foster, true to his image, paused to light his pipe. "There are a number of possibilities, so anything I say will be a guess. Psychiatry is not the science of detection, it's the science of clarification. To do that we need to study the patient, but I know that's not why you called me here so I'll say, based on the small amount of data we have to work from, that he is most likely a schizophrenic with paranoid delusions."

"What the *hell* is that?" said Rafferty.

"Paranoid delusion is pretty well-known. He hallucinates . . . hears things, smells things, sees things that aren't there," he said, thinking for a moment about the patient Margaret described at their lunch, then dismissing it. "Schizophrenia is trickier. Usually it starts in the early twenties, though sometimes later. It's characterized by anxiety, sleep disorder, hallucinations, too, and the tendency to withdraw from others. We tend to think of it as a problem of perception. Among the outward signs are confusing language, compulsive alliteration . . . for example phrases like every exigency for final finesse . . . and a change in eating habits. No one knows for sure what causes it. Some think it is hereditary, some think acquired. Often the two go hand in hand."

"My voodoo expert said schizophrenics were shamen in some societies . . ." said Mercanto.

"Leave the damn voodoo thing alone," Sloan told him.

"No, no, he's right," said Dr. Foster. "Because it's a problem of perception they are often viewed as holy men in primitive societies. In our man's case he may have a genetic predisposition to the disorder but I think it's safe to say it's also somehow tied in with the family. Actually, most schizophrenics exhibit little or no sign of rage. They are more dangerous to themselves than others. With their altered perceptions suicide or death from starvation are more likely. When you do encounter rage, most often it is a result of their abuse as a child, sexually or physically."

"We're checking profiles of people recently released from mental hospitals and known sex offenders," Sloan said.

"A good idea, especially in the first case, possibly not so much in the second. As a Freudian, I believe sex plays a part in most disorders, but in this case I think our man may have very little sexual experience, a low sex drive, and even be impotent. Again, the rage and the nature of the disorder lead me to think that. The denial of his normal urges would close out this avenue of release and tend to fuel his rage."

"Isn't what you just said contradictory? Earlier you said that he might have been married once . . . " Mary Kane put in.

"No, I don't think so. For instance, in this day and age would you classify someone who has only had sex with one person, or even a couple of people as sexually inexperienced?" he said. She nodded, he had a point. "Remember I also said that marital breakup could be a trigger for what's happening now. I'm sure you can see what I mean. His wife, the only woman he's ever slept with, rejects him, maybe humiliates him, then leaves him . . ."

"Then you think he'll do it again . . ." Mary Kane said.

"Definitely, but he's not like a serial killer. The pattern will be much more vague. His victims chosen just because they happen to be there rather than fitting some psychological profile, such as prostitutes in the case of a Jack the Ripper."

"Why did he pick the park for his turf?" Mercanto asked.

"A very good question. And one that I can't answer, except to say that to him there is a valid reason. It may be the offshoot of the disorder . . . the desire to withdraw. In a city where there are not many places where a person can withdraw from human contact, be alone, the park offers an excellent opportunity with its remoteness. Schizophrenics also tend to seek or respond to signs from nature. Their disorders are more likely to be worse during the full noon, or a particular time of the season, or even at high or low tide if they're near the seashore. But it might not be any of these. Don't laugh, but it might be that he's going to the park because he's waiting for a spaceship to pick him up and take him to Mars, outer space. Remember I said it was a problem of perception. Or it might be something as simple as the fact that the park is convenient for him, nearby."

Mercanto suddenly sat up straighter in his chair. He remembered the night he found Hightower's body, the sounds in the woods, and the heavily wooded area where the kid's body was found.

"When he's in one of those states can he drive a car?" he asked.

Foster considered for a moment. "That depends on the severity of the state. It's a matter of degree. Schizophrenics often have trouble with physical dexterity in the more

215

advanced stages, but I would have to say, yes, he could. The question is whether he would want to. It's all a function of his desire, his need to withdraw."

"How likely is it that he's someone from the neighborhood?" asked Sloan.

"Well, certainly not unlikely."

"Do these periods or states come on gradually or all at once?" Mercanto asked.

"Both. They can come of a sudden, but that's rare. Usually there is an incident that triggers it, followed by a build-up in the form of abnormal behavior until it reaches full-blown proportions. As the psychosis progresses it takes less and less time to reach the full-blown stage."

"After he kills, is that the end of the stage, is he normal again?" Mercanto asked.

"No, not at all. As with the build-up, there will be a cooling down period, a time when he will try to put things in perspective again. For instance, after crimes of this type he will be covered in blood. Literally covered, I mean it will be all over him. Psychologically he will have to deal with this in the cooling down period. He probably won't be so-called normal again for several hours, maybe even days in a psychosis this severe, and when he is it will be for shorter and shorter periods of time."

"How can anybody come to terms with something this horrible? It's not like regular crimes, even killings," Mary Kane asked.

"By that ol' debbil repression," Dr. Foster told her, allowing a smile. "His conscious mind will totally reject the incident. Make as if it didn't happen. In all likelihood he will be amnesiac about it, or if he does remember it in any fashion he will treat it as a dream or something that happened to someone else."

"Do you think we can take him alive?" Mercanto asked, not much liking the prospect.

Foster considered his answer. "That depends on you, but I can assure you he won't want you to. For him death may seem the only way out of his predicament."

CHAPTER 20

NEAR DAWN the voice commanded him to go into the park. He changed from his tuxedo into a dark blue sweatsuit and went out. Once in the trees he followed a path that led down to the rocks at Devil's Pool.

Out of sight of the house he no longer felt the presence. If he could just hide, maybe all this would pass. Maybe it was only a dream, a hallucination, after all. He hadn't really done those . . . things. It was only his mind playing tricks on him, an imaginary voice.

He took refuge, squatting in a clump of bushes among the

trees, sure no one could see him. Time moved slowly, he did not know how long he was there, but just when he was beginning to feel safe, he heard it again. As clear and strong and real as the night before.

"There you are, I've been looking for you," and the words were his stepfather's, the same words said when he found him hiding in the closet, trying to escape from what he knew was going to happen. Where to hide now? To escape what he knew was going to happen . . .

He found himself on his feet and running through the trees, branches whipping across his face, underbrush tripping him. He kept on until exhausted and had to stop. Above the rasp of his breath he heard the sound of Wissahickon Creek on his right. That meant he was headed toward the stables or Lincoln Drive beyond. Find other people, then he would be safe . . .

But as he stood there he saw the eyes gleaming in the trees, heard the now too familiar voice say, "If you're going to act like a naughty pet you're going to be treated like one . . ."

He felt his legs collapse under him and fell to the ground. He tried to get up but could not. Finally he managed to get to all fours, the dampness of the ground seeping through the knees of his sweatsuit.

"The way of the wolf, Loring. Once he also walked on two legs . . . until he disobeyed. I know because I made him that way. Now turn and follow me."

Again he tried to stand and could not. He was in his body and out of it, aware and yet beyond any self-control. He followed, crawling on all fours, the gleaming eyes always in front of him, leading. Back they went in the direction he had come. What did he feel? Humiliation, pain, forced down on his knees like an animal, like the wolf he had become. He felt

220

shame. Margaret... he had so badly wanted to love her, instead had felt only lust, like an animal . . .

The rocks and underbrush tore at his knees, making them raw and bloody. The cold dampness of the ground seemed to fill him as he crawled. Was this how his life was to end? A beast, face almost unrecognizable, pulled into distorted features . . . the punishment was mythological. Strange that he could have such thoughts, the way he was now . . .

Memories of missed chances, friendships offered and turned away. Each time he was too afraid they would find out about him . . . There had been no one until Margaret, and now he had hurt her, driven her away . . .

A piece of broken glass cut the palm of his hand, he welcomed the pain. More memories broke in, no longer able to be shut out . . .

His sister's wedding. He ruined that, too. Because of his stepfather, but not for the reasons he'd told himself . . . revulsion, hatred that spread to the whole family, even his sister. The voice was right. He remembered his fantasies. If he saw his stepfather, behind those all-seeing eyes leading him, how would he feel? Would he want it as much as he told himself he hated it . . . ?

Around him dawn was breaking. He saw the eyes staring at him from a bush, heard the voice say, "Penance begins the admission and payment for sins. The next step is obedience. Get to your feet."

Loring saw his body stand, legs and arms trembling from the strain of his crawl. He turned, looked back into the woods. He did not know how far he'd come. There were holes in the knees of his sweatpants, he could feel the stickiness of his blood as it trickled down his shins.

He followed the commands, moving through the woods

again toward the rocks at Devil's Pool. He picked his way across the stream, the water from the small falls chilling his legs.

Yes, the admission of sins . . . memory of the first time with his stepfather came back. He had protested but his stepfather threatened, said he would tell that the bad boy had killed his father, that it was no suicide, he would be taken away and locked up in jail for the rest of his life. Did he want that?

He moved along the bank of the creek until he came to the parking lot by the bridge. Now he remembered, could not exorcise it, what he had done when he found the man in the car. It was crystal clear, no longer could he hide in the pretense of hallucination. That night, too, he had been the wolf, prowling the park until he found his prey—

His stomach went into a spasm, emptied itself, Abaddon's voice scolded him for it. "You are acting like a child. You did it because it was your destiny, it has been since your birth. I've explained that. You are my messenger, through your deeds others will be cleansed and find peace. I have brought you here for that reason. Now see to it."

Loring looked across the parking lot. Less than fifty yards away from where he was concealed, an old Ford station wagon was pulling in at the foot of the steps to the Maison Catherine on the hill above. In the dawn's early light he saw a petite woman with hennaed hair get out and go around to open the tailgate. He recognized her as the owner of the restaurant, although he didn't know her name. As he watched her bend forward to gather some bundles he heard Abaddon's command to go to her, and knew what was expected of him.

For a moment he hesitated, but when he tried to protest he found he could not speak. His voice had been taken from him. What came out was an absurd growl. Not his—"If you resist

222

me I will strike you down and leave you to crawl around on all fours, with no voice. Do you want that?"

Terror convinced him . . . the keeper of the bottomless pit held infinite power. Who was he to oppose him? They were linked together. And as he thought it, he began to move toward the woman.

She did not see him until he was almost on her. She looked up in surprise at the sound, and in that moment he knew *everything* Abaddon said was true. The morning light illuminated her face, and deep in the dark portion of her left eye he saw it clearly . . . the number *13* twinkling like a diamond in the unfolding sunlight.

The mark of the beast.

And he heard Abaddon's voice say, "The new Jerusalem cannot come until those deceived by the mark of the beast are cleansed . . ."

Exhilaration filled him. He was part of the master plan he had begun to perceive in that long-ago Bible class. All his pain had been for a reason . . . so that the beast and the false prophet could be cast into the lake of fire, and Satan bound in chains in the bottomless pit for a thousand years.

The woman knew this, feared it. Before she could speak he grabbed her and smashed her head into the side of the car. Her face split open along her eye. He did it to her again, and again, until she was unconscious. Then he closed the tailgate and picked her up in his arms, walked across the parking lot and back into the woods.

At the stream he switched to a fireman's carry and picked his way across on the rocks. On the other side he found a small clearing in the bushes, put her down, then looked about as he regained his breath.

The sky was overcast now, but he had spared her the gloom

of the day. For her everything hereafter would be bright and shining. His gift to her. The thought made him feel good.

More than "good" as he looked down at the unconscious woman. It was love such as he had never felt before. He knelt over her, all doubt and resistance gone. His role of the wolf was right. Through him, through the momentary pain, the physical would become spiritual. She would no longer bear the mark of the beast. She would be purified, a part of the new Jerusalem, as Abaddon said ...

He ripped her dress open. He had never seen a woman nude before, except his mother. As he touched her breasts and stomach he saw his hands. They looked like thorny claws, which seemed natural, and everywhere he touched, streaks of blood magically appeared, bright red against the whiteness of her flesh. It was so beautiful. For once in his life he was not afraid to give, not afraid to help another—

She stirred, and he saw the look of fright as he bent forward. He was sad that she had to see him so changed, but he understood and soon she would too. Soon, in the next world, she would see many things beyond her understanding now.

He sank his teeth into her throat, feeling the flesh give way. He heard the snap of her windpipe collapsing, the taste of her a sweetness in his mouth. She tried to struggle, feebly, as the blood sprayed over them, sealing their unspoken bargain.

CHƏPTER 21

SLOAN HAD finished making the assignments and everyone had filed out of the conference room. Mercanto stayed to find out why he had been excluded.

Before he could speak, Sloan said, "You've been involved in this case from the start. By now I'd have thought something would have occurred to you, that you'd at least have some decent theories, but all you've got is voodoo and some Germantown Avenue drug dealer."

"What else have you got?" Mercanto challenged. "I've never worked homicide before. Where have you been?"

Anger flashed in Sloan's face, and Mercanto saw him double up his fists. He'd touched a nerve, okay, so be it. "Look, never mind what you feel about me, we should work together. We've got a case to solve. An important one. What do you want me to do?"

Sloan shook his head. "I brought you back into this and all you've given me is cockamamie stuff. You're out."

Before Mercanto could say anything, Mary Kane's voice sounded behind him. "Lieutenant, can I see you for a moment?"

Mercanto turned and stalked out of the room.

Outside he sat in his car trying to cool down. So nothing had changed, all his work was a waste. His career was still shot. Sloan wanted to lay the stigma of Ruth Gunther's death on him no matter what. He pounded the steering wheel. To hell with it, with Sloan. He would not be left out of this case. Erin . . . somewhere in what she'd told him was at least the beginning of a handle on this thing. He had to believe that . . . what the hell else did he have? He pulled away from the curb and headed for the Braddon.

When he found Erin she was supervising the movement of some case of artifacts in the main room during the cleanup after the party.

"Hi," she said, "what brings you out here again?"

"Is there someplace we can talk? Get a cup of coffee or something?"

She hesitated, saw the seriousness in his face. "In my office," she said.

Her office was small and cramped. He took a seat while she went to pour coffee from the pot on top of a filing cabinet. In this light he could see she looked tired. "Hard night?" he asked.

"The opening party."

"Did you have a good time?" he said, making conversation before he got to it.

"I guess so, considering that my date vanished on me."

"What do you mean, vanished?"

"One minute he's there, the next he's gone . . ."

"How did you get home?" He was concerned at the thought of her being stranded, just as he was jealous, admit it, that she'd had a "date." Cut it out, he told himself.

"Friends," she replied . . . "What was it you wanted to see me about?"

"Did you read the morning paper?" When she said no he showed it to her with its gruesome headline. He told her about the boy's body, and what had happened since their last meeting. She listened intently as he went into detail about the wounds, the crime scene.

"The psychiatrist, the lieutenant, nobody buys my theory about the drug dealer. I know what you said about the voodoo, but I feel that there's something else. Something I missed . . ."

She was silent for several moments, then said, "Tell me about the wounds again, in both cases."

He did.

"And what did the psychiatrist think?"

"He said the killer was probably a schizophrenic with paranoid delusions. I'm not too clear on all that."

"Yes, I guess that would figure—"

"What do you mean?"

After several more moments of hesitation she said, "Have you ever heard the term *lycanthropy?*"

He said he hadn't, what was it?

"It's a very rare form of schizophrenia. I saw it once in Haiti . . . You remember I said schizophrenics are often made shamen in primitive societies . . . Well, this one was afflicted with lycanthropy, and he did ultimately kill some people in just the way you've described." She set her coffee down. "Come with me and I'll show you something that belonged to him."

As they went downstairs he said, "Why didn't you tell me about this before?"

"Because you were so specific about Jamaica and voodoo. This happened in Haiti, and it's such a rare thing I didn't see how it could apply . . . not then, at least."

In the main hall there was a glass case with a single mask in it, a mask with tracks of rhinestone tears coming down from the eye holes. "This was his," Erin said.

Mercanto could see the pain in it. "Tell me about it."

"Some people believe lycanthropy is the oldest psychosis known to man, that it dates all the way back to when man made the break between being a farmer and a hunter. When roving bands of men, like wolf packs, preyed on the farmers, killing them, raping their women, cannibalizing them. There's data for both sides, but after seeing this man, I made a small study of it," she said, pointing to the case.

"Go on," he said, more curious than excited by what she was saying.

"The oldest recorded example of it is in the Old Testament book of Daniel when Nebuchadnezzar went into a seven-year depression during which he thought he was an ox and would only eat grass. Some people say that Lot's wife turning into a pillar of salt is another example but I don't see it. Anyway, mention of the disease later turned up in the medical writings of Paulus Aegineta during the Roman Empire—"

"Wait a minute, are you saying the killer thinks he's an animal and acts like one?"

"If he's suffering from lycanthropy, the answer is yes. And

if so, most likely he thinks he's a wolf. That's what this shaman thought he was."

"Why a wolf?"

"Well, there are several theories. In primitive societies the wolf epitomized hunting prowess. It was supposed to bring good luck if the hunter dressed in a wolf pelt. By wearing it he would become like the wolf and be successful in his hunt."

Mercanto remembered the looks of that dead boy, the teeth marks . . . "It sounds pretty farfetched," he said, "but still . . ."

"You haven't heard the half of it. Which is why I didn't want to bring it up . . . In the Middle Ages it became the basis of the werewolf legend. The term lycanthropy comes from the Latin for manwolf . . . Are you bored, still with me?"

"I'm trying, go on."

"Okay . . . well, during this time, especially during the Inquisition, the recorded cases took on a much stronger religious tone. Emphasis shifted from God's punishment, like in the case of Nebuchadnezzar, to demonic possession."

"You mean like witches?"

"Exactly. All throughout Europe there were stories and supposed sightings of men who had become part or wholly wolves, and the idea of the wolf changed from the ultimate hunter endowed with desirable traits to the concept of the wolf as a servant of Satan preying on God's flock . . . And so, the notion of the werewolf. A human cursed, and whose obsessive desire, need, was to kill and eat human flesh."

"It sounds crazy—"

"Yes, I know . . . Of course, these people didn't actually turn into wolves, but they *thought* they did. That's what lycanthropy is all about. There were two especially famous examples. The first, Stubbe Peeter, occurred in Germany in the late 1500s. He supposedly was a cruel man who made a pact with the devil and was given a girdle made from a wolf skin that turned him into one when he wore it."

"What happened to him?"

"Before he was caught he killed animals, over a dozen children and two pregnant women, cannibalizing them all, including the unborn babies. During the trial it came out that he had been committing incest with his daughter. They were both tortured to death as punishment."

"And the other one?" Mercanto asked, not sure he wanted to hear.

"A Frenchman named Jean Grenier. In the early 1600s. His case marked the turning point between the werewolf legend and the idea of lycanthropy. He was tried for murdering and cannibalizing several young girls in his village. Like Stubbe Peeter, he claimed to have been changed into a wolf by the devil. The judge, even then, didn't buy it. He said men could not be turned into wolves. They were imaginings, what we call hallucinations. Rather than send an insane Grenier to prison or execute him, he was sentenced to life in a monastery for religious instruction. That wasn't an easy sentence in those days. He died there two years later, but the important thing is that this was possibly the first time in history when alternative incarceration was used for the mentally unbalanced. Looking back, we can see what a milestone that was."

Mercanto shook his head. "Now tell me about the one *you* saw."

"I told you, he was a shaman of a village in Haiti. They don't call them shamen, but that's what he was. This wasn't the village he was from originally so I don't know much about his past history. One day he just wandered in and began telling everyone about the devil and that he was a wolf ..."

"Wasn't anyone skeptical? I mean, these are the 1980s, not the 1600s."

"You have to understand something about the shaman concept to know what I'm saying." She paused to collect her thoughts. "In the Oriental culture and sometimes in the Caribbean, too, a shaman is believed to be a reincarnate, someone who has had communication with a so-called higher power. Traditionally he's a person of powerful spirituality who has had an emotional experience so strong that it has caused him to . . . to become noticeably different from those around him. And this experience is the basis of his teachings. If people like his teaching they listen. If not, they get rid of him."

"And he was popularizing the devil?"

"Right! It fit in perfectly with a culture that embraces voodoo and zombies . . . you know, the undead. It was just what they wanted to hear . . . that is, until people began disappearing from the village, and they found he was killing them and cannibalizing them . . . exactly like *you* described."

"How did he act when you saw him? I mean, was he crazy all the time or what?"

"I only saw him once. By the time I heard what happened to him he was already dead. The villagers had killed him. When I saw him it was during a ceremony. He didn't go into a trance or anything, but let's just say he wasn't with us. He stalked, howled and in general acted out the part of the wolf. He killed an animal with his hands and ate it. It was, I assure you, scary as hell. There's not much else I can add."

Mercanto shook his head. What she was saying was extreme, weird, but, damn it, it did provide the missing link, the explanation for the mutilations. But he also knew what it was going to sound like when he brought it to Sloan. Still, he had to do it . . .

An idea came to him, he wouldn't start with Sloan. "Would you be willing to go with me and talk about this with the psychiatrist on the case?" he asked.

She hesitated, then agreed.

"This means a lot to me," he said as he took her arm and helped her up. "Have you a phone book handy?"

While she got it for him she wondered just what this man was doing in her life. Was it only professional? Stop worrying it to death, she told herself as he looked up Dr. Foster's number and made the call, asking to see the psychiatrist immediately.

They took the elevator down and went to where Mercanto was parked. His car did not exactly surprise her. A beat-up old Camaro was him. And she liked it. She got in on the passenger side and cleared a place for her feet among the empty coffee cups, Burger King wrappers and newspapers.

He pulled away from the curb in a hurry. As he drove he thought over what she'd just told him. Suddenly something else came to mind. "You said the first guy, this Stubbe Peeter, killed animals too, and you said the same thing about the guy you saw, right?"

She turned to look at him as he drove. "That's right."

"Before we found the first body we had some things happen with animals in the park. Ducks killed. We thought it was a dog from the way they were torn up. But now . . . well, it might have been this guy."

She noted the excitement in his voice, and liked it. "Yes, it might have been," she said.

O

At the psychiatrist's office building near Jefferson Hospital, Mercanto parked beside a fire hydrant and they hurried inside.

Mercanto showed his badge to the receptionist, who said,

"He's waiting for you, go right in." A patient in the waiting room glared at them as they went in.

Dr. Foster looked up from some papers he was reading, his all-purpose pipe in his mouth.

"Sorry to break in on you like this . . ." Mercanto began.

"Quite all right. If it will help us to catch this man . . ."

Mercanto made the introductions, Dr. Foster nodded and asked what they had found out.

"I think Erin, Miss Fraser, can explain it better than I can. She's the one who understands it."

Foster waited.

"I'm an anthropologist, the curator at the Braddon Museum, shamanism is my specialty," she began. "Recently Detective Mercanto came to me for information about voodoo. He said it might be a factor in these murders. I couldn't help him then, but when he came back today he told me some things that lead me to believe I might be helpful . . . Have you ever heard, doctor, of lycanthropy?"

"Certainly," replied Dr. Foster. "Every first-year medical student knows something about lycanthropy and porphyria. It's a joke among the first-year people."

Mercanto gave Erin a quizzical look.

"Porphyria is the Dracula disease," she told him. "It's hereditary, a person's teeth fill up with blood. He also develops acute sensitivity to light. Some think Vlaid the Impaler, the role model for Dracula, had it."

"I'm impressed," Foster said.

She looked hard at him. "Neither one is a joke, doctor. They are both *real* diseases."

"Agreed. Still, the rareness of them . . ."

"The facts of the murders fit the disease," Erin said. And she repeated the story about the Haitian shaman. When she was finished he said, "Yes, they do seem to fit . . . somewhat."

He got up from his desk and went to one of the bookcases lining the wall of his office. "Understand, I've never had any personal experience with lycanthropy. It occurs so infrequently . . ." He took down a volume of bound journals and brought it back to his desk. As he thumbed through it he said, "If memory serves, there have only been two, perhaps three, recorded cases in the last decade or so." When he found what he was looking for he said, "Ah, yes, I thought I remembered an article about it in one of the British journals. Give me a minute to refresh my memory."

They sat while he read. When he was finished he said, "It's certainly controversial. I think we can discount the Navajo Coyote ceremonies and concentrate on the case histories from a Freudian aspect. Although schizophrenics are not commonly the split personalities they are popularized to be, in this case there seems to be a split caused by a traumatic incident during childhood. That does agree with what I suspected about the killer's background."

"You mean a multiple personality?" said Mercanto.

"No, multiple personalities are not usually schizophrenic. They occur because of some terrible abuse, often sexual, that began before age five, the formation of the personality. They're a protective mechanism for the abused . . . In this case the pattern of abuse is the same, the abused is forced into a passive sexual position, but later in life, *after* the formation of the personality. Here is where the difference shows. The abuse produces a conflict and resultant guilt. One part of the person wants it to continue; the other knows it's wrong and wants it to stop. To compensate for the helplessness of it, the part that wants it to stop splits off and takes the personality of a predatory beast, usually, it seems, a wolf, to protect the weaker side from more abuse."

"But all that's in childhood. We're talking about a grown man here. What makes it happen now?" said Mercanto.

234

"There has to be a triggering incident, something that raises up the old conflict in him again." And, surprisingly, this talk brought his lunch with Margaret to mind, when she told him about her patient's shrinking episode after the invitation to his sister's wedding. Just, come to think of it, the sort of incident that could trigger a psychosis . . .

"Why a damn wolf?" Mercanto said. "I know, it goes way back, but I still don't see . . ."

"Because of spirit possession," Erin said. "He thinks, *believes*, he has become a tool of a higher power, probably the devil, that is symbolized by the wolf, the mark of the beast. He's obviously an intelligent person, well-read too."

Dr. Foster picked up his pipe. "You apparently think spirit possession is a reality. I'm afraid I can't go along with that."

"You do admit there are certain things that defy rational explanation, even by the so-called science of psychiatry."

"No, I really don't," he said, but wondering all the same if the answer to the killer's identity could possibly be as simple as that—*a patient of Margaret's* . . . He tried to dismiss the thought, telling himself that Margaret was an insightful, intuitive professional. Still . . .

"Let me put it this way," said Erin. "In my work I have come across literally hundreds of examples of spirit possession, in one degree or another. I've *seen* some personally. I would classify the lycanthropic shaman as one. I'm not saying he's possessed or anything like that. All these examples of spirit possession are explainable according to various disciplines, but *all* the explanations are reduced to fit a particular discipline. *None* can explain the total experience . . . Don't reject the concept of a lycanthropic because it gets into the area of spirit possession . . ."

When she first agreed to come it was to please Mercanto. But now she felt personally involved, it was important to her. She wanted this killer caught, too, and damn well didn't want to be excluded from helping on account of some philosophical disagreement between professions.

Mercanto looked from Erin to Foster. "So what do you suggest?"

Dr. Foster looked at him, half-smiled. "Lieutenant Sloan is at the Park Station. I think you should go out there and tell him what you've found. I'll follow you out because I think you're going to need my backup to support this theory. I'll be a few minutes behind you, though. There's something I have to attend to first . . ."

CHAPTER 22

DR. CHARLES FOSTER dialed Margaret's number. On the fifth ring he heard the answering machine tape begin: "This is Dr. Margaret Priest . . ."

"Damn, she's with a patient," he muttered as he hung up, not waiting for the tape to end. He grabbed up his hat and coat and headed for the door.

In his outer office he told his receptionist, "Cancel my appointments for the rest of the day. Reschedule them." He turned to the waiting patient. "I'm sorry, but something urgent has come up. Please understand."

The patient did not understand. "Look, goddamn it, *I* have important things, too . . ."

"Yes, yes, we'll discuss that at our next session," soothed Dr. Foster, and headed out the door.

Outside he looked around for a taxi. None to be seen. He thought about getting his car but it would take too long, he could more quickly walk the six or eight blocks between their offices. Pulling down his hat against the winter wind he started up Walnut Street, passing the Forrest Theater.

The whole notion was farfetched . . . a modern-day werewolf, he thought, allowing himself the more sensational term rather than the clinical lycanthropic. It couldn't be happening, it was too rare. The very idea conjured up visions of villagers with torches and pitchforks.

At Thirteenth a young woman in a short skirt and fake fur jacket approached him. He waved her away before she could speak, hurrying on. At other times he found the come-on palaver of the neighborhood prostitutes interesting, even provocative. Not today.

If what he suspected was true, which was still a *big* if in his mind, he couldn't help wondering about Margaret not being aware of the condition of her patient. Had she been that bemused by her own emotional attachment?

On Broad Street he turned at Robinson's toward Locust. He remembered the literature he had just been reading, together with Erin's testimony and the facts of the case as laid out by Sloan.

The wolf was a protective mechanism, true, even if to the person suffering it also seemed like Satan's curse. Unlike a multiple personality it would not show itself willy-nilly but would occur only when the patient felt particularly threatened. Assuming her patient returned Margaret's emotion, exceeded it, there would be no reason for that part of him to show itself with her. Being with Margaret would be like a state of grace for him. The time when he was sure nothing bad would happen. He would have to believe Margaret was the cause, and worship her for it.

Walking up Locust he passed a string of restaurants— Mexican, Cajun, Italian. As for Margaret's attachment, professional or not, she like every therapist was human. At their lunch she had said he was an attractive man. At a time when her self-esteem was so shaken by the discovery of Adam's affair, along with this hardly customary intensity of her patient's adoration . . . "Yes, many patients can be seductive," he said aloud, thinking of his advice to her as he entered her building. Any patient in a transference. And *this* one . . .

Margaret's waiting room was empty. Like many therapists she did not have a secretary. No choice but to interrupt her session.

He knew what he was going to say would not endear him to her. Their lunch had ended on a bad note, straining what he had always counted as a most valuable and stable relationship. Since then there had been no communication between them. Appearing now like this, she might consider it outrageous meddling, coming between her and her patient. Well, he would have to risk it, he decided as he opened the door to her private office.

She looked up, shocked. Sitting in front of the desk was a young woman who was thoroughly confused and cut herself off in mid-sentence.

"Charles? What . . . what are you doing here?"

"Doctor, I'm terribly sorry to interrupt, but I must speak to you."

She looked at her patient. "Will it take long?"

"Yes, I'm afraid it might."

What could she do?... It must be important for him to break in this way. To her patient, she said, "Carol, this is Dr. Foster, a colleague. Could we reschedule for eleven tomorrow? That way I can skip lunch and give you extra time to make up for this."

The patient agreed, what could *she* do ... but Margaret saw the anger at the interruption.

She walked the patient to the door while Charles took off his coat and sat down. Behind her desk now, she waited for an explanation.

Foster knew he would have to be careful. Margaret was a fiercely protective person. If he blurted out his suspicions she would get defensive and they would have a repeat of their lunch.

"Margaret, I'm sorry about what happened the last time we were together. Please understand, you're very important to me. When I said what I did it wasn't because I doubted you, it was because I was concerned ..."

He was like the old Charles. Control was so important to him that you could never expect a direct response. Even in an extreme situation like this. "Are your phones out of order, Charles?"

He forced a smile. Obviously there was no good way to start this. "I need to talk to you about that special patient of yours."

Margaret bristled. "Why?"

"Because I'm more concerned than ever," he said, instantly regretting his choice of words.

"Well, doctor, you can put your concern to rest. I'm not his therapist any longer. He fired me."

"What happened?" he said, surprised. This hardly followed his state-of-grace theory. He had felt sure Margaret was the man's only link with his tolerable emotions ... perhaps even reality itself.

"We had an unpleasant incident, a couple of them, to be precise."

"Tell me?"

"I didn't send my patient away just now to give you that satisfaction."

"Come on, Margaret, you know better than that. Give me some credit . . . it *is* important."

The urgency in his tone impressed her. "It happened at a chance meeting . . . at the party for the opening of an exhibit at the museum. Things weren't going well between Adam and me but we went anyway. He was there with a date."

"He?"

"Loring, my patient." He knew damn well who, she thought. "Naturally I was surprised to see him, but these things do happen." She paused. "Adam sort of vanished, which didn't help my mood. Loring asked me to dance. I know I shouldn't have, but I was distracted by Adam, face-to-face with a persistent, terribly vulnerable patient . . . Anyway, we danced. Afterwards, I don't know exactly how it happened, but we wound up in an office together . . . He tried to kiss me and I stopped him. But too late." She hesitated, forced herself to go on. "It wasn't his fault. I tried to tell him that, but it was no use. Charles, I handled it wrong. I let my personal problems mix into my professional. I'm afraid we're both paying for it . . ."

"Margaret, you're being too hard on yourself. From what you've told me there was nothing else you could do . . . You said a couple of incidents. What about the other one?"

She hated to relive it still another time. "Well, when I pushed him away he ran out of the room. I looked for him to try to repair the damage but he was gone." She left out what had happened between her and Adam afterward. "I changed and drove out to his house. I know that was hardly by the book, but he was having a crisis, it couldn't wait for an office appointment. At least that's how I felt at the time."

"What happened?"

"When he finally let me in I could see he had been crying. As he talked he got more and more upset. Not tears, anger. The most deep-seated I've ever experienced. The upshot was he hit me, then in an orgy of shame, self-hate . . . who knows what else? . . . he insisted I leave and said the therapy was over. I guarantee you there was no convincing him otherwise . . . All right, I've answered your questions, now answer mine. Why this sudden appearance?"

"Did you see the morning paper, the story about the murder in the park?" When she said she had, he told her he was working with the police on it.

"What?" And then it dawned on her. "My God, you're telling me you think . . . no, that's not possible. Loring couldn't be responsible for that. God and Sigmund know I may have handled him wrong, but I'm sure I know him too well to believe that. Charles, this man wouldn't kill anyone, let alone commit the kind of killing I read about. What happened between us, even his hitting me, they were my fault, my responsibility. He wouldn't hurt anyone, it's not in his nature—"

"Margaret, you just mentioned his deep-seated anger."

"I know . . . but he still couldn't have done it," she said, her arms folded across her chest.

"Last night I read over everything about the cases." She noted the plural and turned to look at him. "That's right," he continued. "The one in the paper was not the first but the second. The first was a Stanley Hightower, an optometrist."

She shook her head. "I read about his death, too. His office is just down the street, but there was no cannibalization like in today's report . . ."

"Yes, there was. The police managed to keep it quiet. This morning I met with the people from homicide and told them, based on what I was able to piece together, that the killer was probably a paranoid schizophrenic."

When he saw her about to interrupt he raised his hand. "Hear me out. After the meeting one of the detectives, a man named Mercanto, came to see me. He brought along an anthropologist who specializes in shamanism, someone he'd already consulted with about a voodoo angle in the case." He paused. "Do you know anything about lycanthropy?"

Her eyes widened. "At lunch you tried to tell me he was a schizophrenic, now you're trying to tell me he's a . . . a *werewolf*? Charles, please. I may have handled him wrong, but he's neither of these things. He's an hysteric, deeply troubled, I agree, but—"

"I felt the same way at first, but the anthropologist had seen an actual lycanthropic, a Haitian shaman, so I looked it up in the journals. The facts fit the killer too well."

She went back to her desk and lit a cigarette. "Assuming what you're saying is correct, you're talking about the *killer*, not my patient."

"Margaret, believe me, I hope I'm wrong . . . but we can't ignore the possibility that they might be one and the same person—"

"*No*, goddamn it—"

"Forget the term . . . werewolf. Look at the facts with me. We are talking about a psychosis rooted in the guilt of an early passive sexual situation, usually prepubertal or early pubertal. The personality splits off, with one part assuming the identity of a predatory beast, giving it qualities the conscious personality cannot accept—a means of coming to terms with that guilt without acknowledging it. When we talked you said there was a sexual abnormalcy . . ."

243

True, and she thought about what his stepfather had done. But this wasn't enough. "Inexperience is not sexual abnormalcy," she said, choosing not to mention what Loring had told her at his house. "What he attempted with me doesn't fit that pattern at all. To the contrary, it showed him at least striving for a normal relationship. Nearly all of our patients have a sexual problem of one type or another. The statistics have it that one in four women has been sexually abused *and* one in ten men. None of which turns them into lycanthropics."

"But the schizophrenia . . ."

She shook her head. "Charles, I'm surprised. You're trying to do what you lecture against—diagnose from afar. A couple of articles, a lunch conversation, a session with the police and some anthropologist aren't enough. I *know* this man. I've spent time with him. He is not schizophrenic."

"Yes, you've spent time with him, but don't you see, that's just it . . . when he was with you it wouldn't reveal itself. It would only come out when he felt threatened, as the time when he thought he was shrinking. And when you rejected him, he thought but didn't say. With you, he felt protected, even loved. It wouldn't show. You were the one person he could trust." He paused. "I know this is difficult, but I want his name. You won't be involved, we'll see to it that your name never comes up—"

"Absolutely not," she said, sorry now that she had even let his first name slip. "I might not be his therapist any longer but I will not violate his confidence like that, and you shouldn't ask me to."

"Of course, under almost any other circumstances I would agree with you. But sometimes, Margaret, all our fine rules and principles need to be bent for a larger purpose. There will be no railroading. We will check him out carefully. If he is not the one, that is the end of it. If he is, well, he has already killed twice, and will keep on doing it until he is stopped. You do not want that on your conscience."

"There are a few million people in this city. You haven't given me one solid reason to think he's the person responsible," she said.

"Margaret, take off the blinders. This is, as you've said, a severely disturbed person, *and* one who fits the profile. The last time you were together he tried to assault you sexually, then he hit you. You've rebuked and rejected him, or so he must feel, sent him away. To him you are no longer his protector. You know what this means . . . If he is the one he might well come after you next. You owe it to yourself to be sure. Give me his name. He will not be mistreated, I promise, but we must know."

She thought about Loring, the gentleness she had seen in him. The aloneness and fear. Charles was wrong. He could not kill or mutilate. Such were not in his makeup. If there was anyone she was no longer sure about, it was Charles. For some unknown reason he was terribly prejudging a man he had never even met. She would not be a party to it, to the destruction of poor Loring . . .

"I'm sorry," she said. "The answer is no. Period."

CHAPTER 23

AT THE Park Station Detective Mary Kane thought about Sloan's instructions. He had been very specific, no officer was to go out without a partner until the killer was caught. Her usual partner was Spivak, but he was busy at the Roundhouse fielding the calls from worried citizens. If she had her choice Mercanto was the one she would team up with today, but Sloan had already nixed that, banishing him from the case.

She couldn't understand why Sloan was on his back. Everyone knew the details of Rudy Gunther's death. Mercanto wasn't to blame. He was a damn good cop. She only hoped Sloan would come to realize that.

Her temporary partner was a red-haired uniformed officer named Donovan from the Park Squad. Together now they began to help in the house-to-house canvas of the assigned area between the stables and the Valley Green parking lot.

Their section comprised the houses nearest the creek on the West Mt. Airy side. From there the search would move outward. The morning went slowly. Alarmed by the newspaper stories, someone at each house seemed to have something or someone suspicious to report. Mostly noises in the night, but Kane and Donovan dutifully made notes, mainly to reassure the homeowners that the police were on the job and took them seriously.

It was mid-morning when they knocked on the door of a stone colonial and a woman in her mid-forties, dressed in wool slacks, answered. When they explained what they were doing she hesitated for a moment, then invited them in.

"I'm Mona Seidenberg . . . I don't know if this is helpful, but I did see something. Only it wasn't a few nights ago, it was last night, or early this morning to be truthful."

"Tell us about it," Mary Kane said.

She led them to the kitchen and pointed to the window over the sink that faced the park. "I don't know what time it happened *exactly*," she said, "but it was sometime near dawn. Like always, I was having trouble sleeping so I came in here to get something to drink and have a cigarette. I know, I should quit but . . . well, anyway, when I looked out the window I saw, or at least thought I saw, a man out there at the edge of the woods . . ."

"Yes?"

"It scared me. I mean, these days with people getting killed

248

and all, their houses burglarized . . . Anyway, I woke my husband and told him to come and see, but by the time he got here the man was gone." She laughed self-consciously. "He accused me of seeing things, of jumping at shadows, and went back to bed. But I'm *sure* someone was out there."

"Can you describe him?" Mary asked.

"Not very well, I'm afraid. It was pretty dark, and he was wearing dark clothing."

"What about his hair?"

"You mean what color? I couldn't tell. I couldn't even say for sure if he was white or black. I only saw him for a moment, and he was moving. That's probably the only reason I saw him at all . . . the movement caught my eye."

They went into the backyard together and the woman directed them to the spot. From where they were standing it was easy to see she was telling the truth. A crude path of broken branches and trampled bushes led into the woods. Someone had very recently been there, as the woman said, and from the direction it seemed he was headed toward the creek.

Donavan turned to the woman. "You can go back in the house, ma'am. We're just going to have a look around and see where this leads."

After she'd gone Kane said, "Don't you think we should call it in before we do anything?"

"We'd look bad if it turns out to be nothing," he said.

She agreed. Out of sight of the house, each had the same thought and drew a gun. They followed the trail as well as they could, but about two or three hundred yards in the brush thinned out and they lost it.

"Let's try the neighbors, see if they know anything, then we'll call it in," Kane said.

They retraced their steps to the blue-and-white and moved on. No one home at the next house, but two down they met up with a man dressed nattily in a charcoal pin striped suit who was about to get into his Mercedes.

"Hello, there, can we speak to you a moment?" Donovan said as they got out of their car.

The man looked surprised for a moment, then shut the door to his car. He was afraid, but Abaddon's voice told him he had "nothing to fear, the wolf was hidden from them." He felt safe, they could watch all they wanted but they would never see . . .

"Do you live here?" Donovan asked, pointing his nightstick at the cottage.

The man's eyes followed the gesture. "Yes, yes I do."

"Could we have your name, please?"

He hesitated, momentarily startled. But there was nothing to fear. "Weatherby," he said.

"First name, Mr. Weatherby?" Kane asked.

"What? Oh, yes, of course. Loring. Loring Weatherby. Why do you ask, officer?"

"It's routine, Mr. Weatherby. All the excitement around here lately, we're just checking."

Mary Kane watched him closely as they talked. Blond hair, that at least fit the profile, but hardly anything else did. And blond hair was not exactly a crime. "What do you do for a living, Mr. Weatherby?"

"I'm a securities analyst," he said. Sounded better than stock broker, he had always thought.

Just another businessman, hardly a homicidal nut-case who liked to chew on his victims. Still, maybe he had seen or heard something, or his wife had . . . "We're investigating the report of a prowler at one of your neighbors', sir, although that's confidential. Happened around dawn. Did you or your wife happen to notice anything unusual last night?"

He smiled inwardly at the mention of "his wife." Still, why not? He did love Margaret. If only *she* . . .

"Unfortunately my wife, Margaret, is not here just now. She's a psychologist and had an early appointment, but yes, we did have an incident sometime around then. We were both asleep when a loud crash woke us up. Naturally I went to see what was happening . . ." He was enjoying this.

He pointed to the side of the house. "Apparently someone tried to break in. When they did they broke the bird feeder outside the window. That's what the crash was. By the time I got there, whoever did it was gone."

Kane and Donovan looked at each other. This seemed to tie in with the story of the woman down the street.

"Mind if we see?" Donovan said.

"Please, please do," Loring said, intrigued by the abrupt image of horns passing so close to him. Strange. And he felt a sudden chill come over him.

As they walked around the outside of the house Mary Kane asked, "Did you report this disturbance, Mr. Weatherby?"

"No, no, we did not. We considered it, but since nothing was taken, no real damage . . ."

It was the usual and understandable reaction, the officers felt.

On the ground by the window they found the smashed glass of the bird feeder. They did not notice nearby in the tall grass the headless body of an arrogant blackbird. Loring remembered, pleased with himself, knowing it was the only way to keep the other birds safe from the other's hateful presence.

"Yeah, well, after the noise scared him off, that's when your neighbor saw him on the edge of the woods," Donovan said.

As they walked back to the car Loring said, "This seems quite a lot of trouble to go to over a prowler." He was reluctant to give up the exhilaration from this close contact with his enemies.

"Have you seen the papers yet?" Mary asked.

"Only the Wall Street *Journal*," he said. "Why?"

"Well, sir," Donovan said, "we don't want to upset you, but you should know that another person was killed in the park. A teen-age boy. We have to track down any possible lead."

"Yes, yes, and you think this prowler might be . . ." Loring allowed himself the memory of the boy's struggles, and the cleansing good of it.

The officers got into the blue-and-white and Donovan said, "We're not sure, probably not, but to be on the safe side it'd be a good idea to keep your doors and windows locked, and be sure to report anything suspicious."

"We will," Loring assured him.

○

He watched them drive away, then got into his own car, his thoughts on his "wife," on Margaret. Abaddon's command sounded again . . . She, too, had the mark on her, she too had been corrupted. How else could she have tricked him into believing she was his mother. If he loved her, there was no alternative. His course of action was clear.

CHAPTER 24

ERIN HAD to admit she was excited as they neared the police station—it seemed her experience and background might help the investigation. She looked at Mercanto driving, and felt exhilarated to be with this man, even be part of his work. Whenever he was around, things certainly seemed to happen. A relief from the static environs of museums and academia.

"What do you think they'll do when you tell them about what we've found out?" she asked, curious about how their information would be used.

Mercanto glanced at her out of the corner of his eye. "Don't know. I've never had any experience with this sort of thing before. It's another piece of the puzzle, a reason for what he's doing, but it doesn't identify him. It helps, though ..."

One of the things she liked best about him was his lack of pretense. If he knew something he said it, if he didn't he said that too.

As they passed the turn-off to the parking lot in the Valley Green section he pointed. "Down there is where I found the first body."

She shivered slightly at the memory of his description of that night.

O

At the station house he told her that he and Lieutenant Sloan didn't get on too well. He didn't elaborate. Once inside, Mercanto asked the desk sergeant where Sloan was. "Upstairs with the drug people, they just brought in the stuff on your boy Rashid," the sergeant told him.

Maybe the case was finally breaking. "Come on," he told Erin, taking her by the arm.

They hurried upstairs to where Sloan was talking to two detectives Mercanto did not recognize. Both were in their late twenties, unshaven and dressed for the street. One wore a leather jacket, the other a dirty navy peacoat.

When Sloan spotted Mercanto he said, "Come on in, I want you to hear this," and added when he'd taken in the young woman with the schoolboy glasses, "who's that?"

Mercanto introduced Erin, saying that she was the Caribbean expert from the museum.

"Ask her to wait outside."

Erin could understand why Mercanto and this Sloan didn't get along, but she did as she was asked.

After she had gone, Sloan said to the other two detectives, "Okay, let's have it, what have you got on this Rashid."

The one in the peacoat said, "They found him earlier this week in a crack house near Twentieth and Diamond. Somebody had pumped a couple of .357's into him. The reason for the delay is that nobody identified the body until today. For such a high roller he was a low-profile guy."

Mercanto held his breath as Sloan asked, "What about the body, was it mutilated?"

"Not more than you would expect from a couple of .357's," said the one in the peacoat.

Disappointment crossed Sloan's face. Mercanto felt the same way.

The leather jacket said, "Hey, lieutenant, what's the big deal? You're looking for a blond. This guy was anything but a blond."

"I think we know that already from his name," Sloan said. "What we were *hoping* was to tie it in to one of his associates. Both victims were users. We're sure in the first he was the seller. In the second we're not so sure but it looks right."

"Believe me, lieutenant," said the one in the leather jacket, "this guy had no blond companions. In the circles he traveled in a blond would stick out like Rudolph the Red-Nosed Reindeer."

"You're sure?"

"Positive," said peacoat. "Is that all you need from us?" When Sloan nodded they stood up. "We'll be going then. Good luck on this case. Everyone wants to see this guy caught. If you need anything more from us, give a holler."

When they had gone Sloan rubbed his hand over his bald head, as though there was still some hair there. "A damned dead-end. There goes the closest thing we've had to a lead."

He looked at Mercanto. In spite of what he'd felt since the Rudy Gunther investigation, he did have to admire Mercanto's thick-skinned, bulldog tenacity. "Look, Mercanto, I was rough on you this morning. Forget it."

"Yeah, we both just want this guy caught."

Sloan nodded. "Why did you bring that woman here?"

"We've just come from the psychiatrist's office. He's on his way here to confirm what she's going to tell you."

"Okay, bring her in." Hell, at this point he was willing to listen to anything. Time was their enemy. The psychiatrist had said the killer's rational periods would get shorter and shorter. Which meant he would soon be ready to kill again— maybe even tonight.

O

"I know the voodoo angle didn't work out, but after this morning I felt there was still something I was missing so I went back to the museum," Mercanto said when Erin had joined them. "Where I'd gone wrong was, I wasn't asking the right questions. I was concentrating on Jamaica instead of Haiti."

None of this was making any sense to Sloan. "Wait, you said you told this to the psychiatrist and he's coming out to confirm it . . ."

"That's right, Dr. Foster. Why don't you pick it up, Erin?"

For the third time in as many hours Erin went through her story about the Haitian shaman, his ceremony, and what he had done that ended in his death by the villagers, being very careful not to use the word "werewolf." She was just finishing the story of Jean Grenier, the French boy who had been sentenced to the monastery instead of prison, when Dr. Foster arrived.

"You've heard all this . . ." Sloan said.

Foster nodded. "Yes, and because of the rareness of the disorder I have to admit it didn't occur to me, but everything she says makes very good sense. In fact, I'm sure she's right. It's a very unusual form of schizophrenia, only two or three known cases in the past decade or so."

Sloan looked at Erin. "You say the killer believes he's some sort of beast, a wolf? Come on, I can't buy that. It's out of an old Lon Chaney flick."

Dr. Foster got up and made sure the door was securely closed. "It's no Lon Chaney movie, believe me. We're talking about the *disease* the werewolf legend is based on."

"Are you crazy? The three of you are sitting here trying to tell me we have a damned werewolf loose in Fairmount Park? I've got days, maybe only hours to stop a nut before he kills again, and you come to me with a cockamamie story about some guy covered in hair howling at the moon. This is bullshit."

Foster raised a hand. "You misunderstand. We said this disorder is what the werewolf legend is *based* on, not that he *was* one. He does not grow hair or fangs. You were right, that's in the movies. But schizophrenia in this form is a problem of perception accompanied by hallucinations. When, for example, he looks in the mirror he *thinks* he is actually turning into a wolf, with hair and the rest, but of course he is not. It is in his mind, in his altered perception of reality. That's what the disease is about," he said. As he talked he could not help thinking about Margaret's patient, the incident in the clothing store . . . He hoped she was right in her defense of him. But if not . . .

Sloan sat back in his chair. "Okay, I don't believe it, but assuming what you say is true, how does it help us catch him? Does it, say, make him any more predictable?"

"Explainable, not necessarily more predictable. There is a cause and effect relationship not always present in other paranoid schizophrenics. The wolf aspect takes over only when he feels threatened by guilt, usually associated with early sexual experiences."

"So he might have longer periods when he's normal than you thought this morning? As long as he's not threatened?" asked Sloan.

"Yes, that's right."

"Well, I guess that's something . . . The only thing to do is continue with our plans for the park and hope if he tries it again we can catch him at it. Meanwhile, I don't want this stuff to leave this room. You can imagine what the papers would do with it. First a cannibal, now a werewolf. Sweet Jesus."

As they were about to leave Sloan said, "Mercanto, I want to see you a minute . . . alone." After Erin and the doctor were gone, he said, "There's nothing I can do to keep you out of this case, is there? Okay, you're back in it. Officially. Be back here at midnight in plain clothes. You're going into the park. Maybe if I keep you up all night I can stop you from bringing in some other crackpot scientist to tell us Frankenstein's monster is our killer."

Mercanto smiled. "I'll be here."

Erin was waiting for him in the hallway. Dr. Foster had already gone.

"Where's the doctor?" he asked.

"He said something about doing more research, then he's coming back. Well, what did the lieutenant want?"

"Just to give me my orders. I have to be back at midnight to go on patrol."

"Patrol where?"

"The park, maybe I can turn up Frankenstein's monster."

"Don't joke." She took his arm in an instinctive gesture, the hard muscle beneath his sleeve felt reassuring. Ordinarily she had no doubt he could take care of himself, but this was different. She had, after all, seen the type of man they were after. "Be careful," she said. "I mean it."

"I will . . . Now, how about some lunch?"

"You're on."

Downstairs the desk sergeant stopped them. "Mercanto, there's a phone call for you. Line four."

On the line he heard the voice of DeBray, the man who worked for his brother.

"Nate, I'm at the hospital. When I got to the garage Frank was in a bad way. After I got him here he wanted me to call you. Nate . . . he's not going to make it. They've called for the priest. You'd better hurry. The last thing he said was to tell you to stop by his place and pick up his rosary, the one that belonged to your mother."

He had known all along this day was coming, but now that it was here he was no more prepared for it than if it happened out of the blue. "I'm on my way," he managed to get out, hung up and told Erin.

"I'm going with you," she said, "and you're not driving either. Give me the keys."

O

Spring Garden Street was the quickest way to Frank's garage but she had to slow down to twenty-five to make the lights. As they passed the Fraternal Order of Police building near Broad he thought of how he and Frank had celebrated his reinstatement to duty there with two many beers at the

conclusion of the Rudy Gunther business. How proud he was
...

"God, we had some times," he said, then was silent again.
She didn't try to make him say more, only gave his knee a
squeeze.

They parked in front of Frank's garage. "Want to wait here?"

"You're not getting rid of me so just forget it."

All in Frank's apartment was clean, in its place, unlike the
last few times he'd been there. It was as if Frank had known,
used his last strength to be sure no one would see it that way.

She waited while he went to the bedroom, and in a moment
heard him saying, "No ... no ..." She ran in to see him standing
in front of an old bureau. One of the small drawers at the top
was open. In his hand was a wallet. She looked inside the
drawer and saw pictures, of Mercanto and Frank, the rosary
and a pearl-handled derringer.

"What's wrong?" she said, then looked down at the wallet.
It was open to a driver's license with a picture.

The name on the driver's license was Stanley Hightower.

"But that's the name of the dead man? What does it mean?"

He shook his head, remembering the day he found Frank's
phone number in Hightower's address book. "I don't know."
He pocketed the wallet and started for the door. Erin took up
the rosary and followed.

At the hospital they were met outside the intensive care
unit by a black man dressed in work clothes and a cap
advertising Colt .45 Malt Liquor.

"Nate, thank God you made it ... You can't go in yet," he
said, pointing to the door. "The doctor is with him now. They
had to put him on a respirator."

Mercanto looked around. The sights and smell of hospitals
was nothing new to him, dating back to their parents' death

and continuing through his years on the police force. He'd been in corridors like this too many times.

"Where's the priest?"

"Father Dom . . . he's in there with him," DeBray said.

Mercanto looked at him in silence for a moment, then: "Come over here, I need to speak to you."

Erin remained while they went out of earshot. Mercanto took out the wallet. "You know Frank better than anyone, me included. What does this mean?" he said, handing it to him.

DeBray looked at the wallet. "I promised I wouldn't tell . . . I guess in the end he couldn't stand to get rid of it."

"Don't do this to me. I have to know . . ."

"On one condition . . . when you see Frank you can't let on you know. You have to do that or there's nothing you can do that will make me tell."

"All right, I promise . . ."

DeBray sighed. "He and Stanley, they were . . . were real close."

"I don't believe that, not Frank—"

"They met while Frank was working on his car. He showed him his paintings and I guess it went from there . . . Who do you think paid his doctor bills and his chemotherapy and—"

"His insurance."

"Frank didn't have insurance. Stanley paid them, that's who." He paused, then: "Being straight, you wouldn't understand—"

"He had me . . ."

"Not the same. It was something he needed. When he found it he recognized it."

"What about the wallet, how'd he get that."

"The chemotherapy wasn't working. You know it, he was

getting worse by the day. Stanley called late one night and asked Frank to meet him in the park. It was one of Frank's good days when he could get around. When he got there they must have had a scene. Stanley couldn't face the idea of a life without Frank. I mean, he'd divorced his wife, changed his life around to be with him, then this. Frank tried to talk some sense into him but it was no good. He pulled out that little derringer and shot himself before Frank could stop him. It's true, Frank told me . . ."

Mercanto was numb, but knew it had to be like he said . . . it explained Hightower's mood change, the withdrawals, everything, except the mutilation that must have happened after Frank left and the . . . whatever it was . . . found the body. "Why did Frank take the wallet and gun?"

"The wallet because he wanted something of Stanley's to keep near him. They were so careful they didn't even have a picture of each other. The gun because he was going to use it on himself when he couldn't stand the pain anymore. But he couldn't, he was too much of a Catholic for that."

"Why did he tell *you* this, not me? I'm his brother, damn it . . ."

DeBray looked down at the floor. "There was a whole side, that side of Frank, you didn't know about. He was afraid he would lose your respect if you knew. That would have killed him quicker than the cancer. Why me? We were friends for a long time. He gave me a job, got me out of the ghetto. I would have done anything for him."

Erin came down to them then: "The doctor wants you."

They turned and followed her. The doctor, a tall gray-haired man, looked tired. "It won't be long . . . I'm sorry . . ."

Frank died less than an hour later.

○

They left the hospital together and she drove again.

At his apartment she said, "Have you got any liquor?"

He pointed to the kitchen, and she poured him one. While he drank it she went into the bedroom and turned down the bedcovers, then brought him in and began to undress him. When he tried to help she stopped him. "Let me."

She got him into bed, took off her glasses and undressed too. What he was going through was not new to her. She remembered it all too well from her own parents' death, and wanted to give him a closeness and sharing in whatever way he needed.

He held her, but said, "I don't think I can. Not now."

She put her arms around him. In a few minutes the exhaustion of the day took him over and he fell asleep. She stayed beside him, awake, watching him, marveling at this man who in such a short time had come to mean so much to her. A cop . . . It made her smile.

Later he woke and told her what he had learned from DeBray.

"What are you going to do about it?"

"Nothing. He was my brother. Family comes first." She liked that.

This time when she reached for him he was ready. He also was surprised. They were from different worlds . . . he from South Philly, she probably Main Line, Ardmore, Swarthmore . . . but the desires he felt, and the way she returned it, drove all such thoughts from his mind. Their intensity, and the newness of it, at first made them awkward in their lovemaking, but their need overcame that too, with a promise of more, and better . . .

She looked now at his face, bags of exhaustion under his eyes, and urged him to sleep again.

"If you'll promise me one thing," he said. "I have to go to

work at midnight. Be here for me when I get home in the morning."

His words were what she wanted to hear. "I will, but now sleep, and as he rolled over on his side she fitted herself to him, savoring the feel and strength of him, marveling that this had happened to her, and grateful for it.

The sound of the telephone woke them. Mercanto reached for it. "Hello," in a voice thick with sleep. "Okay, I'll be there," he said, sleep suddenly gone from his voice.

"What is it," Erin said, resting on one elbow, the covers around her waist.

Mercanto was up and pulling on his clothes. "It was Sloan. They've just found another body. Catherine Poydras, the owner of the Maison Catherine."

CHAPTER 25

RAIN BEGAN to fall as Loring sat in his car and watched Margaret's house. It was a familiar sight. He had driven by it many times, imagining her inside with him . . .

The rain splattering on the windshield brought back the night he found the man's body in the park. How their paths crossed had been a mystery to him, though now he assumed Abaddon led him there. The man was sitting in the black BMW alone. A dark presence in a dark place, a servant of the devil preying on the unsuspecting.

It was the first time he had tasted human flesh, and had

blacked out completely afterward. Not now, though. Now he remembered, and understood . . .

Finally he got out of the car, walked up the street and around the house. At the rear was a glassed-in porch with wicker furniture. A nice room. We could have had such nice evenings here, he thought as he broke a pane of glass in the door with his fist and reached through to open it.

The glass cut his hand but he took no notice of it as he went from room to room, taking his time, touching things, taking in the feeling of Margaret.

He came to the study, and stood there for a moment, unsure. Something was wrong with this room. It wasn't Margaret at all. Nothing about it spoke of her. Why?

He heard the front door open. No, it was not her room. It was *his* . . . the one who had hurt her at the party. The one he felt in the house now. His heart began to pound, he stepped behind the door, out of sight. And saw the sofa, and remebered the night, his mother's nudity . . .

Desire, fear, quickly displaced by overriding anger. But this time he was not helpless. This time he was the one with power . . . the power of the bottomless pit . . . Wolf, his boyhood friend and protector part of him now . . .

He picked up a liquor bottle from the top of the bookcase, waited to hear footsteps in the hallway. He looked down at his hand holding the bottle . . . a thorny claw. It reassured him.

The man, the stepfather, came through the doorway. Loring stepped into his view, swung the bottle with all his might. It exploded against his old enemy's face, shattering, and as it did, opening bloody zippers in the flesh.

Adam Priest sank to the carpet. With a low snarl Loring was on top of him, his teeth bared, feeling the ecstasy of revenge finally come. He sank his teeth in, ripping, tearing, the face, the throat, the stomach, skin coming away with the sound of cheap cloth. Childhood memories tinged in red played across his mind like a flickering, grainy home movie.

When it was over, Adam's life dissolving in sticky puddles around him, Loring moved back and looked on. He was satisfied, it was deserved . . .

He stayed beside the body, squatting on his haunches. Through the windows he could see the trees and the rain. What he had done was the way of the wolf, he had obeyed the laws of nature, an inviolate code to cleanse the herd by, to purge it. His stepfather would no longer spread his sickness, tainting everyone that came too close.

Now he noticed the picture on the table. It was of a much younger Margaret leaning against a railing, wind blowing her hair in her face, water in the background. She had been tainted, too, but for her, through him, there was still hope. The happiness of that time, gone now from her face, would return.

CHAPTER 26

AS HE drove he hoped Erin would keep her promise and still be there when he came home. Now that he'd found her, even the thought of losing her was not something he wanted to think about.

The rain made traffic worse, turning Kelly Drive into a series of slick curves, slowing cars to a nightmarish crawl. He tried to pick his spots, weaving in and out, moving ahead wherever possible.

The phone call, Sloan's words . . . Catherine Poydras? There was no way she should be a victim, not her. She was too full of life. He remembered their last meeting, waking up in the hospital after the shooting and seeing the worried look on her face. The comfort it had given him.

The Valley Green parking lot was filled with blue-and-whites. Policemen in slickers were milling about. He thought of the night when it started, when he found Hightower's body there, then over near the steps to Maison Catherine he saw her old Ford station wagon. A dumb witness.

He parked and got out, grief pushed aside by anger. Unlike with Frank's death, he could *do* something about this one. See that it was avenged. If he had anything to say about it her killer would never make it to trial.

"Where did it happen?" he asked.

"On the other side, in the bushes right at Devil's Pool," the cop said, pointing across the creek.

He started down Forbidden Drive, the rain pelting him. At Devil's Pool he stopped. Across the creek he could see people moving about in the trees. He knew there was direct access to that spot from either side. After a moment he climbed down the steep embankment and waded across the rocks of the falls, ice-cold water soaking his feet and trouser legs to the knees.

On the other side one of the officers helped him up the slippery bank. "Nate, another bad one. If you're looking for Sloan he's over there." The officer pointed further into the bushes. "We've had a hell of a time maneuvering down here. Whoever did it had to know these woods like the back of his hand."

Mercanto started toward the spot.

Sloan was watching as the Medical Examiner's people wrestled with the body bag. When he saw Mercanto he nodded. No words.

"What have you got?" Mercanto asked.

"This morning just after you left we got a call from one of

the restaurant staff, said they found her car and she was missing. We put out a search."

"That was mid-morning," said Mercanto. "Why didn't they call sooner? She usually came to work early."

"Good question. Even I thought of it. They said sometimes after she finished whatever she usually did she would walk across the bridge and have breakfast with some friends who live on the West Mt. Airy side. It was a routine thing for her, so when they didn't find her, that's where they assumed she was. But after three or four hours they began to get worried. That's when they called us . . . It took us all day to find her."

"The same as the others?"

"Yeah, only worse," Sloan said, rain dripping from the brim of his hat. "What he did to her makes the others . . . He really tore her up. Jesus, one of her arms was missing. What we talked about this morning, I'm a believer."

Sloan looked at his watch. "We've done all we can here. We're losing the light and it's too far to bring in portables. The shift is due back at the station and I need to get their reports. Come on."

"My car is in the parking lot," Mercanto said.

"I'll drop you off, you can follow me."

$$\bigcirc$$

At the station house they gathered on the second floor, some taking coffee, some sodas. Sloan and Dr. Foster sat at the head of the table that was the command post. The other officers either sat or lounged wherever they could find a place, including Captain Zinkowsky. Everyone was wet, tired, and disgusted.

"All right, let's have it," Sloan said.

271

Team by team they gave their results. Busywork that added to a big zero.

When Donovan and Kane's turn came, it was Mary who spoke for them. "Nothing, other than what we called in before lunch," she said.

Sloan was about to move on to the next team, then her words registered. "What *did* you call in before lunch?"

"I guess everybody was out on the search. That's why you didn't hear. It might not be anything, but I'll go over it again. This morning was moving along like everyone else's. Nothing. Then we stopped at a house and spoke to a Mrs." . . . she paused to consult her notebook . . . "Mona Seidenberg."

"And . . ."

"She reported a prowler in her backyard sometime near dawn this morning. She couldn't give a description, other than that he was wearing dark clothes. When she woke up her husband the man was gone. We checked the backyard and she was right. There were signs that someone had gone into the woods there. We followed the trail for a couple of hundred yards, then it petered out. But there was definitely someone there."

The room went quiet. "That was around the time Catherine Poydras went to work," Sloan said, voicing everyone's thoughts.

"Yes, right. After that we checked the neighbors. Two houses down" . . . again she checked her notebook . . . "a man named Loring Weatherby said he and his wife were awakened around the same time by someone trying to break in. The prowler smashed a glass bird feeder attached to the window. That's what woke them, but they didn't get a look at him either."

Dr. Foster, who had been drawing doodles on a pad, suddenly

looked up. "Excuse me. What did you say this neighbor's name was?"

Mary Kane checked again. "Loring Weatherby."

"Please describe him."

"Early thirties, above medium height, slight build. Wearing a charcoal business suit. Handsome, blond hair ..."

Every eye in the room was on her now.

"You say he mentioned his wife ... ?" Dr. Foster said.

Mary checked once again. "Yes, name was Margaret. He said she wasn't home because she was a psychologist and had early appointments today."

Foster took a deep breath, let it out slowly. "You are *sure* that's what he said? Did he say anything else?"

"I'm *sure*, and that's all he said."

He turned to Sloan. "Is there someplace we can talk?"

Sloan understood. "Right here ..." In a louder voice to the group: "That'll be it for now, we'll take this up again at roll call."

Reluctantly the group filed out, except the Captain Zinkowsky. She hadn't been there much during the lycanthropy talk earlier and he didn't much want her to hear what was going to be said, but he had no choice. She was, after all, the captain of the station.

As Mercanto started to go Dr. Foster said, "Detective, it might be helpful if you stay, too."

Mercanto closed the door and joined them.

"The coincidence is too great..." Dr. Foster began, as if trying to convince himself to say what he was thinking.

"Go on," Sloan said.

Looking at Mercanto, he said, "This morning when you were leaving my office, remember I said I had something to do before coming out here ... ?"

Mercanto nodded.

"I went to see a colleague of mine, a psychologist who has been treating a very disturbed patient, one suffering from hallucinations similar to the profile of a lycanthropic. I went to convince her to give me his name." He added quickly, "Not that I exactly believed he was the killer, but to be on the safe side ... schizophrenia is a highly individualized disorder that often resembles many other disturbances we treat. Still, it worried me ..."

"What did she say?" Sloan said.

"She refused. I expected that, but during our talk she mentioned his first name ... an unusual one, the same that Detective Kane just mentioned. Loring."

He paused. "That's why I asked about the wife. I'm confident our killer is single, but you heard what he said ... his wife's name was Margaret and she was a psychologist ... Margaret is the name of my colleague ..."

Sloan was on his feet. "Goddamn, you're right, it sure does sound like too great a coincidence. Same first name, blond hair, and from the neighborhood." He crossed the room in a couple of strides and opened the door, yelling, "Kane, in here."

As soon as she gave the address, Mercanto was out the door, the others close behind. He got in his car and took off, not waiting for Sloan to assemble the backup. As he drove he checked his revolver, made sure it was loaded, anger boiling inside for the killer who now had a name.

O

He pulled to a stop in front of the cottage.

The drive was empty, the house gloomy dark in the rain. Before he had approached the front door Sloan arrived with two blue-and-whites, lights flashing.

Kane and Dr. Foster piled out of Sloan's car with him. Sloan took charge. "You two wait here," he said, indicating Mary and the doctor. "Two of you take the front. Two go around to the rear," he said to the uniformed officers armed with shotguns. "And be careful. Don't get trigger happy, but remember what this guy could be."

Sloan and Mercanto followed the team to the front door, guns drawn. Standing out of the line of fire, Sloan rapped on the door with the butt of his revolver. "Police, open up. We want to talk to you."

No sound from the house. Sloan repeated it, no results. One of the uniformed officers hustled around from the rear of the house, rain streaming on his slicker.

"Lieutenant, there's a bunch of windows on the back. Looks like nobody's home."

"Wait here," he said to the team at the front door, and he and Mercanto followed the officer to the rear of the house.

They peered in but couldn't make out much because of the darkness inside. "Looks like he's not here," Sloan said, "and we don't have a search warrant."

Mercanto stepped forward and smashed one of the windows with his revolver, the sound of the breaking glass loud in the late afternoon. "Looks like we just discovered a burglary in progress. Probable cause."

Sloan gave him a look of grudging approval. "Okay, Mercanto, go around front and alert the other team so they don't start shooting."

As he hurried around the side of the house, he heard them entering the house.

In a moment Sloan came through and let them in, motioning for Mary Kane and Dr. Foster to join him. "He's our man..."

They followed him into the house. In the living room the

other team of uniformed officers was standing by the fireplace, staring down. On the mirror above the mantlepiece someone had written in large red letters . . . ABADDON.

"Search the place," Sloan said. "Now, get a move on."

As the men began to move about the house, Sloan said, "Come over here."

Mercanto, Kane and Dr. Foster followed him to the fireplace, and he pointed down at it. There, nestled among the burned logs, was the remains of Catherine Poydras' arm.

Dr. Foster backed away to the sofa. Sloan was all business, in his element. "Looks like he wrote it in blood. What do you think it means?"

"No idea," Mercanto said, staring at the word on the mirror.

Dr. Foster spoke up behind them. "It's from the book of Revelation . . . the Hebrew name for the angel who is the keeper of the keys to the bottomless pit where Satan is to be ultimately imprisoned . . . It helps to know that book when you treat disturbed patients," he said, thinking of Margaret's deep involvement with the man.

The officers came back then from the other rooms. "Nothing," one of them said.

Dr. Foster got to his feet. "Margaret Priest is his psychologist. During his treatment he's become obsessed with her. It's very possible that's where he's gone—"

Sloan turned to Mary Kane. "You stay here with one team. If he comes back you make sure nothing goes wrong with the arrest. We don't want to blow this case . . ." Looking back at Dr. Foster, he said, "Where will this Margaret Priest be now?"

"Probably at home, although she could be seeing patients late at her office," he said, and gave them both addresses.

Sloan told the other team of officers, "You take her office . . . Kane, get on the phone to Spivak and have him meet them there. Mercanto and I will take the house."

CHAPTER 27

MARGARET PARKED in front of her house and sat for a moment. Her last appointment had been a group session, which always left her exhausted. Charles' earlier appearance in her office made it worse.

After he left she had tried to deal with what he had said. At lunch she had even gone so far as to look up the articles on lycanthropy he had mentioned. Even though there was much in them that fit Loring's behavior, at least on the surface, she still was not convinced. She felt she knew the man too well to believe him capable of such . . . well, atrocities.

Still, it frightened her. She needed to talk to him and called his office. He had not come in today, they said. Then his home, no answer. Should she have given Charles Loring's name? Prove to him she was right? No, it would have been too traumatic for Loring to go through such an interrogation. It could push him over the edge, beyond any help by anybody . . .

She got out and started for the house, too tired even to hurry in the rain. Adam's car was across the street. Good, he was home. She didn't want to be alone. And since what had happened at that party he'd been at least trying to make amends. Not that she had much hope there, but still . . .

She used her key to open the door, surprised that the house was dark? "Adam? Where are you?" No answer. He must be upstairs, maybe taking a nap. She turned on the hall-table light, hung up her raincoat, started upstairs . . .

In the study Loring heard her voice and moved out of sight behind the door. He didn't want to startle her. But he was eager to tell her what he'd done, that with Abaddon's help he had finally rid himself of his old enemy, that his life now had a purpose as never before . . .

Upstairs she walked into the bedroom, and even in the darkness saw the bed was empty. Maybe he was in the study, he sometimes took catnaps on the sofa there . . .

Loring heard her footsteps on the stairs. There was so much to say, to tell her, to prepare her before he gave her eternal life. He was glad for that, but he also didn't like to think about losing her. He would be lonely, but was still willing to do it for her . . .

Margaret flipped the switch at the entrance to the study that operated the light on the table at the end of the sofa, and in its glow she saw Adam's body on the floor.

The carnage was surreal, and so much so it took time to register before her hands went to her face and she screamed.

Loring moved forward now from behind the door. "Margaret, don't . . . it's all right." He kept coming, his arms outstretched.

She backed away. "No . . . *no* . . ." Oh God, Charles, he was so right . . .

"Please, Margaret, calm yourself. We have to talk. There are so many things I want to tell you."

She looked at him, couldn't stand the sight, blood all over him. Not a word from her . . . at least she knew enough for that.

He smiled. More a rictus in his blood-smeared face, like the mask she had seen at the museum that night with Adam.

"It was all part of the Plan," he was saying. "That's why I wanted to talk to you, to make you understand. It was all revealed to me that night after you left my house," he said, his eyes blank, looking more through her than at her. "Abaddon came to me and did what you were never able to do. He let me see my past, and future . . ."

She fought for breath, and the strength to mask her fear. There was no doubt she was to be his next. No escape, nothing to defend herself with.

Get a grip on yourself. Talk to him, try to reach him. You've got to bring him down, get through to him somehow. Use your skills, what you know. Your life depends on it . . .

"I don't understand, who is Abaddon?" Get him talking, try to distract and get to him.

He smiled again, a smile that was terrifying with the unrealness of his eyes. "He's my angel, Margaret. My Angel Margaret." He was pleased with his cleverness. "He keeps the keys to the bottomless pit."

She managed to say, "The bottomless pit?"

At least he made no move toward her as he shook his head. "Yes, where Satan is to be imprisoned, but not until the new Jerusalem. That can't happen until all those with the mark of the beast are cleansed. That's what I'm doing, helping to cleanse them. Then Abaddon and I will stand guard over Satan for a thousand years. It's my reward."

Too clearly, she realized, he thinks when he kills it's in some higher service.

"Tell me more about Abaddon."

Loring remembered the comfort, the *relief* he had felt since he surrendered himself. A note of . . . of near-tenderness was detectable in his voice as he said, "He is the changer of men's shapes, he can make men seek death but keep it from them. He is very powerful . . ."

She noticed the change. It was a step, a small one, but seemingly away from the murderous anger. Abaddon was the changer of men's shapes, he said, and she began to remember what she had read at lunch about lycanthropy . . . "Did he change your shape?"

He looked across the room to the windows, where he saw the reflection of his face, changed feral in its wolf shape, and was no longer frightened by it, welcomed it . . . "He allowed me to become the wolf, the cleanser of the herd."

And with the word "wolf" she remembered the picture on his mantelpiece. "Like your friend Wolf, your dog . . ."

Yes, yes, Margaret understood, and the old feeling of just the two of them alone in her office began to come back to him. Margaret was the only one who had ever even tried to understand what he thought, what he felt. That made what he had to do especially hard, but he knew that was her only way, her only hope for real salvation.

She noticed his eyes seemed to clear slightly when she

asked about his dog. But she knew that one wrong word, one wrong gesture could retrigger him.

"Tell me what it's like when you're the wolf," she said, trying to let him know that to her he was still human, still Loring . . .

"Words can't describe it, Margaret. It's beyond . . ." He stopped, the blankness back in his eyes. Then: "At first I was afraid, that's why I didn't remember, but Abaddon explained it to me."

"What did he say?"

He looked down at Adam's body. "That I was selfish, self-centered, that I was jealous of my mother and even wanted my stepfather to do those things to me. He *made* me remember, told me it was the first step to redemption. The second was to obey."

Obviously he was seeing Adam as his stepfather. She must try to keep him from the next transference, seeing her as mother. She pushed away thoughts of the consequences of *that* . . .

"You are not selfish, Loring. You're a good man. Do you think I could care about you, as you know I do, if you weren't?"

He looked at her, eyes suddenly sharp. "You're afraid of me, aren't you?"

Be careful, he goes in and out of reality. Don't lie. "Yes."

Her reply hurt him. Didn't she understand he was her only hope? He loved her, didn't she *know* that?

And then he said it.

"I know you do, Loring. Let me help you. Sit down, please." Her words sounded like whispers. Could she go on with this charade? She'd better, her life depended on it.

Loring felt the old pull of emotions. She did care for him, even knowing so many of his secrets. With her he didn't have to be stronger than he was. He looked down at the body on the floor. His enemy was gone.

"Let's sit here, like we've done before." If only she could get him to do this simple thing it could mean he was beginning to respond to her.

Her voice was so soothing, he wanted to capitulate—as soon as his mind formed the word he knew he felt tricked, deceived. He looked up and there it was, twinkling deep in her left eye. The number 13. The mark of the beast.

Margaret saw the change. Something had gone wrong. Something she said, or something he thought had brought back the anger. She saw his muscles tense. She hurried on to say, "You didn't want your stepfather to do those things, we both know that."

The urgency in her tone stopped him for a moment, then he repeated Abaddon's words. "It was my punishment."

She was losing him again. "But why? You did nothing to be punished for."

He shook his head. "Yes, I did. He was right all along."

"About what?"

He didn't want to tell her, he'd never told anyone before.

"Please help me understand . . ."

Finally he said, "He was right when he said I killed my father . . . even though he didn't know it."

He saw the look on her face, knew he had disappointed her. "But that's all over now. I have my orders, and my redemption." He said it proudly.

Margaret stared in disbelief. There was no end to it, the layer upon layer of horror that made up his life.

"Surely it was an accident," she said automatically.

"No." Said in a quiet tone that chilled her. "I was eight. One night he and my mother quarreled, he made her cry. I promised myself he would never make her cry like that again. The next day when we were alone in the house I took his gun. I went to his office where he was working and I shot him. Then I put it in his hand. They thought it was suicide."

He looked down at Adam's, his stepfather's body. "That's how he made me do it. He knew I was alone in the house with my father that day. He said he would tell the police I killed him and I'd be locked up until I died if I didn't do what he wanted . . . Don't you see the joke? He was right, only he didn't know it. I thought about killing *him*, too, a thousand times, but I knew if I did my mother would go out and marry another one like him and it would start all over again. I knew that. It was easier to let it happen. After all, it was my punishment . . ."

Loring saw the understanding in her face. He had been right to tell her—

A loud pounding on the front door. "Police, open up."

Loring looked in the direction of the hallway, knew what was happening. They were trying to stop him from giving Margaret her salvation. He heard Abaddon's voice . . . "Do it now while there is still time. For her. For yourself . . . It's the only way she can be saved from eternal damnation . . ."

With a growl he sprang forward, teeth bared, his hands now shaped like gnarled claws, knocking Margaret down, climbing on top of her.

"Dear God, no!" she screamed, feeling his breath. She twisted under him, fighting, trying to keep his teeth from reaching her throat.

His hands were squeezing. Everything was becoming a blur. There was a ringing in her ears, a coldness seeping through her. The fight was going out of her as his face came closer

Faraway, like down a long tunnel, she heard the door burst open, the sound of running feet, but in her oxygen-deprived brain they no longer mattered.

Nor did they matter to Loring. The only thing that mattered

was his love for Margaret, using his power to protect her from
... from them ...

Mercanto, first in the room, grabbed Loring's hair, jerking
his head back before his teeth could find their mark. With
visions of Catherine Poydras's body etched in his mind, he
smashed Loring in the face with his pistol until Sloan finally
pulled him away from the unconscious body.

Margaret turned on her side, pulled herself into a fetal
position. Charles Foster hurried to her and held her, rocking
her like she was a child.

Loring was manacled and taken away to the psychiatric
wing of the Detention Center. Mercanto went along, staying
until he saw him sedated and handcuffed to his bed. As he
looked at him for the last time, his thoughts went back to
Loring's forerunners—Stubbe Peeter and Jean Grenier. Even
though all that Erin had said about the disease was true,
something he rationally understood, it was too much to find
sympathy. Not for a man who had done what Loring had done.

Fortunately, he thought as he turned to go, that was all up
to a judge, not to him. He was just a cop. And never more glad
of it.

EPILOGUE

DR. FOSTER took Margaret home to his house and kept her there for the next two weeks, staying with her until she began to regain something of her old strength, physically and emotionally.

It wasn't easy. On the fourth day following her ordeal, in one of her low points, she said, "I'm giving it up, Charles. All those people, dead because I couldn't handle the case—"

"Margaret, it's time we both came down from our pedestals. Me the all-knowing mentor, you the Fallen Doctor. And stop chewing on the guilt. You don't deserve it, and if you were your patient you'd tell yourself so. What it's really about is the old Greek *hubris*, pride, and you know what it went before—a fall. You're too human to be beyond a mistake, a bad one, I grant you. But you're also too valuable a therapist to run and hide in an orgy of guilt and self-pity."

"I appreciate what you're saying, Charles, but—"

"But bullshit. There, a good scientific term. Just about as scientific as our knowledge of the worst of ourselves. We've got a lot to learn, but we've no right to stop trying. Sorry, I'm lecturing again, but I can't help it. And you know I'm right about this, or you will once you give yourself a chance to recover . . . from Adam . . . from Loring Weatherby . . ."

"We'll see," she said, more to appease him than believing.

O

On the sixth day she dreamed she was walking through a green field filled with tall grass and spring flowers. The day was sunny. She was wearing a spring dress and carrying a straw hat with a wide brim. Near the edge of the field she heard a whimpering sound. When she went to investigate, on the road nearby she saw the body of a large dog. One that had been run over by a car. The whimpering was coming from it. Moving closer, she saw the dog had no face. In its place was Loring Weatherby's face

O

The sound of the phone woke her and she walked to the door, where she could see Charles. When he hung up he turned to her. "That was Detective Sloan. There's a problem. I have to go out"

"About Loring?" The dream returning to her. He nodded. "I'm coming, too," she said

○

Sloan was waiting for them. An attendant unlocked a series of steel doors, one after another, until they were beside Loring's bed.

He lay on top of it uncovered, dead, his unseeing eyes staring into space, his teeth still bared. Somehow he had gotten one hand free of its handcuff. No one offered an explanation about how it happened. But he hadn't been able to free the other one. In his desperation, fury, or whatever, he had gnawed it until his teeth had found their mark, ripping out veins and arteries alike, bleeding to death. Like a wolf caught in a trap.

Written in blood on the wall beside his bed was the word—"Margaret"